I0763455

MY DEAR MARGARET

K.M.Bishop

—Shellville Press—

Printed by Shellville Press in the United States of America

Cover by Shelly Connor

ISBN: 978-1-7334487-1-0

Shellville Press
a division of Shellville Design LLC
www.shellvillepress.com

10 9 8 7 6 5 4 3 2 1

To all those who believed in me.
You are loved more than you know.

1

Margaret Hepworth sighed as she looked out from the balcony of Sir Walter's estate. The June night air was crisp and warm, but she shuddered as the noises from the ball floated outside.

Another ball, she thought. *There is always a ball.*

A servant drifted her way with a tray of champagne, but she politely declined. She had already had one and it had left her head spinning. A squealing of laughter hit her ears and she cringed. She wanted to leave. She wanted to *escape*.

She looked up at the stars and gave a weak smile. At least she could rely on them. Constant, beautiful, and silent. Movement caught her eye and she turned her head to see two young lovers sneaking through the yard for somewhere more private. She watched them head out to the lake just ahead, where the moon reflected brilliantly on its surface and the young woman's long skirts rustled in the grass.

She continued to watch them as they disappeared into the darkness and her heart began to ache. She had once stolen away into the darkness for a few minutes of privacy with the one she loved. She had once found solace in the night, looking up at the stars and whispering hopes and dreams into the air, wishing they would come true. She had once boldly stolen a kiss and had received another in return.

Margaret dabbed at the tears that had formed in the corner of her eyes and bit her lip to keep it from quivering.

She had once been loved and loved in return. But now it was gone. The hope from that love was gone, but not the pain she felt from its absence.

"Margaret?" came a familiar voice. "Margaret, what are you doing sulking by yourself out here in the dark?"

Margaret only half turned her head to see her friend Celeste Willoughby coming toward her, a half full glass of wine in her hand. "Thinking."

"Oh, for heaven's sake, what would you want to do that for?" Celeste replied. "You are at a ball, Margaret! Why do you not come inside and dance? Lord what's-his-face has been looking for you, though I would not let you dance with him for a hundred pounds. His hands are always sweaty, and you are not wearing gloves tonight."

"Lord Culver is looking for me?" Margaret asked skeptically.

Celeste nodded as she took a sip from her wine. "He is not an awful man. Though I sometimes cannot tear my eyes away from that strange mole on his neck."

Margaret gave a slight laugh and looked back out toward the lake, trying to guess which way the lovers went. Perhaps where the willow's branches just touched the surface of the water. She gave a sad smile to herself as she remembered.

It didn't matter now. Nothing did.

Celeste stretched her arms up and took a deep breath in. "I am glad the weather finally broke," she said resting her back against the railing of the balcony so she could see inside to the dance floor. "I was getting tired of all of that rain."

Margaret gave a one-worded response.

"Charles looks rather dapper tonight," Celeste continued. "I wonder who he is trying to impress. I hope it is not that Wilmington girl. She is much too boring for him."

Margaret didn't reply, she just kept staring out into the darkness.

"Oh, Amanda Haderly is here," Celeste exclaimed. "She is quite adorable. I like her. I think I shall invite her to tea tomorrow. Are you coming?"

Margaret nodded. "Yes," she replied distantly.

Celeste turned her head to look at her. "Margaret, my love, my darling, my dear," she said taking her friend's hand, "why are you so quiet this evening? I cannot have you sulking around in this lugubrious manner. Sir Walter only throws a ball once a year and they are the most luxurious. Have you had the wine?"

"No, I have not the taste for it tonight."

Celeste turned back to the balcony doors. "Well, if you do not want to drink and you do not want to dance, and you obviously are not interested in talking, what do you want to do?"

"Right now, think."

"Should I not have urged you to come tonight?"

Margaret shook her head. "No, I *did* want to come," she assured her. "But being here is different."

There was a brief silence.

"So, what are you thinking about?" Celeste asked, sipping her wine lazily, mentally judging and laughing at the dancing young couples fumbling through the rules of courtship. She gave a small chuckle as one the young men she had been watching went in the wrong direction and bumped into another dancer.

"A lot of things." Margaret swallowed and cleared her throat. "But quite frequently and often I have been thinking I might become a nun."

Celeste spit out her wine to keep from choking on it. "Where-the-fuck-fore?" she replied loudly, wiping away red droplets from her chin.

A few other guests further down the balcony looked their way, their brows raised in curiosity.

Margaret flushed, abashed at her friend's outburst. "I cannot go on living like this, Celeste," she replied in a quieter tone than her friend. "I am drowning in my own thoughts. I need a distraction."

Celeste nodded. "Yes, you do, but joining a convent?" she asked incredulously. "How in the world would that make sense? How would that be a distraction?"

Margaret gave a sad smile. "Perhaps I cannot explain it."

"My dear Margaret," started Celeste, "I am at a loss as to what to say or what I *should* say." She shook her head. "Honestly, I cannot agree with this." She grabbed another glass of wine from a servant as he passed by them, replacing it with her own empty one and took a gulp. "This is so," she thought for a moment, "permanent."

Margaret nodded. "Yes, it would be, but I see no other course for myself to take."

Celeste put her hand to her mouth and regarded her friend. "No other course to take?" she repeated. "What other courses did you even consider?" She held a hand out palm up.

Margaret sighed. “I cannot live like— like— like this,” she said opening her arms to motion toward the entire ball, “anymore and pretend I am not affected by it all.” She shook her head. “I am in torment, Celeste, and every day is a reminder.”

Celeste scoffed. “All of this because of that stupid boy running off with that wretch of a woman.”

Margaret flinched.

“And to make matters worse, they are cousins. He ran off with his cousin!” Celeste exclaimed.

Margaret looked back out to the lake. “You do not approve of cousins marrying?” she asked trying to smile.

“Oh, heavens, no!” Celeste replied. “Far too strange for me.”

“Yet, it is not uncommon,” Margaret told her. “A lot of royals marry their cousins. They have been doing so for centuries.”

“Yes, and a lot of good it does them. Half of them have unusually large chins,” Celeste retorted. “No, it is not sound.”

Margaret gave a small laugh.

“Seriously, Margaret, why?” Celeste continued waving away a handsome young man who came to ask her to dance. “Not now, Joseph, you simpleton. Can you not see that Margaret and I are in the middle of a very important conversation?” she scolded him.

The young man blushed and bowed an apology before scampering away.

“Celeste, that was rude,” Margaret chided. “You did not have to send him away like that.”

Celeste adjusted a fallen curl, indifferent to Joseph’s plight. “Yes, I did. Poor Joseph cannot take a hint. I have been avoiding him all night! And do *not* change the subject! I want an answer. Why do you feel as if hiding yourself away from the rest of the world is the only course you can take? Surely, that is what you would call this, nothing more than running away from the issue."

Margaret gently touched her friend's arm. "I know you are concerned, but this is not something I can just explain. It is a feeling."

Celeste looked at her friend unblinking for a few moments. "So, are you to France then? Or Scotland, or Ireland?"

"I do not know yet," Margaret told her.

"Honestly, your mother cannot have agreed with this. Her only daughter joining a convent? I do not see her welcoming the idea."

"I have not told her yet. It was just something I have been thinking for a few weeks now."

Celeste drained her glass and took her friend by the hand. "Well, then let it be just a thought for tonight as well," she insisted. "For right now, I will have you dance."

Margaret smiled at her. "I will dance, but only if you find Mr. Sharpe and dance with him."

Celeste made a face. "Joseph?" she groaned. "You are a cruel friend, Margaret, but I will make this sacrifice for you. Come, let us find you a worthy partner first."

2

The next morning, Celeste sent a hasty note to Charles Pratt, a man she always depended on, and, within the hour, he burst into the parlor, his face red with exertion, wiping sweat from his face.

Celeste started when she saw him. "Charles, you look awful!"

"Are you alright?" he asked coming up to her, breathing heavily.

"Of course, I am alright," she replied looking him up and down. "Did you run all the way here? You came rather fast."

"Your note had but three words, Celeste," he explained, running a hand through his light brown hair to smooth it down. "'*Emergency. Come now.*'"

"Yes, because I am in dire need of your advice and I knew not how to convey my urgency on a piece of paper in any other way."

He blinked at her in disbelief. "I ran my horse the entire way here."

"That was very kind of you to come so quickly."

"I thought you had taken ill or that perhaps your

father had died."

"Well, if my father had died would you not have triumphed?"

He peeled off his now sweat-soaked jacket and flopped down on a couch opposite her.

"Gerald, bring Mr. Pratt a water," Celeste said over her shoulder to her servant.

"You are impossible," Charles told her taking a deep breath and letting it out in a huff.

She smiled at him coyly. "You are too easy," she retorted.

"So, are you going to tell me what this great emergency is?" Charles asked half annoyed.

"Yes," Celeste began, "it is a matter of extreme importance and will very likely negatively affect the life of someone we both hold very dear."

Charles stared at her.

"I am talking about Margaret, of course."

"Of course."

"She has told me something of the most alarming nature last night and— well, I am almost ashamed to say it."

"She is with child!" Charles exclaimed leaning forward in his seat.

"What?"

"I always knew behind that prudish exterior was a vixen waiting to be set free!"

"Do not be vulgar, Charles," Celeste scolded. "She is not with child."

"Oh," Charles replied almost looking disappointed.

"What I am about to tell you is far worse than that."

"Celeste, you have a propensity to drag things out," Charles told her rubbing his brow. "I would much prefer you would just get to the point."

Celeste frowned. "Margaret has it in her head to join a convent."

Charles pressed a hand to his mouth to suppress a smile which he did unsuccessfully.

"This is not a joke!" Celeste proclaimed. "She was quite serious about it."

"My apologies," Charles said trying to regain his composure, "but this is your big emergency?"

Celeste looked at him earnestly. "Of course, this is my big emergency! My most intimate friend is about to throw her life away—"

"That's slightly sacrilegious."

"—and become a nun! A nun, Charles!" Celeste bowed her head and pressed the back of her hand against her forehead. "I cannot allow her to go through with it," she said after a moment, sitting back up.

"And you are telling me because—"

"Obviously, you are to help me."

"—you expect me to help," Charles said with a nod. "Obviously. So, what do you propose we should do?" He tilted his head a bit. "You're not going to ask me to seduce her, are you?"

Celeste blinked at him. "Absolutely not," she replied half laughing.

Charles frowned. "Why are you laughing? Do you not think I could?" he asked, dejected more by her laughter than her refusal.

She gave him a half serious look. "I am not so terrible as to allow something like that to happen to a soul as pure as Margaret's," she explained to him. "Besides, you are much too tainted and she knows you too well." She shook her head. "No, if we are to find someone to replace that useless man she still pines for, we need to find someone with similar likes and tastes."

"And get him to seduce her?" Charles asked skeptically.

"Dear Lord, what is it with you and seducing her?" she asked. "Is it my uncovered sofa legs? Does their delicate design remind you of the female form as I was warned it might?" she teased. "Perhaps, Mrs. Bard was right and I should buy sleeves for them."

Charles did not appear amused.

Celeste sighed. "I am not trying to have her deflowered," she informed him. "I just want her to fall in love or," she struggled for another word, "whatever."

Charles gave a small laugh. "Love or whatever," he repeated. "You are quite the romantic, Celeste."

"Yes, a real dreamer," she agreed sarcastically.

Charles sipped on the water Gerald snuck in a few minutes earlier. "Speaking of 'love or whatever,'" he started looking around to make sure they were alone, "what are you doing later this evening?"

Celeste smirked at him. "Why?"

He leaned in closer to her. "The weather has been fine, and I thought we could make our way to the clearing in your father's woods."

"Charles," Celeste said in an even tone.

"I will bring a blanket this time, and some of that Spanish wine you love so much."

"Charles, as lovely as that all might sound, you know we agreed not to bed one another anymore."

Charles sat back up in his seat. "I do not remember *agreeing* to anything," he replied. "You will not even tell me why."

"Yes, but that is not why I called you here."

Charles stood and walked over to a table beside the

mantle where Celeste's father kept bottles of port and canary. He poured himself a glass and moved to do the same for Celeste, but she declined.

"So, how are we to show Margaret what she will possibly be missing by joining a convent if we cannot get her to lie with a man first?" Charles asked after taking a sip.

"Well, for one, you will not be showing her what she would be missing, but showing her what kind of disappointment she can spare herself from."

Charles lifted a brow at her. "That was a little mean."

"Life is mean," Celeste told him. "That was truth."

Charles let out a sigh as he took a gulp from his glass. "Mh, there is a new preacher that has moved into old man Richard's house. I have heard he is quite godly."

"Is he not a Methodist?"

Charles shrugged. "I am not sure, I never asked."

"Well, Margaret is a Catholic. She would never go for a Methodist preacher."

He huffed. "Well, we certainly cannot set her up with a priest, now can we?"

She gave a small smile. "A shame, is it not?"

Charles nodded in agreement.

There was brief silence.

"Celeste," Charles started.

"Yes?"

"Why did you want us to not—" Charles stopped and took a step closer to the window, peering out. "Why is Joseph Sharpe riding up to your house right now?"

"You are not serious?" Celeste said getting up and looking out the window herself. She let out an annoyed huff.

"He looks extremely happy to be here," Charles goaded. "Look at that grin on his—" He turned to look at her, a knowing look on his face. "Did you lie with him?"

Celeste avoided his gaze.

"You did, did you not?" He almost laughed. "I cannot believe you would lie with him. He is so—"

"It was not *ideal*, but it was not the worst," she said interrupting him.

"Was it just the once?"

Celeste didn't answer.

"More than once?" Charles asked incredulously. "I cannot believe you slept with him more than once." He laughed seeing her irritation rise. "He is such a clumsy fool."

"It was his first time."

Charles laughed harder. "Even better."

Celeste groaned and flopped back down on the couch. "What could he possibly want?"

Charles looked at her skeptically. "I do not know, Celeste, what could he want?"

"Do not tease," she replied tetchily. "This poor puppy follows me everywhere; he is utterly relentless. You should have seen him last night at Sir Walter's. Poor louse was practically drooling over me. I would have told him off but cruel little Margaret made me dance with him."

"So, when did this little 'event' take place?" Charles teased.

Celeste narrowed her eyes at him. "He may have visited me last week for tea right after father and I got into one of our *disagreements*." She coughed. "He is so innocent and sweet; it was almost too easy."

"And when was the second time?" Charles goaded, picking his jacket up from the couch and putting it back on.

She scowled at him. "Well, the first ended so quickly

it hardly counted."

"So, right after, then?" he surmised. He sighed. "I am almost offended. No," he held a finger up, "I *am* offended that you would choose to lie with the laughably inept Joseph Sharpe and not myself."

"So, you are saying you *are not* laughably inept, then?" Celeste replied with a raised eyebrow.

Charles opened his mouth to speak when the door to the room opened and one of Celeste's maids informed them that Mr. Sharpe was at the door.

Celeste turned to her maid. "Tell him I am on the rag and cannot be seen by anyone."

Her maid turned a deep shade of red at the suggestion, looking uncomfortable and confused by the request.

"I am joking, of course, Madeline," Celeste reassured her.

The maid gave a sigh of relief. "Yes, ma'am."

"I will be out to meet him shortly, but do not let him in or—"

But before she could finish her sentence, Joseph stepped through the door, a large smile on his face. The smile faltered when he saw Charles, but only for a moment.

"Forgive me," he said with a bow. "I did not realize you had company. How are you Mr. Pratt?"

Charles gave a slight bow. "Mr. Sharpe, how is your sister?"

"Well, thank you." Joseph turned to Celeste. "I merely came to ask if you wanted to join me for a ride, it is such lovely weather, but I, of course, did not know you had company."

"Yes, that was very kind of you to think of me, but—"

"I was just leaving, Mr. Sharpe," Charles broke in. "So,

there is no harm done. You can ask away."

Celeste shot him a glare before returning a smile to her face. "Charles, did you not just tell me you were going to stay for tea?"

Charles looked pensive for a moment before shaking his head. "No, I did not."

"Funny, I could have sworn you did." She pleaded with her eyes, but she could see he was in no mood to placate her.

Charles shook his head. "I did not." He poured himself another glass of canary. "In fact, I think you were just telling me how wonderful a ride would be today."

Celeste turned and gave a forced smile to Joseph. "I did, but I am expecting Miss Hepworth and Miss Haderly for tea any minute, so it would be rude of me to go."

"You can have my share of the tea, Mr. Sharpe," Charles told him raising his glass to him. "But, to be honest, it is the dessert that you should really stay for." He winked at Celeste who shook with anger.

Joseph bowed and thanked them for the invitation, the innuendo surpassing him completely. "I would love to stay for tea, but I am to dine with the Wakefields and do not want to risk being late." He walked over to Celeste and took her hand. "I shall hopefully be more successful the next time I call." He kissed her hand and bowed his way out of the room.

Charles laughed as he sipped from his glass, but his joy was short lived as Celeste hurled a pillow at him, hitting him in the face and spilling the contents of the glass all over him.

"Now, why would you do that?" he asked her, surveying the mess she had caused.

"I could kill you for what you pulled just now," she

replied.

He laughed. "How could I resist?" he retorted. "He was so eager for another go."

"Well, apparently so are you, but that scene surely did not help your cause."

Charles's smile fell from his face.

Celeste sighed. "Let us not quarrel, Charles."

"Were we quarrelling?" he replied. "I thought we were just being mean to one another."

Celeste stood and took his face in her hands. "You are very dear to me, Charles," she told him earnestly. "And though I might miss our," she paused for a moment, "bedroom escapades, I just feel it is the best thing for our friendship if we keep it," again she paused and took a step back, hands falling at her sides, "somewhat normal."

"Nothing about our friendship is normal, Celeste."

She gave a slight shrug. "At any rate, I feel it is simply for the best, for now anyway."

"Does it have anything to do with your father?" he asked her.

Celeste laughed. "No," she told him firmly. "You know I defy him any chance I can get. No, this is all my doing."

As if their speaking of him summoned him, Celeste's father's voice could be heard in the hall talking sternly with one of the servants.

"The devil himself," Charles mumbled.

Celeste gave him a small smile.

"I should go before he sees me then," he told her, planting a kiss on her forehead. "I will be thinking about you later."

"A whole thirty seconds?" Celeste retorted. "You really know how to make a girl blush."

Charles gave a laugh as he opened a window and

jumped out.

Celeste smiled after him and watched him go until her father came through the doors.

"Ah, you are here," her father, Andrew Willoughby, said in greeting.

"Strange having a daughter living in the same house as you and seeing her from time to time, is it not?" she replied turning to him.

He forced a small smile. "As loving as ever."

Celeste looked her father up and down. "You are dressed for travel," she observed. "Where are you going?"

"To London," he replied.

"Oh," Celeste replied unfeelingly.

"I was invited by the widowed Duchess Natasha to stay with her for a few weeks."

"Ah, the lonely widow," Celeste responded. "Your favorite prey."

Her father gave her a stern look. "Seems her brother, Count Orkoff, is visiting her for a few months from Russia."

"How wonderfully droll sounding, father. I hope you have an amazing time."

"Yes, well, if all goes well, I will be inviting them to stay with us for a month," he told her.

"A month?" Celeste repeated, her face contorted in displeasure. "A whole month with people in our house?"

"Yes, in our house," he replied. "That is what you do when you invite people to stay with you."

Celeste poured herself a port at the thought. "But a month?" she repeated taking a long sip. "Seems excessive, does it not?"

"I think it a fair amount of time."

Celeste gave a small nod. "And how long are *you* gone

for?"

"A fortnight, perhaps more," he replied. "Short enough so as not to give you enough time to throw another masquerade while I am away."

Celeste waved her hand. "There is always enough time to throw a masquerade, father," she told him with a sly smile. "I keep partially filled out invitations just for occasions such as this."

Her father let out a sigh. "I wish one day you would grow up, Celeste."

"Father, please," she started, taking another sip, "we both know you do not want me to grow up. You just want me married and out of your life."

Her father's face twitched. "And, yet, here you are, a woman of twenty-five and still no husband!" he started.

Celeste refrained from rolling her eyes in a bored manner.

"You should have been married years ago! How many proposals have you turned down over the years? Three?"

"Four, no, five," she told him.

"Five?" Her father's face went red.

"I guess I forgot to tell you about a couple," Celeste said with a shrug. "The latest one was the Earl, the one that was going bankrupt due to his gambling debts and bad investments." She gave a shrug and small sigh. "Going bankrupt seems the fashion these days. Men with old money squandering their family's fortunes that their ancestors spent decades killing for."

"Are you speaking of Earl Winstead?" her father asked in a shaky voice. "Earl Winstead proposed to you and you refused?"

Celeste took another sip from her glass and savored the flavor. "Yes," she finally replied.

Her father put a hand on the back of a chair to steady himself. "He comes from an ancient family, Celeste. His family name can be traced back to the Norman invasion."

"No one cares about ancient family names anymore, father." She drained her glass and put it down on a side table. "Besides, I am not so pathetic as not to realize he only wanted my money so he could save that precious family name." She rolled her eyes this time.

"You are a most aggravating child!" her father exclaimed. "You will never find a husband you consider worthy of you and will die an old maid!"

Celeste grinned at her father. "I might die old, yes, but not a maid."

Her father's face turned even redder as he let out a scream of frustration. "Must you constantly rub your bed hopping in my face?"

"Must you constantly rub yours in mine?" Celeste shot back.

"No one will ever want to marry such a woman as you!" he yelled at her.

Celeste laughed. "Trust me, father, with as much money as I will receive upon your death, there is not a man out there who truly cares whether I have lain with one or a thousand men."

"I swear, child, I will have you locked away and the key to release you destroyed!"

Celeste walked up to her father and kissed him on his forehead. "Now, we both know you would never do such a thing. How would the Willoughby name be perceived by others if you had your own daughter sent to the mad house?"

Her father breathed quickly in and out of his nose, anger flashing in his eyes. "Mark my words, child," he proclaimed, stamping a foot and pointing a finger at her. "If you are not engaged by the year's end, I will have you thrown away for promiscuity!"

Celeste took a step back from her father, giving a small laugh. "Same threat, different day."

"I mean it this time!" he all but shouted. "I am tired of your flitting about and doing as you please, so maybe a stint in the asylum will straighten you out."

Celeste regarded her father with caution. He was keen on making similar empty threats, but this time was different. She knew her father's moods, knew what to say or do to get him riled up, but she had never seen him as determined as this before.

After a few moments, she forced a smile on her face. "Better hurry, father, your lonely widow will be wanting you." She walked stiffly past him to the doors.

"I mean it, Celeste," her father called after her in a softer, yet stern tone. "I *will* have you locked away."

"Have a safe journey to London, sir. Do have the widow pick me out that fine muslin from last time," she replied not turning to look at him.

Her father huffed. "No parties while I am gone!"

Celeste waved a hand as she left the room without a response.

3

"You are throwing a ball?" Amanda Haderly asked excitedly when Celeste handed her an invitation later that day.

"Yes," Celeste replied putting her tea cup back down. "A week from today."

"Such short notice?" Margaret asked.

"You know how I love spontaneity, and the whim to throw my own ball ran away with me this morning," Celeste told her.

Amanda Haderly, a young girl of seventeen, having just come out into society a few months before, beamed at her invitation. Margaret, on the other hand, put it down with nothing more than a polite smile.

The gesture was not lost on Celeste. "I hope you both will come as my guests of honor," she told them. "I will have the best rooms for you to stay the night and we can all get ready together." She turned to Amanda. "I might even have a dress from Paris you could wear, Amanda, if you would like."

"Really?" Amanda asked almost breathlessly.

"It is a few years old, but Parisian dresses never go out of style."

The young girl's eyes sparkled at the thought.

"For you, Margaret," Celeste continued, turning to her friend, "I am going to take you to Mrs. Parson's shop and have a whole new dress made."

"Celeste," Margaret replied softly, "is that all not a bit too much?"

"No," Celeste replied defiantly. "I think it just enough."

Tea continued in almost the same fashion with Celeste doing most of the talking. She talked about her dresses and what food she expected to serve at her ball and even all of the men she was going to invite.

"Amanda, this must be exciting for you," Celeste continued. "Was not Sir Walter's ball your first?"

The young girl nodded gleefully. "It was very diverting. I have never been half so entertained before."

"I remember *my* first ball," Celeste told her. "It was at Mr. and Mrs. Farrell's. I danced half the night away. I can still remember how my feet ached."

"Yes!" Amanda exclaimed. "I thought I would finally die from exhaustion when I got home!"

"Well, let us hope your second ball is just as successful!"

"Two balls in less than a month!" Amanda almost squealed. "What luck!"

Celeste looked at the young girl, satisfied with herself.

"It does seem rather close to the other ball, Celeste," Margaret finally chimed in. "It will only be just over a week since Sir Walter's. Are you sure people will want to attend?"

Celeste tried to hide her disappointment at her friend's remark. "I cannot see why not. I have invited several people who were not there last night or even invited."

Margaret nodded, but gave her friend a strange look, sensing something was going on.

Celeste shifted uncomfortably in her seat, ignoring Margaret's looks. "Was there anyone you danced with last night in whom you took a particular interest, Amanda?" she asked, sipping her tea again.

Amanda blushed. "Well, there were a few men I found more interesting than the others."

"Oh?" Celeste said, her interest piqued.

"Mr. Prescott was quite charming, I thought."

"Oh, he is a very sweet young man," Celeste informed her. "I have never heard a harsh word about him or from him."

"But I believe I fancied Mr. Browning more."

Margaret choked on her tea at the mention of the name.

"Stephen Browning?" Celeste asked a little surprised. "He is a character."

"He danced with me twice last night."

Celeste cleared her throat with a smile. "That is quite adventurous for Mr. Browning."

Margaret nudged Celeste under the table.

"Do you not like him?" Amanda asked sheepishly.

"Stephen?" Celeste said. "Stephen and I get along very well. I have known him for a long time. And if you wish it, I will insist on him being at my ball."

A large smile rose from the young girl's lips, not an attractive smile, but the hideous kind one sometimes gets when they are unable to fully control their facial expressions. It made her small features look hollowed out and dark. She was not usually unattractive, no, normally the young girl had a brightness to her, a sense of wonderment and awe that livened her features. But that fool's smile has a way of distorting one's face and making it seem half formed and the owner simple. Celeste decided she must show her how to control it.

Amanda left soon after tea, but Celeste had convinced Margaret to stay for supper, claiming she would be "awful lonely" eating by herself. So, her friend dutifully stayed.

"Are you angry with Mr. Browning?" Margaret asked her, watching Amanda ride away on her horse.

"Should I be?" Celeste replied.

"Well, do you not like him?"

"Did I not express that earlier?"

Margaret lifted a brow at her. "I mean *like* him," she clarified.

"Ah," Celeste said catching on. "He has his attractions, but it is far from *like* that I feel for Mr. Browning."

Margaret shook her head. "I fail to understand you sometimes, Celeste."

Celeste hooked her arm in her friend's and led her back into the house. "Perhaps, I do not want to be understood, Margaret."

Margaret looked at her friend. "Do we not all wish to be understood by at least someone?"

Celeste looked at her as well. "Sometimes it is just best to be understood by ourselves."

Margaret shifted her gaze down a bit and nodded. "I agree," she replied softly.

"At any rate, I believe I must speak with Stephen about Amanda. I know how he can be."

"Amanda seems like a very sweet girl," Margaret replied.

Celeste nodded. "Yes, and young, and naïve, and completely ignorant about the wiles of men." Celeste thought for a moment. "Perhaps I will make her my creature."

"Your creature?" Margaret repeated with a small laugh.

"Yes, I shall teach her everything I know about capturing a man's interest and then leaving him in the wind when she is done with him."

"You have never tried to do so with me," Margaret told her more as a remark than out of jealousy.

"That is because I prefer you just the way you are, Margaret," Celeste told her genuinely. "You are the too good to my too bad. You balance me."

Margaret laughed.

"Now, I fully expect you to entertain me on the piano while we wait for dinner."

"You want me to back off of Miss Haderly?" Stephen asked Celeste the next evening.

Celeste took his cigar from him and took a puff, nodding as she blew out the smoke. "I do," she replied.

Stephen smiled as he ran his hand over her bare skin. "Are you jealous?" he teased.

Celeste arched an eyebrow when his hand reached lower. "Stephen, you know I have not a jealous bone in my body," she responded. "I am a free spirit. If you want to bed another woman, I will not care. I will not share you, of course, but I will not be broken hearted."

"Then why ask me to back off?" he asked leaning in to kiss her neck.

Celeste closed her eyes and tilted her head, allowing his lips to roam her skin. "Because she is a sweet girl and I will not see you ruin her. Bedding young girls is not a game."

"Oh, yes, it is," he replied, continuing to caress her under the sheets. "And it is a game I very much enjoy."

Celeste gave a small gasp as his fingers slipped inside

her. She took another puff of the cigar before putting it down in the holder and allowing him free range of her body. "It might be a game to you, but, to her, it is not."

"No more talking," he said softly, but sternly. "You know how I abhor it while I am in action." He pulled her closer.

"Were you not already 'in action'?" she asked with an amused smirk.

He kissed her breast and flicked her nipple with his tongue. "You know I have to have you at least twice," he replied pushing himself up and moving toward her.

Stephen was on top of her now, spreading her legs so he could enter. As he lowered himself to her, Celeste wrapped her legs around his waist and pulled him in, making him let out a small moan. She held him there for a moment before she pushed off with her hip and, with him still inside of her, flipped him over on his back.

He uttered a small cry of surprise but grinned playfully when he looked up at her on top of him. "Oh," he said moving his hands to her hips, "a new move. I like it." He sat up to try and kiss her, but she put a hand on his chest to stop him.

"Miss Haderly is not one of those poor foxes you hunt, Stephen," she told him sternly. "I will not see you ruin the poor girl. She is too sweet for you."

Stephen laughed. "Alright," he replied laying back and manually moving Celeste back and forth. "If I can still have you in my bed from time to time, I promise I will abandon my hunt of Miss Haderly."

Celeste squeezed her thighs against him and peeled his hands away, entwining her fingers in his. "You will be no more than friendly?" she asked lifting herself up slightly and coming back down slowly.

Stephen breathed in sharply through his nose, laying his head back further. "Yes," he replied almost breathlessly as Celeste continued that movement. "I promise."

"Touching will go no further than dancing?"

Stephen nodded, his eyes closed as he moaned. "No touching."

"Good," Celeste replied, lowering herself down and biting his neck playfully. "Then, shall we finish?"

Stephen opened his eyes, wrapping his arms around her and sitting up, kissing her hard. "Absolutely."

4

It always confused and sometimes appalled Celeste that she could have become such close friends with someone so different from her. It was not appalling to her that *she* was friends with someone like Margaret, but that someone like Margaret could be friends with *her*.

Margaret was reserved, kind, unassuming, and as non-judgmental as a human could be, while Celeste, except for the occasional random act of kindness, was none of those things. She was as free a spirit as one could be in the Victorian era, an age marked with sexual frustration and murderous intentions.

In a time when women of means were expected to remain pure until the bonds of marriage gave them the opportunity to explore the missionary position, Celeste found herself giving into her physical desires and the men who stirred them. She was not an emotional person. Of course, she had her monthly mood swings, but it rarely roused more than a few tears from her at a time.

No, she was a stalwart flirt, able to charm and choose from the men around her. She was not so licentious, however, to just give herself so easily, but was nowhere near prudish enough to always care when the urge hit her.

That is why Margaret and her being so close confused her so much. Margaret was by no means ignorant of Celeste's exploits. Celeste never went into full detail about them, for Margaret's gentle nature could not withstand the particulars, her face flushing the color of crimson every time, but she shared enough to not keep her in the dark. And even though Margaret was rather devout in her faith (and only gently scolded Celeste on occasion) she did not always object to her friend's impropriety.

It was true; Margaret did not, *could* not, understand how her friend seemed to be so unattached to these men she gave herself to no more than Celeste could understand how Margaret was still heartbroken over that worthless man who had left her for another. But, they set their differences aside for one another.

Yes, they were different. Socially, they were in different classes. Celeste was of a higher social standing, living lavishly, while Margaret lived more modestly in the upper-middle class. In most cases, Margaret's stern Catholic upbringing would certainly clash with Celeste's live-by-your-fancy lifestyle, but it was their differences that truly bound them together. Margaret helped stabilize Celeste, while Celeste helped broaden Margaret's social circle and encourage her to open up.

They both saw each other as guarded, though in different ways. Celeste saw Margaret too guarded in her thoughts, while Margaret saw Celeste too guarded in her feelings.

Celeste's feelings for Charles was an example.

Charles had been Celeste's first when she was only Amanda Haderly's age. It was not long after her loving mother passed away, and Charles, though willing, was hesitant, but Celeste had insisted. After that, they began to meet frequently in secret, sneaking out into the night and climbing through windows or up balconies to meet.

Celeste assured Margaret, who had not known of this affair for a full year, that it was not love, but a different kind of longing that kept her going back to Charles. It went on and off for years and did not stop even when her father had caught them in the act.

Curses and fists had flown as her father threw the young man across the room and threatened his life with violence of the most extreme kind, but it did nothing to stop their meetings. If anything, it put in Celeste the want to venture even further with other men and gave her a lack of subtlety toward it.

She knew it boiled her father's blood, but if ever he mentioned her misdoings, she threw his own back in his face; his lack of loyalty toward her mother was her favorite weapon to hurl. Their arguments were often heated, fueled by stubbornness on both sides.

Margaret had witnessed such an argument once. She had called on Celeste when the shouting started and Mr. Willoughby stormed out of the room threatening to have his daughter carried away to the asylum. It had been a terrifying display for Margaret, but Celeste laughed it off as if it were nothing.

For the most part, Celeste was an open book. She said what she thought and did almost as she pleased. Margaret did neither of those things. Often enough, Celeste had to pry her open to get her to say anything she was thinking and even then, she believed Margaret was not always telling her the full story.

There was a somber mystery with Margaret.

It had never been so apparent how mysterious

Margaret was until she met John Howard. Celeste had never seen her friend show interest in anyone before he came around. He was all smiles and bows and polite conversations which Celeste found rather tiresome, but Margaret seemed enamored. They often went on long walks together or rode their horses. They were never fully alone of course. That would have been improper. No, they were constantly chaperoned by Mr. Howard's beautiful, young widowed cousin, Irene Samson.

She was the interesting one, Celeste had always thought. She was witty and quick, and, right up to the point she ran off with John, Celeste had liked her. But Irene had hurt her friend in the cruelest of ways and was doomed to be cursed by Celeste until her dying breath. Celeste half believed the woman had killed her husband herself, and secretly wished she would do the same to John for using her friend so ill.

The worst of it was that Margaret, who had finally began to blossom, illuminated by the aura that love gives off, had dug herself deeper into her hole almost refusing to come out at all.

Celeste hurt for her. It was true, she did not fully understand the heartache a lost love can give you, her mother being the only person she lost whom she cared for, but seeing her friend suffer stirred something in her she couldn't explain. A bitter taste in her mouth, perhaps, or an uncomfortableness.

And now, her only true friend, other than Charles, wanted to leave her for a convent, to surround herself with prude, bitter old women. It was not sound. Margaret was the only level-headed voice in her life. She was the only one whose advice—though Celeste rarely followed it—made sense.

There was honestly no reason for it other than to run away, to hide herself from the rest of the world. Well, Celeste could not have it. She could not lose her friend to such foolishness, to such strictness of rules, to such—such— such a hideous wardrobe.

Celeste knew little about love, but knew that with time, heartaches do heal. So that was all she needed, to buy herself a little time.

Celeste was not sure what she could do to stop her friend, but she knew she had to do something. Thus, she did the only thing she knew how to do better than anyone else; she threw a party. And whatever Celeste did she did it well and she did it with the utmost extravagance.

5

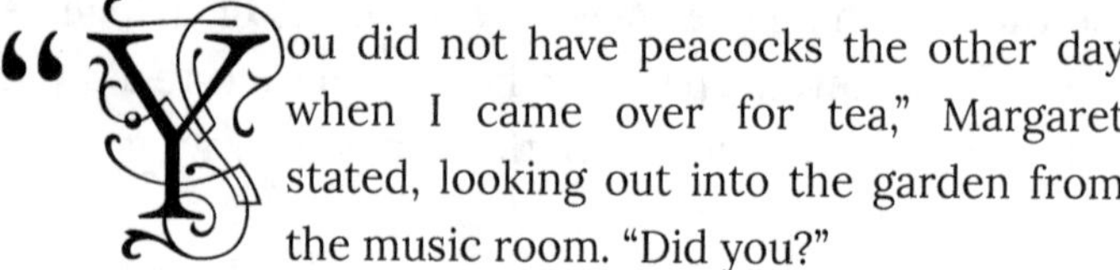

“You did not have peacocks the other day when I came over for tea,” Margaret stated, looking out into the garden from the music room. “Did you?”

“I did not,” Celeste informed her. “And, technically, I still do not. Those are Sir Edwards’s birds.”

“Why are Sir Edwards’s peacocks in your garden?”

“I am borrowing them for my ball,” Celeste replied. “I visited with him for two hours yesterday. He called me the most industrious flirt he has ever met.” She smiled to herself.

“You have not,” Margaret paused and turned to her, “you know, had *relations* with Sir Edwards, have you?”

Celeste laughed. “Absolutely not!” she proclaimed trying to catch her breath. “Oh, heavens, Margaret, you do amuse me. ‘*Relations*,’ you said with such emphasis, yet you whispered it as if anyone was here to hear you.”

Margaret only blinked at her friend, unsure what was so amusing.

“Rest assured though,” Celeste began, “I have never, and will never, bed Sir Edwards. The man is a toad.”

“He has always been kind to me,” Margaret said.

"Well, yes, he is kind to all the young pretty women and girls," Celeste replied. "But he expects too much from them." She stretched and stood, joining her friend by the window.

Margaret nodded staring at the peacocks. "What do you need them for though?"

"Live decoration."

Margaret lifted a brow at her friend. "You do not think them too excessive?"

"Excessive is *not* a term I am familiar with," Celeste replied with a smile. "They are beautiful creatures but make the most awful noises."

As if on cue, one of the birds let out a loud squawking noise causing both of the women to jump.

Celeste pressed her hand to her chest. "Awful things."

Margaret gave a small laugh.

"Now, we have to discuss what you will be wearing to my ball," Celeste said turning to Margaret. "If you will not let me buy you a new dress, at least let me give you one of my newer ones."

Margaret lifted a brow and pursed her lips at her friend. "I am not sure it will fit."

"Of course, we will have to take it out some around the bust area, but we can make it work," she reassured her.

"Celeste, why can I not wear one of my dresses?" Margaret asked.

"Because," Celeste replied taking the champagne one of her servants brought over and handing Margaret the other glass, "you have not bought a new dress in over a year."

"That is not true."

"Mh," Celeste started taking a sip. "The last dress you

bought was for Arabelle Weston's wedding *last* May. It is now June the following year and I have yet to see you in anything new since then."

Margaret gaped at her friend. "How can you possibly know that?"

"I know because I care, my dear," Celeste replied gently touching Margaret's arm. "I know because I have seen you in the same five, no," she held up a finger, "six dresses, I try to forget about the one with that terribly high neck. So, six dresses for the week, then you have your two Sunday dresses, and maybe three party dresses."

"I like that dress with the high neck; it is modest."

"It is an abomination."

Margaret frowned pitifully.

"At any rate, I want to gift you with another party dress, and maybe even a few more if you wish. I have at least two I have never worn."

"Celeste, you are very generous, but-"

"Good, because I believe I hear Gerald coming to announce that Mrs. Parson is here to refit the dresses for you."

"What?" Margaret said turning around just as the door to the room was opened.

It was indeed Gerald announcing the seamstress and several other servants carrying a partition, and a number of Celeste's dresses for Margaret to try.

"Are we to do it in here?" Margaret asked looking around.

"Well, the lighting is better in this room," Celeste explained motioning to all of the windows, "making adjustments a lot easier than if it were in the dimly lit rooms upstairs."

Margaret, whose eyes were wide with hesitation,

looked around the room at all of the people.

"Oh, do not worry about them," Celeste said with a wave of her hand. "Once they are done setting up, it will only be you, Mrs. Parson, and myself."

"But the windows," Margaret whispered. "What if someone were to walk by?"

Celeste put her hands up. "You are not to worry. No one is working on this side of the house. So, you are safe from anyone trying to steal a peek. Except for the peacocks, perhaps."

Margaret blushed from her neck to her forehead. "Do not tease me so, Celeste," she replied.

Celeste repressed a laugh by gently pressing the back of her hand to her lips. "I promise, you will not be shamed on my watch."

"Are we to start? Or are we just going to stand about going over the rules of modesty?" came the impatient voice of Mrs. Parson, a middle-aged hard looking woman. Celeste always found it sad that her personality never reflected the same beauty as her dresses. She was a harsh, down-to-brass-tacks kind of woman who did not appreciate her time being wasted.

"Yes, Mrs. Parson," Celeste told her. "We are going to start."

"Good," the stoic, little woman beside them said. "Then dress so I can adjust."

Celeste exchanged a glance with Margaret, trying to hide a smirk at the woman's bossiness.

"Move, don't just stand there!" Mrs. Parson said again. "We have work to do."

"Yes," Celeste said stepping forward and picking up a dark green dress with a subtle lace trim. "I believe this will brighten your brown eyes and complement the almond coloring in your hair."

Margaret took the dress in her hands and blinked at it. "Celeste, this is so intricate. Are you sure you wish to give it to me?"

"Absolutely," she replied. "The color, though beautiful, does nothing for my complexion." She turned to Mrs. Parson. "We will start with this one."

The woman nodded and hastily took Margaret by the arm, pulling her behind the partition to help undress and dress her. Margaret gave a small squeal of surprise as she was all but dragged across the room to the corner where her makeshift dressing room was set up.

Celeste snorted into her champagne as she watched it all.

"First, I will take your measurements," Mrs. Parson told her aggressively. "Then you will put on the dress and I will make note of what needs to be altered on it."

"Yes," Margaret said sheepishly to the woman who was used to taking charge.

"Then, I will take the dresses back to my shop and make the necessary alterations."

Margaret nodded.

Celeste listened to it all trying her best to keep a straight face, but it was no use. She could not help but laugh at the situation in which she had put her friend. Mrs. Parson could certainly be a very frightful woman.

"Is it fitting alright?" Celeste asked after a few minutes.

"Your friend is quite bustier than you," Mrs. Parson responded without hesitation. "I will need to re-hem all of the dresses as well since she is also shorter by several inches."

"Are the alterations doable?"

Mrs. Parson stepped out from behind the partition so

she could give Celeste her most serious of looks. "Yes, of course," she replied with more contempt than Celeste had ever heard before, her eyes daring her to question her again.

Celeste forced a smile. "Yes, of course," she repeated. "I would not have hired you for the job if I thought you were not capable."

Mrs. Parson gave a curt nod and vanished once again behind the partition to finish her job. A few minutes later, she asked for the next dress which Celeste handed over as quickly as she could.

"Do you need anything, Margaret?" Celeste asked. "Your champagne is still out here barely touched."

"No drinking while I am working on you!" Mrs. Parson shot back without letting Margaret say anything.

Celeste shrugged and drained the remainder of her glass before picking up Margaret's and sipping on hers.

"After you are done being fitted, I thought we could take a walk to the clearing and have a picnic," Celeste said, watching the peacocks strut to-and-fro, pecking at the ground and dragging their incandescent tails behind them.

"That sounds won—"

"Do not talk!" Mrs. Parson barked. "You will ruin my measurements. You can talk when I am done."

Celeste pressed her lips together to keep from laughing, remaining over by the window until she was ordered to bring the next dress to Mrs. Parson.

When the fittings were over, about an hour and five dresses later, Mrs. Parson hurriedly gathered her things.

"I will send my bill," she replied as she moved to the door. "The dresses will be done in about two weeks."

"Oh, except—"

"Except the dark green dress which you have already requested to have done in five days," Mrs. Parson continued, cutting her off.

"You are most efficient, Mrs. Parson," Celeste told her. "And you are now to—"

"I am now to Miss Haderly's to fit her for a dress," Mrs. Parson said, again cutting her off. "The dress is in the carriage you provided for me then?"

"No, I had it sent over this morning to her house. It is already there waiting for you."

"Good," she said, her hand on the door handle.

"Thank you, Mrs. Parson, for your help!"

The woman waved, her reply cut off by the shutting of the door.

"I very much like that woman," Celeste said still looking at the door she had exited.

"She is truly terrifying," Margaret replied. "I scarce took a full breath while she worked on me. She is very fierce."

Celeste laughed through her nose. "Come," she said taking her friend by the arm. "I had Gerald prepare our picnic while we waited, so we only need to get there." Celeste led her out of the doors leading to the gardens and breathed in the warm summer air.

"Your father's roses are starting to bud already," Margaret pointed out.

Celeste nodded. "Yes, he is very proud of them as you know."

It was Margaret's turn to nod.

"He is off to London for two weeks," Celeste informed her.

"I assumed he was away," Margaret replied. "You only ever throw parties when your father is absent and most certainly after he has told you not to."

Celeste smiled at this caricature of herself.

"You both are quite hard on each other."

Celeste shot her friend a sideways glance. "Perhaps we do not have the typical father-daughter relationship, but it is the only way we know how to show affection."

Margaret blinked at her friend. "I am not sure you understand the word 'affection,'" she replied.

Celeste gave a sigh wanting to bring up the one topic of conversation she didn't know how to. She wanted to talk about Margaret's desire to join a convent. No, not *desire*; it couldn't possibly be that. Could she even use the word want? She was not even sure how to define this situation, because if it wasn't a *want* and it certainly wasn't a *need*, what could she classify this as? A curiosity? A whim? A momentary lapse in judgment?

She decided it could be nothing other than that and was resolved to finally bring it up when, after reaching the end of the row of hedges a horrible squall broke through their silence.

The two women screamed, hitching up their skirts to run when one of Sir Edwards's peacocks walked out in front of them.

"Oh, wretched birds!" Celeste yelled shooing it away while Margaret laughed.

Celeste turned at the sound.

"That is the first genuine laugh I have heard come from you in several months," she told her.

Margaret smiled sheepishly. "I know I have been rather melancholy lately."

"You have been positively depressing."

Margaret didn't reply.

"I do not blame you, of course," Celeste told her.

"I know."

There was another brief silence.

"Are you truly thinking about taking the veil?" Celeste finally asked.

There was a short pause. "I am," Margaret replied with soft conviction. "I think it is only right that I should."

"But why should you think that?" Celeste pressed. "I am trying to understand, but there is just no reason for it."

Margaret sighed. "Does one really *need* a reason to want to be closer to God?"

"Of course not," Celeste replied. "But how does shutting yourself off from the world and the pleasures provided for us *by* God bring you any closer to him?"

"There is no shame in humbling yourself and doing God's work."

Celeste patted her hand. "No, I agree, there is no shame, but can you not do God's work without promising yourself to a life of celibacy and boredom?"

"I do not believe it will be a life of boredom," Margaret told her firmly, "but a life of solitude from life's distractions, a life of service."

Celeste pouted.

"And there is a convent in Scotland up in the mountains where the air is fresh, and the trees are plentiful, and the sunrises and sunsets are magnificent."

"Do we not have trees?" Celeste started. "Do we not have sunrises or sunsets? We might not have mountains so close by, but we do have some very tall hills."

Margaret softly laughed and squeezed her friend's arm. "It warms me to know you are so hesitant to let me leave."

"Should I not?" Celeste asked her, pausing in their

walk for a moment to turn and look at her. “You are my most intimate friend and I cannot bear to think you so far away being miserable and surrounded by miserable old women.”

“Nuns are not miserable!” Margaret almost laughed. “They are humble.”

Celeste sighed and resumed walking. “Honestly, I do not know how they cannot be miserable.”

“Why?” Margaret asked raising a brow at her friend. “Because they cannot lie with a man?”

Celeste waved a hand. “Oh, no, I am sure one can live without that just fine,” she responded. “But you will not be allowed to go to balls, or gamble, or wear clothes to show off the glorious figure the Lord has blessed you with.”

Margaret laughed again. “Though I am fond of dancing, I believe I can live well enough without the latter two.”

“But what about me?” Celeste almost whined. “I shall miss you. I will have no one to ground me if you leave.”

“Oh, Celeste, I would miss you too, but I cannot pretend that I am happy.”

“Oh, who is actually happy?” Celeste blurted out. “What is life but suffering and pretending to be happy.”

“*You* are not happy?”

Celeste gave a shake of her head. “I was generalizing, of course.”

“Of course,” Margaret repeated.

“I just do not know why you would go so far away to serve God,” Celeste continued. “You can serve God anywhere, including here.”

“Perhaps, Celeste, you need to learn what it is to serve God,” Margaret told her. “Maybe you should try visiting with the vicar more often and talk about it."

Celeste failed to suppress a smile. "Oh, I have," she replied coyly. "Four times, though I would not call it 'talking.'"

Margaret stopped walking to gape at her friend. "You cannot be serious?" she asked incredulously. "Tell me you have not!"

Celeste presented another one of her famous waves of the hand. "Oh, do not be so surprised, my dear." She tilted her head slightly and trailed her fingertips along her neck as she looked back on her 'visit.' "I was rather amazed to be honest. I did not think the vicar would be so," she bit her lip for a moment, "fervent."

Margaret pressed her hands to her cheeks as the color rose in them. "I cannot believe it. Vicar Harris?"

"Of course, Vicar Harris!" Celeste told her. "You do not suppose I would have lain with his predecessor Vicar James, do you? That man was at least a hundred when I was born."

Margaret shook her head. "Vicar Harris. I cannot believe it."

Celeste smirked at her friend. "If it makes you feel better, you can think of it as me having done the Lord's work."

Margaret looked sharply at her friend. "I cannot see how."

Celeste pursed her lips at her. "Religious men need a *release* every bit as much as regular men do."

Margaret pressed her hand to her forehead as the flushing of her face rose. "Celeste, honestly, you are incorrigible."

"Yes, well, so was the vicar," she replied with a grin. "I found the act a lot more pleasurable than I thought I would. I guess all of his suppressed desires fueled him. What he lacked in experience, he surely made up in enthusiasm."

Margaret fanned her face with her hand. "And is he not to wed soon?"

"Do not fret, Margaret," Celeste reassured her. "This was over a year ago before he proposed to Miss Smith. I do make it a point not to mess with attached men."

Margaret shook her head again. "I cannot believe you do not blush when you are telling me these things."

Celeste laughed. "Why should I when I have you to do all of the blushing for me?" She took her friend's arm again and gently pulled her along the path. "And, I dare say, you look all the prettier for it. You should be thanking me for doing nothing more than enhancing your beauty."

Margaret gave her friend a side glance.

"Now, instead of you joining a convent, I would very much like to use that enhancement to help you find a husband."

Margaret huffed out of her nose. "Why must I marry when it has never been good enough for you?"

"Is marriage not a godly constitution?" Celeste shot back.

"Yes, but—"

"Is it not supposed to save us from the sin of fornication?"

"Well, you are one to talk," Margaret stated delicately. "And why should I marry to save myself from fornication if you, who has received at least five proposals, refuse to do so?"

"We are a different breed," Celeste told her.

"What if I do not want to marry anyone as you do?"

"Oh, Margaret, you are too good of a person not to

find happiness in married life," Celeste explained.

Margaret shook her head. "I disagree," she replied. "I deserve no more than the next person."

"See!" Celeste exclaimed. "That right there proves my point. You are destined to wed a handsome man and have impossibly handsome children. I will bet on it."

Margaret grew silent.

"Give me until the end of the year," Celeste finally said, breaking into Margaret's thoughts. "That is just over six months. Give me that long to find you someone."

"Celeste, please—"

"No, Margaret, I am serious," she insisted. "This whole joining a convent thing came about because of your broken heart. Well, let me find someone who can mend it and if by the end of the year I cannot," she paused, "and you still want to throw your life away, I will not stand in your way."

"You mean it?"

Celeste gave a single nod. "I do. I will not stop you if that is truly what you wish by the end of this year."

Margaret smiled at her friend. "Alright," she agreed. "You have until the end of the year."

"And who knows what six months can bring," Celeste continued. "Perhaps we will both be engaged."

Margaret looked at her curiously.

"But that is a small matter. It is you I am worried about."

"Will you be able to find me a man with whom you have not lain?" Margaret asked her teasingly.

Celeste, taking no offense, simply nodded pensively. "We might have to look a few counties out, but I am sure I can manage."

Margaret gasped. "Verily, you must be joking!" she

exclaimed.

Celeste could not help but laugh at her. "Of course, I am only teasing!" she replied. "I do have standards, you know? I do not let every man walk through my door."

Margaret gave an exasperated sigh. "You are unbelievable."

Celeste grinned. "I know."

"Do you not worry about your soul or God's judgment in all of this?" she asked in an agitated voice.

Celeste narrowed her eyes pensively and gave a small shrug. "Is God not a forgiving god?" she replied.

"Yes, you know he is."

"Then I do not see the problem," Celeste told her matter-of-factly. "I ask for forgiveness regularly and if you ask, does God not provide?"

"Yes, but that is not how the Lord works!" Margaret proclaimed. "You are supposed to resist sin, not give into temptation."

"If that is not how the Lord works then he is not a forgiving God, is he?" Celeste retorted. "I am but a frail human, Margaret. What can you or anyone expect?"

Margaret gave her a cross look.

"Besides," Celeste continued, "if fornication was so awful, it would be one of the ten commandments. The eleventh, perhaps." She gave an approving nod and smirked. "Thou shall not fornicate before thou hast wed."

Margaret gave another fretful sigh. "You are impossible," she said, shaking her head. "There is not an argument I make that you do not have an answer for."

Celeste smiled triumphantly. "Father tells me if I were a man, I would have made a great solicitor."

"I am inclined to agree with him."

"Ah, finally, there is Gerald waiting for us," Celeste

said pointing to the opening in the woods. "I am quite famished."

6

harles looked at Celeste, a confused expression on his face. "What are you doing in my house?" he asked her as she walked into his parlor.

Celeste raised a brow at him. "Am I not allowed?" she asked in reply.

"You are," Charles started hesitantly. "I just cannot remember the last time I saw you here."

Celeste rolled her eyes. "It has only been about two months," she informed him.

"Two months is a long time not to come to a friend's house when they live but a few miles, is it not? Especially when said friend goes to your house so often."

"Would you prefer that I leave?" Celeste asked him, pointing at the door.

He narrowed his eyes at her. "No, but I do wish to know why you are here. It must be something important or completely ridiculous."

"And I shall tell you, but first, will you not offer me something to drink?"

He pointed to a cabinet along the wall with several

bottles and glasses on it. "Drinks are over there, where they normally are."

"Well," Celeste said in a scolding tone, "that is one way to treat a lady."

"You never offer me a drink when I am at your house," he told her.

"I never have to," she retorted moving to the cabinet and choosing one of the carafes. "You make your own drink without hesitation."

"Yes, well," he paused thinking of what to say, "you are just as capable of making your own."

Celeste walked back over handing him a drink. "You are in a rare mood," she said. "Can I ask what is the matter or are you going to make me come up with that myself as well?"

Charles crossed his arms over his chest in a guarded manner, ignoring the proffered drink. "I would prefer neither to tell you nor have you guess."

Celeste put his drink down on a side table and took a sip from hers. "Fine," she told him. "This certainly does not make me want to come back here."

"I am not obligated to share anything with you."

"Yes, I agree, but you do not have to treat me so rudely either," she retorted. "Am I the cause of these ill feelings or was it something else and you are just taking everything out on me?"

Charles shifted uncomfortably where he stood. "You went to see Stephen Browning again," he finally stated.

Celeste looked at him, unblinking. "Yes, I have," she replied. "How did you get wind of it?"

"I thought you were done with him."

Celeste frowned at him. "We sometimes dabble."

Charles shook his head. "Browning is bad news,

Celeste," he informed her sternly.

"Stephen is harmless," Celeste replied. "And you still did not answer me as to how you knew I went to see him."

Charles fidgeted. "I was on my way to see him the other day and I saw you walking out. Your face was flushed and your hair unusually blowsy."

"I have never hid my relations with Stephen from you," Celeste said.

"Yes, but I thought you would stop seeing him after I told you about his parties with the women of the night."

Celeste grinned. "You are telling me you have never dabbled in the occasional prostitute?"

Charles gave her a stern look. "I told you that one time in Paris was a mistake. I was completely drunk, and she did not tell me she was a whore until after the act."

Celeste laughed into her glass. "I am sure."

"But it was not the fact he was 'dabbling,' as you say, but how he was treating them," Charles explained. "He was abusive and disrespectful."

Celeste smiled approvingly at him. "Charles, you surprise me," she told him. "I did not know you were so progressive toward women's rights."

"It has nothing to do with all that," he told her. "It has everything to do with common decency that of which Browning has none."

"You are adorable when you are angry."

"Do not tease me," he said half pouting.

Celeste walked over to him and took his hand, giving it a squeeze. "I promise, I am not. I am very proud of you and your speech. But if you disapprove so of Stephen, why were *you* going to see him the other day?"

Charles looked down at her hand holding his and stroked it with his thumb. The strangeness of the action made Celeste take her hand back, though slowly.

"Browning had a card party the other week and he still owes me money," Charles finally told her. "I was hoping to collect on that debt."

"And did you?"

"No," he replied finally moving to pick up the drink she had poured for him. "I could not bring myself to go in."

"All because you saw me leave?" she asked skeptically. "I cannot imagine why that would have stopped you."

He cleared his throat. "What brought you here today?" he asked after a few sips of his drink.

Celeste batted her eyes at him. "Can I come here for nothing more than the pleasure of your company?"

"That would be nice, but I know you too well," Charles responded sipping from his glass.

She sighed. "Fine. I am here because I have yet to receive a reply from you about whether or not you are attending my party."

"I only received the invitation two days ago."

"Is that not a sufficient amount of time to reply?" she retorted.

"I suppose you expect me to come?"

She blinked at him. "Should I not?" she asked him hesitantly.

It was his turn to sigh. "Do you want me there?"

"Do I make it a habit of inviting people to my house whom I do not want there?"

He gave a small nod. "Then I will come."

"Good."

"Good."

Celeste looked about the room. "What happened to that new sofa your mother bought not a year ago?" she asked. "The other one that was over here?" She pointed to an empty spot in the arrangement of chairs and sofas.

Charles paled. “It, uh, needed cleaning,” he replied. “My mother spilled wine on it. It was a horrible stain.” He cleared his throat.

“Oh, how unusually clumsy of your mother,” Celeste replied. “Pity, it was quite comfortable.”

There was a strange awkward silence between them.

“Is there another reason you are here?” Charles asked her.

Celeste finally took a seat. “My father and I are at odds again,” she started. “He had told me that if I am not engaged by the end of this year, he will send me away to the mad house.”

“He has made such threats before.”

Celeste shook her head and looked down into her glass. “This was different,” she told him. “I could see the conviction and determination in his eyes, written all over his body language.” She paused to look back up at him. “I am inclined to think he might actually half mean it this time.”

“What are you to do?” he asked her, scratching the back of his neck. “Are you going to seriously look for a husband now?”

Celeste gave a weak smile. “I suppose I might have to,” she told him.

There was a brief pause.

“Perhaps we could marry?” Charles slowly suggested.

Celeste looked back down into her glass and gave a small laugh, failing to notice the hurt look on Charles’s face.

“Now you are teasing, Charles,” she scolded lightly. “I do not know what I am to do. But by the end of the year I have to find two men.”

"Two?"

She nodded. "One for Margaret, who promised if she were to fall in love with another man by the end of the year, she will not join a convent. And one for me, to keep me from being shipped off to some wretched place unworthy of my wit, beauty, and humor."

Charles opened his mouth like he wanted to say something but closed it again.

"I am at an utter loss as to what I should do," Celeste continued. "For Margaret, it will be easier, but for myself?" She shook her head. "I am a whole different story. I hold no stock in love and all of that."

"Your father did not say *you* had to fall in love, did he?" Charles asked.

"My father would not care if the man I married had a hump on his back, warts on his face, and beat me every Sunday just as long as his name meant something, and it took me off of *his* hands." She shook her head again. "No, my father does not care for my happiness in marriage. He just wants me married. One less problem for him to deal with."

"What if you married someone he disapproved of?"

"Oh, I suppose he would just disinherit me," she replied. "At any rate, he will make sure I am miserable no matter what the situation."

Charles put his glass back down, half full. "You and I—"

"Will have to figure something out together," Celeste said finishing what she thought he was going to say.

Charles nodded. "Yes, we will."

Celeste slipped her shoes off and stretched her legs out on the couch. She leaned back against the arm rest and sipped from her glass as if she had always belonged there. Charles watched her. He watched her stretch her long elegant legs out on his sofa and bring the amber liquid to her soft, red lips. He watched as her other hand trailed the pale skin of her neck as she often did when she was deep in thought. And he watched as her long, golden-orange hair, which she obviously refused to put up that morning, moved about her as if it had a life of its own.

He used to lose himself in that hair.

"Are you alright?" Celeste asked, breaking him from his thoughts.

Charles quickly looked away. "Why would I not be?" he replied as he picked his glass back up and drained it.

"You look rather flushed."

"It is *rather* warm in here," he responded.

"Then take your jacket off, Charles," she told him, lifting her hair off her neck and letting it cascade back down her shoulders. "It is only me here. There is no need to perambulate the rules of propriety."

Charles huffed as he watched her once again lift her hair off her neck and let it crash back down in waves. He swallowed hard.

"By the way," Celeste started turning on her side so she could look at him, "I forgot to ask you the other day, did you sleep with that Wilmington girl?"

Charles blushed again. "Why would you say that?"

"I saw you trying to pursue her at Sir Walter's ball," Celeste explained. "She is a cute little thing, but completely boring and not very bright." She now began to twirl a lock of her hair around her finger. "And her fashion sense is rather lacking." Celeste chuckled softly. "I am sure you noticed her headpiece, how could you not? Someone needs to tell the poor girl that sometimes more is less. She was practically wearing an entire bird on her head."

Charles cleared his throat and moved to pour himself another glass.

"She is very sweet, however, if I am being honest, I think your mother's pug has more intelligent things to say."

Charles did not reply.

"How is your mother anyway?" Celeste asked digressing. "I did not get a chance to see her before she left."

"She is well," Charles told her. "I received a letter from her a couple of days ago. She asked about you."

Celeste pressed a hand on her chest tenderly. "I do adore your mother. She is in Bath, is she not?"

He nodded.

"I think I will plan a trip to Bath next year; I have not been in ages. But back to what we were speaking about before."

He turned to her. "*We* were not speaking of anything. *You* were the one doing all of the talking."

"Semantics, Charles," she replied with an indifferent wave of the hand. She put her glass on the side table so she could pull herself up a little more on the couch. She gracefully tucked her legs in front of her and rested one arm on the armrest before continuing to play with her hair, the color of dying embers. Beautiful, but still hot to the touch. "Now, did you?"

"Did I what?"

Celeste sighed and frowned at him. "Did you sleep with Sarah Wilmington?"

Charles cleared his throat. "No, I did not," he finally replied. He tapped his fingers on the side of his leg in an agitated manner.

"For your sake, I am glad," Celeste told him reaching

for her glass to take another sip. "You could do much better than her."

"She is not as bad as you think," Charles retorted. "She is a sweet girl as you said yourself."

Celeste smiled teasingly. "Do you like her?"

"No more than you like Joseph Sharpe," he shot back.

Celeste's smile fell. "I had a temporary lapse of judgment with him during a moment of weakness." She shook her head. "It will not happen again."

"Huh."

"Did you try with Sarah at all?" Celeste continued, pushing the subject.

"You will not drop this until I give you all of the particulars, will you?" he asked her in a bland tone.

Celeste gave him a confused look. "Is this not what we do?" she replied. "Do we not talk about our exploits together?"

Charles swirled his glass. "Yes, usually we do," he said solemnly.

She looked at him, concerned. "What is wrong? Has something happened?"

He shook his head slowly. "No, not really anyway." He frowned into his glass as he took a sip. "She had been willing, but I found that," he paused, "I had not been."

Celeste blinked at him. "I am at a loss here," she started. "Miss Wilmington had offered herself to you and *you* refused?"

Charles let out a sigh. "No, I found, after tender kisses and soft caresses, I," he made a hand gesture, indicating himself, "was not *willing*."

After what he had told her finally sank in, a smile slowly spread across Celeste's face. She pressed her lips together to contain it. When that wasn't enough, she hid her mouth with her hand, but her eyes said it all.

"You are laughing at me," he said bitterly. "Now you see why I hesitated to tell you."

"Oh, Charles, no," Celeste replied still trying to get her smile under control. "I would never laugh at such a thing."

"You are laughing now."

"Well, would you prefer me to tell you about one of my recent bedroom disasters?" Celeste asked him. "I can tell you what an awful time I had with Joseph if that would brighten your mood."

Charles shook his head. "It would not."

"Then what can I do to help?"

He turned fully to look at her still laying sideways on the couch. She looked like a roman sculpture. Her pale skin glowing in the rays of sun that floated in through the windows; her tilted head resting on her delicate hand; her full chest rising and falling with each breath. His heart pounded as he looked at her.

He shifted his gaze away. "I do not believe there is anything you can do," he finally replied.

Celeste drew her feet from under her and stood, her hair swishing around her, like it had used to envelope him during their throes of heated pass—

Charles cleared his throat and took another sip of his drink as Celeste approached him. She gently put a hand on his arm, causing him to shudder slightly. She smelled of peppermint.

"Charles, you are my dearest friend, and I hope to always be close to you," she told him. "I would also hope that nothing I say or do ever hurts you."

He looked down into her wavering eyes and gently placed his hand over hers. "Celeste," he said softly, "I want to help you with the situation with your father. I think I—"

"Oh, I do not want to talk about that right now," she replied pulling her hand away and moving to the window where her skin continued to glow. "I am not afraid of his threats," she told him after a few moments. "I have gotten through the other ones; I can get through this."

Charles closed his eyes and sighed. "I think I need to go and lie down," he said, rubbing his forehead with his fingertips.

Celeste turned to him.

"I have a headache," he continued.

Celeste nodded. "Alright," she said placing her glass on the table. "I shall see you in a few days then? At my party?"

He nodded. "I never miss a chance to scorn your father."

She smiled. "That is the spirit." She gave him a quick peck on the cheek and sashayed her way out of the room.

When she was gone, Charles placed his hand over his pounding heart.

"Shit," he said softly.

He was in trouble.

7

The days flew by and the day of the ball finally arrived. Celeste was in high spirits as she flitted around her house giving orders and taste testing all of the food and wine that was to be served.

She breathed a sigh of satisfaction as she thought about the grand event she was going to throw. Almost everyone had replied they were coming, so she expected a full house.

The band had been chosen carefully, not the same one that played at Sir Walter's ball. The cellist was sloppy, and they didn't know the right songs. No, she made sure she hired the best. The one from Mrs. Albert's winter party last year would do nicely. Celeste was a little disappointed they had a new violinist, but after hearing a few songs, she was satisfied.

Everything was going perfectly, or as perfectly as anything can go. At any rate, Celeste was in her element. It had been far too long since she had thrown a ball and she was ready and willing to play hostess to the nicest, or the least boring, families in the neighborhood.

Rooms were readied at her request for some of her

guests who were from out of town, and Margaret and Amanda had theirs as well.

She smiled satisfactorily throughout the day as she mentally checked off her checklist. The evening would mostly take place in the music room where the doors opened to the garden. The bushes had recently been trimmed and lanterns were strategically placed along the paths. She had taken on several extra hands for the evening to make sure that guests, both inside and out, were supplied with drink. The peacocks had been fed and somewhat contained in the garden. Margaret's and Amanda's dresses had been picked up the day before and were ready for an evening of wonder. Celeste made sure to invite all of the unattached men in the neighborhood and encouraged each to bring a friend if they could.

Yes, everything was ready. This night would be a new beginning for Margaret, and Celeste, its engineer.

"Are you sure this is suitable to wear?" Margaret asked timidly from behind the dressing partition, her voice slightly panicked.

"Oh, let me see!" Celeste said gleefully.

Margaret walked around the screen, her hands covering her pale cleavage.

Celeste gasped. "My dear Margaret," she said almost breathlessly. "You are a vision."

"I feel rather indecent," Margaret told her, uncomfortable, still hiding her exposed chest.

Celeste glided over to her and took her hands, pulling her over to the mirror. "Just look at you," she said pointing at her reflection, beaming. She stood behind her friend to gauge her reaction.

Margaret looked wide eyed at her likeness. "Goodness," she whispered. "I *am* indecent." She tried covering herself again when Celeste took her hands and held them down gently.

"You are not indecent," she corrected her. "You are free! I knew this dress was the one for you. You are beyond beautiful."

Margaret blinked at herself still unsure, but she had to admit that the dress was stunning on her. The color somehow brought out the color in her eyes and the sheen of her hair. She twitched a bit. The only problem was how revealing it was. Her breasts almost seemed to flow over the brim of her neckline. It was not the style she was accustomed to, her dresses usually having a lot more material to them. But her image was striking, she had to admit that herself.

"Do you not like it?" Celeste asked when Margaret didn't say anything.

"No," she said slowly, "I do. I just—" She took a deep breath surprised that the dress was not more restricting than it looked. "Is there not a way I could," she put a hand on her breasts again, "hide this?"

Celeste smirked at her friend before walking over to her vanity and pulling a fan from the drawer. She handed it to her. "This is about all that I can do," she told her. "But it is better than nothing."

Suddenly, the doors to the room burst open and Amanda came dancing in. "This dress is the most beautiful I have ever seen!" she exclaimed as she flitted around them. "It is so light and wonderful; I almost feel as if I could fly!"

Celeste laughed at the young girl's exuberance. "I am very glad you like it."

"Like it?" Amanda repeated, not stopping in her twirling. "I love it! It is the most beautiful dress I think I shall ever own, and I never want to take it off!"

"Well, I am glad at least one of you is happy," Celeste said.

"One of us?" Amanda repeated. She finally paused enough to look at Margaret standing in front of the mirror in her dark green, silken dress. "Are *you* not happy, Miss Hepworth?"

"I did not say that," Margaret replied shooting Celeste a look.

"And you should not be," Amanda told her, placing her hands over her cheeks. "I have never seen a dress look so well on anyone."

"See?" Celeste said triumphantly.

"You truly look beautiful," Amanda continued.

"I did not say that I do not look beautiful," Margaret replied a little irritated. "I am only concerned with my lack of neckline."

Neither Celeste or Amanda replied.

"I feel like a lady of the night. A— a whore."

Amanda blushed and giggled.

Celeste only gave her friend a playfully cross look. "You most certainly do not look like one. And as Amanda said, a dress has never looked so well on anyone as this one does on you."

Margaret shifted uncomfortably. "It is not really the fashion."

"No," Celeste agreed, "it will be a fashion statement."

"Oh, yes!" Amanda agreed.

"The point of this evening is to have everyone look at you and with that dress they will most certainly look twice," Celeste told her.

"You will be the death of me, Celeste," Margaret finally said.

Celeste lifted a brow. "My father says that on a regular basis and he is still alive."

The guests began to arrive at an alarming rate. There was a long line of people waiting to get into the house and be introduced that snaked its way along the front of the house. Margaret was overwhelmed; Amanda was ecstatic; Celeste was satisfied with herself.

After the last of the guests had arrived and Celeste's job of greeting everyone was over, she slipped back upstairs to ready Margaret and Amanda for their entrance.

"Now, you will each be introduced as you glide beautifully down the stairs," Celeste informed them.

"That is a bit dramatic, do you not think?" Margaret asked, her anxiety rising having watched the hoards of people filing into the house from an upstairs window.

"Of course, it is dramatic," Celeste informed her. "That is the whole point."

"It sounds like a dream!" Amanda chirped happily. "A grand entrance with everyone looking at you!"

Margaret pressed her hand to her stomach and took several deep, slow breaths.

"Yes!" Celeste said clapping her hands. "I am very glad you are so excited, but we must not let that excitement show."

Amanda furrowed her brows. "No?"

"No," Celeste repeated. "Now, you are to wait at the top of the stairs until your name is called with your back straight and your chin held high." Celeste paused to show them. "You will then put one hand delicately on the railing while the other hand elegantly hikes up your dress." Again, she demonstrated. "But the most important, no, the most crucial part of your entrance is your facial expression."

Amanda looked at Celeste wide eyed, taking in every word, while Margaret fanned herself and paced the room.

"You must not smile."

"I must *not* smile?" Amanda asked, a little confused.

"No," Celeste told her, one finger raised. "Your face must maintain soft, neutral lines, and your eyes should not be searching the room. It is imperative you do not make eye contact with anyone. You should look distant, a little indifferent, and mysterious." She stood there posing as if she herself was about to descend the stairs. She took a few steps forward, her gaze straight, her face hiding every thought or emotion. "Do you see?"

"Oh, yes!" Amanda exclaimed.

"Good! Now, let me see you take a turn, Amanda," Celeste told her motioning with her hand.

Amanda took a deep breath to fill her chest and poised herself just as Celeste had shown her. After a few moments, she took a few steps forward, her eyes looking over an imaginary crowd.

"Amanda, you are a natural!" Celeste exclaimed proudly.

The young girl beamed gleefully.

"Now, Margaret, it is your turn," Celeste coaxed.

"Must I really do this?" she asked. "We are already here. Why must we be introduced?"

"You are my special guests," Celeste explained. "And special guests get special introductions."

Margaret held back a groan. "Why did I agree to this? It seems silly. And daunting."

"It is alright to be nervous," Celeste assured her. "But that is why I am here. If you descend the stairs with the thought that *everyone* is looking at you, then you will be anxious. But," Celeste continued holding up a finger, "if you descend the stairs with the thought that the party cannot or will not start without you, then it gives you a sense of importance. You *are* the party."

Margaret stared at her friend, an eyebrow raised. "That in no way makes sense *nor* does it make me feel better."

"Trust me for once, will you?" Celeste pleaded.

Margaret sighed before giving a hesitant nod. "Fine."

Amanda clapped her hands together. "This will be an amazing night!" she exclaimed. "Just wait and see!"

Celeste gave a nod. "Exactly. Now, Margaret, let us see how you will descend the stairs."

Celeste was soon back down with the other guests searching the room for Charles. She finally found him somewhat sulking in a corner, a full glass of brandy in his hand.

"I need to borrow you for a moment," she told him, taking his glass and setting it on the tray of a servant as he walked by.

"For what?" Charles asked skeptically with a frown, watching his brandy disappear into the crowd.

She began pulling him through the other guests, navigating him to a spot near the stairs Amanda and Margaret were to descend.

"I need you to be the first to dance with Margaret when she comes down," she replied.

"Why must I ask her?"

"Because I have already asked Joseph to ask Amanda, and you know Margaret. She is extremely nervous, so I feel that if you were the first one to ask her to dance, it would make her feel more at ease."

"I hate dancing. I am terrible at it and you know it."

"Yes, I do, but it is for Margaret and you do have a high social standing, so if other men see that you are interested, then *they* will show interest as well."

He blinked at Celeste a moment. "I sometimes forget how conniving you are until I hear you speak and then I am both impressed and terrified by how your mind works."

She winked at him. "Thank you."

"What are you wearing, by the way?" he asked her, finally taking her in. She was in a pale brown dress with barely any lace or anything to embellish it. The poor garment looked as if the seamstress had forgotten about it, or simply given up. "I have never seen you in such a drab, lifeless dress before."

"Yes, I know," she replied smoothing out her skirts. "It is rather hideous, but tonight is not about me, it is about Margaret. So, being the wonderfully good friend that I am, I sacrificed my taste for good fashion so that she might stand out more than myself."

"How truly selfless of you," Charles replied blandly, smiling at her golden-orange hair bunched up on the top of her head. "You look like a tree in the middle of fall."

"But a beautiful tree," she added.

He gave a small laugh. "Yes, a beautiful tree."

"Sh! They are about to come down the stairs," Celeste whispered, ignoring his sarcastic remark.

The music, being played just as background noise before the dancing began, ceased and one of Celeste's servants dressed in an obnoxiously bright, yet, elegant uniform cleared his throat.

Everyone turned to look at him.

"Miss Amanda Haderly," he said.

Amanda who had been patiently waiting at the top of the stairs, poised with one hand on the banister, the other hand slightly hitching up her dress, slowly began to descend the stairs. Her young face looking out, beyond everyone, as if she were the only person in the room. Gracefully, she walked down the stairs, almost gliding. Celeste smiled to herself looking amongst her guests.

The effect was noticeable; everyone was enamored by the young beauty floating down the stairs who emanated a calm, mysterious indifference.

When she finally made it down to the bottom of the stairs, Joseph Sharpe, as instructed, bowed and asked her for the first dance which she gratefully, yet, dispassionately accepted.

Celeste's heart swelled in her chest as she watched her young pupil make her way to the dance floor.

It was now Margaret's turn to be introduced.

Again, the servant cleared his throat, calling to attention the other guests, who upon seeing Margaret, her pale skin glowing against the dark contrast of the dress, gasped.

"Is that truly Margaret?" Charles whispered in surprise.

"Is she not a vision?" Celeste replied.

"Miss Margaret Hepworth."

Margaret, though she did not look as confident as Amanda, came down the stairs just as elegantly. Her eyes sparkled with tears of anxiety and her cheeks were flushed with embarrassment enhancing her natural beauty and modesty.

"You have outdone yourself, Celeste," Charles whispered to her. "I have never seen her look more beautiful."

"If that was not the effect I wanted," Celeste started with a coy smile, "I might be jealous."

The room stirred with whispers as Margaret continued her descent. Everyone seemed taken by her beauty.

Celeste was about to silently applaud herself for her success when, misjudging the last step, Margaret tumbled and fell, letting out a squeal of equal surprise and terror.

"Oh, shit," Charles said pressing his hand over his mouth.

Gasps filled the room as Margaret laid still on the floor.

Celeste hit Charles in the chest with the back of her hand. "Go and ask her to dance, you idiot," she hissed.

Charles quickly walked over and helped Margaret up whose shoe had gotten caught in the hem of her dress. It was a small disaster, but was quickly resolved with Margaret only slightly limping onto the dance floor.

Celeste held in a groan and pressed her hand to her forehead, but soon the music picked back up and everyone began to dance as if nothing had happened.

"I am sure that did not go as planned," came a laughing voice beside her.

"No, it did not," Celeste replied looking over at Stephen who was handing her a glass of champagne. She let out a sigh. "Was it so horrible?" she asked taking the glass.

Stephen coughed to keep from laughing. "Well, I am not sure if others did, but I certainly caught a glimpse of her undergarments as she tumbled."

Celeste's eyes grew wide as she sipped from her glass.

"Do *not* tell her that," she pleaded. "She will never forgive me for putting her on display if she knew that happened."

Stephen chuckled. "I think the sound of her squeal as she went down will forever be in my head."

Celeste coughed back a laugh as well. "Stop it!" she demanded playfully. "I cannot be laughing at my friend's embarrassment. She was obviously mortified."

He nodded as he drank.

"Would you do me a favor and ask her to dance tonight?"

"For you, I will," he replied, sliding his hand down her back in an all too familiar manner causing her to swat his hand away.

Celeste shot him a playfully stern look and he laughed.

"Am I allowed to ask Miss Haderly to dance or am I forbidden to?" he asked her after a moment.

Celeste pursed her lips at him. "You are not forbidden from dancing with her, but you are forbidden from forming an attachment," Celeste replied.

Stephen huffed. "Sounds serious."

"It *is* serious," she told him. "She seems fond of you, so it would be cruel to take advantage of her feelings."

"Not if it got me what I wanted," he replied sneeringly.

"Stephen, trust me," Celeste warned, "I am sparing both her and yourself. Amanda is a sweet girl, but immature and naïve. She will not understand your intentions and will take them to mean something entirely different."

"Like what?" He asked with a raised brow.

"Like *love*," Celeste replied.

"Huh," Stephen breathed as he gulped from his glass. "That is serious."

"At this stage in her life, if you were to kiss her on the cheek, she would expect a marriage proposal the next day." Celeste smoothed out her dull dress. "I dare say the child even knows how babies are made. She probably believes that, after you are wed, a baby just falls in your lap." She took another sip of her drink. "No, she would not know what to do with your manhood if you gave her written out and illustrated instructions."

Stephen choked on his drink and went into a coughing fit. He pulled out his handkerchief and wiped his chin, laughing. "I see your point," he finally said after catching his breath. "She is too young for me."

"Thank you. I rather like the girl and do not want to see her hopes dashed too harshly."

"Too harshly?"

"Well, everyone needs a dose of reality," Celeste explained. "One should learn disappointment at a young age. When you are young, your skin is not as thin but more pliable and you can easily bounce back."

"You are saying I should do that to Miss Haderly?" Stephen asked her.

"You specifically?" She shook her head. "No, I am merely saying it is good for young girls to learn how the world is while they *are* young. Whether or not it is you that does it, well, that is out of my hands."

Stephen laughed through his nose. "Well, I shall try my best to neither encourage nor disappoint the poor girl."

Celeste smiled and nodded.

"Am I allowed to ask *you* to dance?" Stephen asked after a moment, holding out his hand.

"You are," Celeste replied finishing her drink and taking his hand.

"Though you are in a hideous thing of a dress, I do rather like what is underneath it," Stephen replied with a grin as he led her to the dance floor.

Celeste huffed. "Always the gentleman, are we not?"

Margaret's fall was soon forgotten as the night was filled with dancing and gambling. The couples swirled around each other, exchanging partners when the music changed or taking a moment to rest on the chairs that lined the walls. Some of the men drifted to the game tables, while some of the women found their way to the garden.

After resting herself for a few moments, Celeste found Margaret without a partner. She spied her friend standing next to Charles, nervously fanning herself and looking about the room.

Celeste searched the room herself, trying to find someone she could get to ask Margaret to dance. Her eyes grazed over the men left in the room when she came across a dashing young man sitting alone watching the crowds himself. She smiled as she walked over to him.

"Mr. Wilde, you are looking rather handsome tonight," Celeste told him, handing him a glass of wine.

The man smiled and stood, his dark hair framing his boyish face, though he was in his late twenties by now. He took the glass offered to him. "Thank you, Miss Willoughby," he replied taking a sip. "You are looking beautiful as you always do."

"You are too kind," she said feigning a blush by putting a hand to her cheek. "I was actually wondering if you were engaged for the next dance."

Mr. Wilde looked surprised. "I have never had a woman ask me to dance before."

"Oh, no, not for me," she explained, giving a small laugh and gently touching his arm. "I mean for my friend

Margaret. She is standing by the window over there."

"The unfortunate young woman who fell down the stairs and is now standing next to Mr. Pratt?"

Celeste pressed her lips together. "Yes," she replied curtly.

"Will Mr. Pratt not ask her to dance?"

"Mr. Pratt has two left feet and often steps on his partner's toes. Margaret, who is such a beautiful dancer, needs a partner with more elegance than that." She smiled playfully. "I heard *you* were an elegant dancer yourself. And she does love your poetry."

Mr. Wilde gave a soft bow. "Ah, I do hate to disappoint a fan. I would love to—" he paused as a young blonde man walked by, pausing to shoot Mr. Wilde a smile which caused his face to flush. He cleared his throat. "I would love to dance with your beautiful friend, but, unfortunately, I have a prior engagement," he told her, his voice distant as he watched the blonde man leave the room but not before he shot him a wink.

"Oh?" Celeste responded trying not to sound disappointed. "Well, you do look rather flushed. Are you quite well?"

Mr. Wilde nodded taking a large gulp of his wine before putting it down. "Quite well." He took Celeste's hand and kissed it. "It has been a pleasure, Miss Willoughby, as always."

Celeste pouted as she watched Mr. Wilde leave in the direction of the blonde man and moved to stand with Margaret when she noticed a group of men hovering around her friend. Sir Walter's son Elliot, his cousin William Gardener, Stephen Kelly, and the Edison twins enclosed around her. Satisfied after all, Celeste turned to walk the other way when she bumped into Joseph

Sharpe.

Celeste gasped in surprise and took a step back, slipping. She thought for a moment she was going to fall, when Joseph caught her by the arm and pulled her into him.

"Are you alright?" he asked her.

"Why, Joseph, you scared the devil out of me!" Celeste exclaimed.

He gently tightened his grip on her. "Miss Willoughby, there is no devil in you to scare out."

Celeste gave a weak smile. "You are very kind," she replied. "I think I am no longer in danger of falling though."

"Yes, I apologize." Joseph loosened his grip on her and took a step back. "I came over here to ask if you would honor me with your company."

"Well, I am here," she told him.

"Sorry, I mean, would you mind taking a walk with me?" He offered her his arm.

Celeste hesitated, but took it.

"I was worried it might rain this evening since the morning was quite wet, but I am glad it held off," Joseph said as he led her out to the gardens.

Celeste nodded. "Yes, it would have been a great disappointment."

"You have truly outdone yourself tonight, Miss Willoughby."

"Thank you."

"Honestly, I find your capabilities endless. You dance beautifully, you organize beautiful parties, you sing beautifully, you play the harp beautifully." He stopped and turned to her. "There is not an aspect about you that is not beautiful." His eyes searched hers in the glow of the lanterns. "You are the most beautiful person, inside and out."

Celeste knew where this was going. She had been there five times before.

"You are a very sweet friend to say so, Joseph," she replied. "It is good to hear reassurances about yourself and who better to give them than friends?" She patted his arm and slowly slipped hers out of his. "Did you hear someone call for me?" she asked looking about them.

Joseph shook his head. "I hear nothing, save for the sound of your musical voice."

Celeste refrained from groaning. "Perhaps it was Amanda. She might need me for something."

"She was dancing with Michael Wilmington when we walked out," Joseph informed her. "I believe she is happily occupied." He offered his arm again.

"I do not remember inviting the Wilmingtons," Celeste thought to herself as they continued to walk. "Amanda is a very sweet young woman," she said aloud to him, trying to change the subject.

He nodded. "She is the most exuberant of girls," he agreed.

"I thank you for dancing with her this evening."

"It was my pleasure. I would do anything for you."

"Margaret looks very well tonight, does she not?" she asked, again, trying to shift the subject away from her.

"I have never seen her look so handsome."

They fell into silence. One of them trying to muster up the courage to say what he felt, and the other one trying to plan a mode of escape.

"Perhaps, I should just make up some random emergency," Celeste thought as they headed further into the garden. She knew where he was trying to take her. It was a secluded spot where a large, ancient tree grew. It was surrounded by tall hedges with only one entrance in and out of the small enclosure. The tree was in a large enough area to allow a small group to gather there, but small enough to give a party of two privacy for clandestine conversations.

It was an area where she had stolen away several times to meet Charles in the middle of the night. It was where she had first given herself to him. Her skin tingled at the memory of his lips on the nape of her neck and she shivered.

"Are you cold?" Joseph asked.

Celeste shook her head. "No, no, I am fine," she quickly replied. "I am just getting a little tired. I have not sat down all night. Perhaps we should return."

"Are there not benches just over there?"

Celeste saw he was pointing at the tree. "Yes, but I am sure they must be wet from the rain earlier today." She applauded herself on her quick thinking. "I would hate to get my dress wet."

"Yes!" he told her almost laughingly. "I am a fool. I did not even think about that."

"Do not be too hard on yourself," she said in a comforting tone. "Men never think of such things." She moved to steer them back to the house, but Joseph did not budge.

"Then I shall have to do it here," he mumbled to himself. He closed his eyes and took a deep breath, appearing to be gathering his courage.

Celeste slipped her arm out of his again and started walking back to the house. "Come now, Joseph," she goaded not waiting and moving faster. "I believe I promised Charles a dance and would hate to be rude."

"Miss Willoughby," Joseph called out, coming out of his

trance. "Wait, please! I have something I would like to ask you!" He started to run after her, but only got a few steps in the dimly lit path when he tripped over something.

An awful squawking sound broke through the silence of the night followed by the screams of Joseph.

Celeste turned and could just make out Joseph appearing to wrestle with something on the ground as his screams and the yowling of some animal filled the night air.

"The peacocks!" Celeste exclaimed running back to Joseph.

"Help me!" he yelled rolling on the ground and trying to shield his face as the bird pecked and scratched at him. "Help!"

"Joseph!" Celeste yelled. "Do not hurt it!"

"It is hurting me!" he yelled as the squealing bird continued to bite at him. "Make it stop!" He tried batting at the bird, but it was no use; it continued to ravage him.

By now, a crowd of guests had gathered hearing the commotion as they were walking the gardens. They all watched, some in horror, others in amusement, as poor Joseph cried out for help while the evil bird continued in his assault.

Celeste pressed her hands to her mouth as she watched, trying to figure out what to do. Finally, Celeste saw what was wrong.

"For heaven's sake, Joseph, you are lying on the poor thing's tail!" she exclaimed. "Roll to the left!"

Joseph did as she had commanded, releasing the peacock's long tail out from under him. The triumphant bird gave one more yell of complaint before strutting off in victory down the path.

"Joseph, are you alright?" Celeste asked coming closer.

Joseph rolled back over into the light of the lanterns and the sight of him stopped Celeste where she stood.

She gave a small scream. "You are covered in blood! He is covered in blood!" she shouted to the spectators. "Someone, send for a doctor!"

No one dared to move, not wanting to miss any more of the display.

"Seriously?" Celeste said putting her hand on her hip. "This man is hurt, and no one cares to go have a doctor sent for?"

Again, no one moved.

Joseph moaned in pain on the ground.

Celeste gave an irritated sigh. "John Whitmore, I see you there in the crowd," she said in a stern voice. "You go and send for a doctor this instant or I will tell your wife just how much you lost tonight at the gaming tables!"

The man stood alert and gave a quick nod of the head before running to the house.

"Alex Stern, and Harry Locke, you help carry Joseph to one of the rooms upstairs," she commanded. "Everyone else, go back to dancing. There is nothing more to see!" She made a shooing gesture with her hands. "Go on! There is more wine to be had inside."

Everyone finally began to move, looking disappointed that the entertainment had ended so soon.

"Do not go that way, you two!" Celeste shouted. "What? Are you to drag his bloody body through the dance floor?"

The two men paused, holding a pathetic looking Joseph under the arms.

"Obviously, I want you to use the servants' entrance." She shook her head and led them into the house through the back entrance where she was able to order hot water from the kitchen as they made their way to a room in the back of the house.

"Put him on the bed," Celeste ordered once they made their way upstairs. "Thank you, gentlemen, you can return to the party, I shall stay with him until the doctor arrives."

"Miss Willoughby," Joseph whispered, wincing with pain.

Celeste pressed one hand to her stomach and one over her mouth at the sight of him. It was quite gruesome.

From what she could see through the blood, Joseph had several cuts on his face; a chunk of his nose was hanging loosely, his lip was split in two places and his cheeks were shredded. His hands were also torn in several places having tried to defend his face.

Blood covered the front of his jacket and shirt and was still trickling down his face.

"Miss Willoughby," he whispered again, stretching out a ragged, bloody hand. "Take my hand."

"Ugh." Celeste grimaced at the sight of it. "Joseph, I think it is best that you just lie still and not speak. A doctor is being summoned." She sat on the bed, a safe distance from his hand's reach and patted his shin with the tips of her fingers.

"You are so kind to take care of me," he said sending himself into a coughing fit. Blood sprayed from his lips, shooting a few droplets which landed on Celeste's chest.

Celeste froze. "Oh, heavens no," she whispered, slowly looking down and seeing the red splatter coloring her pale skin. She stood from the bed trying to breathe slowly in and out of her mouth to keep her from panicking when a servant came in with the hot water and rags she had ordered. "Oh, thank God!" she exclaimed taking one of the rags and dipping it in the water before the servant had a chance to place it anywhere. "Gross," she said as she wiped away the blood from her chest and neck. "Help clean his wounds, would you, Samantha?" she ordered the maid.

The older woman nodded. "Aye, ma'am."

Just then Charles burst into the room, a panicked look on his face. "Celeste, I heard there was an accident. Are you—" His face paled when he saw Joseph. "Oh, dear Lord," he whispered as he fell to his knees and passed out.

Celeste lifted her hands up in helpless frustration. "Really?" she said aloud going over to him. She pulled his head onto her lap and slapped his face to revive him.

Charles slowly came around, looking about the room. "So much blood," he murmured. "Celeste, I thought you were hurt."

"Well, if I were, it is nice to know that my oldest friend is capable of running to my aid," she said mordantly.

"Who it that?" Charles asked sitting himself up.

"That is Joseph."

Joseph groaned on cue as Samantha cleaned his wounds.

"What on earth happened?"

"That is a story for another day," she told him. "Can you stand, or do you need help?"

"I think I am alright," he told her pushing off of the floor. He swayed a moment, but soon gained his bearings. He held out his hand to help Celeste up when he caught sight of Joseph again. "I think I need to sit down," he said putting his hand on the wall for support.

Celeste rolled her eyes and put his arm over her shoulder so she could support him to a chair. "This is a new side of you, Charles, I have never seen," she told him as she sat him down gently. "I did not know the sight of blood made you so girlish."

Charles nodded in reply.

"It would be very selfish of you to pass out again with poor Joseph cut to pieces on the bed."

"Describing it to me does not help," he replied taking a deep breath.

Celeste walked over to the bell and rang it. "I will order you some wine," she told him when the manservant entered a minute later.

Just then Margaret came through the door in a panic. "Celeste, what has happened? Everyone is in such an uproar downstairs; I cannot make sense of it!" Like Charles, Margaret paled when she saw Joseph's sad state. Her eyes fluttered and her breathing came in short bursts.

Celeste moved to catch her when another figure came through the door scooping her in his arms before she fell. Celeste's breath caught in her throat when she saw the man who saved her friend. He was one of the handsomest men she had ever seen with his dark hair, tall, yet, muscular stature. His cheekbones were high, and his eyes seemed to be a deep mysterious pool of blue.

Joseph's groans filled the background.

"Sir," Celeste said breathlessly, "I believe you have saved my friend. What is your name?"

The man looked at her and Celeste could feel her heart skip a beat.

"I am Doctor Digsby," he replied in a deep, melodically soothing voice. "I was told there was someone who was hurt?"

Celeste looked at him for a moment without

answering.

Charles cleared his throat.

"Yes, Mr. Sharpe is on the bed over there," Celeste replied pointing but not breaking eye contact.

Margaret finally came to and gasped, realizing she was being held. Her cheeks colored when the man looked down at her.

"Are you alright to stand?" he asked her.

Margaret swallowed hard and nodded slowly.

Celeste watched with great interest as the man gracefully and effortlessly placed Margaret safely on the floor and then gave an elegant bow.

Joseph groaned yet again.

"I think it best if you sit down," the doctor told her gently.

"Thank you," Margaret whispered.

Celeste took her friend by the arm and helped her to a chair next to Charles who looked at her reproachfully, but Celeste did not notice; she was formulating a scheme.

Poor Joseph was finally tended to by the vigilant and handsome Doctor Digsby. His wounds were cleaned, and a garlic-scented salve was put on them. His nose was bandaged so the piece of flesh hanging off could hopefully reattach.

When everything was said and done, Joseph was given a sedative so he could sleep and rest properly.

"None of his wounds are truly serious," the doctor told them. "I rubbed a salve of my own making on them to keep them from festering. I will come back and clean them again and reapply the salve tomorrow."

"He should not be moved then?" Celeste asked.

The doctor shook his head. "I would not tempt it.

He needs rest as it appears he has lost a fair amount of blood."

"He shall have the best care while he is here," Celeste assured him. "Thank you so much for your help, Doctor Digsby. And it was so good of you to come so quickly."

He smiled. "Fortunately, I had just arrived. A late add-on to the Edison party. They are neighbors to my aunt whom I am visiting."

"Then, you are most welcome," Celeste replied.

"I apologize, I did not get any of your names upon my entrance," he replied, his eyes shifting to Margaret who blushed and immediately looked away.

The look was not lost on Celeste who smiled to herself.

"I am Celeste Willoughby," she started, pointing to herself. "This is Charles Pratt and this," she paused holding a hand toward her friend, "is Margaret Hepworth."

The doctor bowed again. "It has been my pleasure serving you," he said.

Charles huffed.

"I will see you tomorrow then?" he asked still looking at Margaret.

"Yes," Celeste answered quickly. "We shall be here. Do you need someone to show you the way back downstairs?"

"Please, I am not sure of the way," he replied.

"Down the hallway, you cannot miss the stairs," Charles mumbled.

"Margaret can show you," Celeste said giving her friend a gentle push. "I just want to stay with Joseph a few minutes longer to make sure he is resting."

Margaret gave her an alarmed look.

"I would be honored, Miss Hepworth," the doctor said.

Slowly Margaret stepped forward taking the doctor's arm. "It is just down here," she said softly as she led him out of the room.

"Oh, Charles!" Celeste exclaimed once the two had disappeared. "Did you see that man?"

"I have been here this entire time," he told her blandly.

"He is unbelievably handsome, is he not? And tall and, and wonderful!"

Charles shrugged. "I see nothing special about him," he replied finishing his glass of wine.

Celeste fanned herself. "You cannot say I am not a good friend," she continued. "Any other time, I would have pursued him myself."

"Why did you not?" Charles asked bitterly.

"Did you not see how he looked at Margaret and how Margaret blushed at him?" she replied, her voice full of hope for her friend. "He was taken by her and I believe she might be taken with him too."

"Ah, so this was another one of your selfless acts?" he asked sardonically as he stood.

"Well, I did promise her someone I have never bedded," she told him. She sighed after a moment. "What a pity."

Joseph babbled something in his delirium of drugs and sleep.

"Shall we return to what is left of my party?" she asked Charles, hugging his arm. "Perhaps there are a few people left for us to choose from."

8

Celeste blinked her way down the stairs the next morning, her eyes dry. She yawned, covering her mouth with the back of her hand.

"Gerald, is anyone else awake?" she asked before entering the breakfast parlor.

"Yes, ma'am. Miss Haderly and Miss Hepworth are both out walking, and the Gilfords left jus' after dawn."

She nodded. "Is breakfast still out?" she asked turning the corner.

"Yes, ma'am, but I must tell ya—"

"I need very strong coffee, Gerald. Make sure we have some."

"Of course, ma'am, but I must warn ya—"

"Has Joseph been attended to?"

Gerald sighed at being interrupted again. "Yes, he's well, but—"

"Good. That poor man, it was such an awful thing to happen to him."

"Ma'am, before you enter the breakfast parlor, I must tell you—"

"We are not out of bacon, are we?"

Gerald shook his head. "No there is plenty of food, but

there's a—"

"Then you can tell me later whatever it is." Celeste put her hand on the door and entered the room.

"Good morning," came an unfamiliar voice from an unfamiliar man sitting in her father's usual seat.

Celeste started and then stood there blinking at the man for a moment. She promptly stepped back out into the hallway.

"Gerald, there is a strange man sitting at my table," she told him.

Gerald gave a nervous nod. "I did try tuh tell ya, ma'am."

Celeste nodded. "Who is he?"

"Sent by your father, ma'am."

"Huh. Well, this should be interesting." Celeste went back into the room a little more collected.

"Miss Willoughby, I presume," said the strange man. He was a thin, pale thing with a crooked smile and dark wispy hair.

Celeste detested the sight of him, but seated herself not far from him. "You presume correctly, sir, which puts you at an advantage, for I have no idea who you are."

The man's smile broadened, showing surprisingly straight teeth. "I am Mr. Stanley," he replied. "I am here for an interview with you."

"Interview?" Celeste repeated. "I was not aware we were looking to hire a personal undertaker."

The man huffed and pulled out a notebook from a bag slumped next to his chair then a pen from his jacket. He opened his notebook and scribbled a few lines.

"Actually, Miss Willoughby, I am here to interview you," Mr. Stanley told her.

She lifted a brow at him. "For what?"

The man pulled a letter out of his jacket and handed it to her.

Celeste flinched at his long, gangly fingers, but she took the letter, instantly recognizing her father's hand.

"Your father sent for me," he told her triumphantly.

Celeste perused the first few lines of the letter before she tossed it on the table in an indifferent manner. "It appears he has," she said with a shrug, trying to seem unbothered when her insides were boiling with anger.

The man, this Mr. Stanley, turned out to be the head director of the South London Asylum. Her father, who had sent him a letter when he first arrived in London, had asked this wretch of a man to talk with his daughter and gauge his opinion on whether the asylum would be the right choice. In the letter, he described his daughter as stubborn, licentious, and utterly disinterested in following the rules of being a lady defined by society.

"And I suppose you could not wait until after breakfast for this ridiculous interview?" she asked, piling food on her plate.

He arched a thick eyebrow at her. "It is nearly ten thirty," he replied. "I believe most people have breakfasted by now."

"I have trouble sleeping," she explained indifferently, putting jam on a piece of toast. "So, when I finally do fall asleep, it is terribly late which, in turn, makes me sleep later than *most* people." She took a bite of her toast.

Mr. Stanley stared at her, unblinking for a few moments. "Your father told me a great deal about you in that letter," he said with a nod of the head.

"I am sure he did," Celeste replied cutting into a sausage and forking it into her mouth. "My father talks about me often, no doubt, to anyone who would listen."

"He made some interesting observations about you."

"Do you often make house visits so far from your facility?" Celeste asked ignoring his statement. "Seems a rather long way to meet with someone you have no connection to."

"You father is paying me."

Celeste laughed. "My father offered you money to come here?"

The man nodded. "He did. That is how concerned he is with your behavior."

"Did you receive payment yet?" Celeste asked taking another bite of her toast.

The man opened his mouth to say something but paused. "I am to receive it after I write my assessment."

"Fool," she said shaking her head. "My father is the cheapest man I have ever known. He has not bought himself a new jacket in three years and his idea of a gift is a book he purchased from the traveling library that has several unexplainable stains and has been handled by countless people." She sighed. "How he has ever managed to keep any of his mistresses happy I do not know."

She laughed at the man's dumfounded expression.

"You should have received payment *before* you left. So, you are either a man lacking substantial common sense, or you are not so much the head director of your asylum, but the head idiot." She shrugged. "Do they allow excursions for their non-violent inmates at your treatment center?" She smiled coyly.

The man's face twitched as he scribbled a few more notes into his book. "You are rather rude, Miss Willoughby," he told her.

"Forgive me," she replied between bites. "Being questioned by a man who wants to see me locked away in a cell does not incite warm, civil feelings inside of me. I will try to do better." She rang the bell to order coffee.

Mr. Stanley cleared his throat. "Do you view yourself as exempt from certain laws?" he asked her.

Celeste huffed. "Laws or rules?" she challenged, moving to a table in the corner of a room. "For example, I would not exempt myself from the law of murder. Murder is a terrible thing and I know, understand, and adhere to that belief." She opened a small box that was on the table and pulled out a cigar. "But do I believe that I should not behave in a certain way because I am a woman even though men around me are doing that exact same thing I am taught I should not do?" She put the cigar in her mouth and lit it, taking a few small puffs to get it started. She blew out the smoke and shook her head. "If that were the case, then, yes. Though, I do not necessarily say I am 'exempt,'" she took another puff of the cigar. "I just do not care to follow that 'rule.'"

"And what about your feelings toward marriage?" he continued.

Celeste walked back over to him, an eyebrow raised and a grin on her lips. "Why? Are you looking?"

Mr. Stanley's cheeks blushed slightly.

She laughed again as she sat back down. "How old are you, Mr. Stanley? About fifty-five?"

"I am forty-two," he replied bitterly.

"And I see that *you* are not married," she continued. "Why should it be so different for me than it is for you?" She shrugged. "I do not want to marry because I do not want to give up the freedom of my youth. *You* do not marry because you look like something Victor Frankenstein brought to life."

The man shook with anger.

Celeste hid her smile by taking another draw from the cigar.

A maid finally came in with a pot of coffee. Celeste thanked her.

"I would offer you some, but it might encourage you to stay longer and drink it," she told him pouring herself a cup.

He did not reply. He just watched her with a grim look on his face.

"Is this interview over, then?" she asked him.

"I have a few more things to go over," he replied curling his thin lips into a smile.

"Please," she said holding out a hand, "by all means, continue."

"Your father does not trust you. He believes you are irresponsible and need to grow up."

Celeste held her hand up. "He has been gone almost two weeks and the house still stands. I have not burned it down yet."

"He says you live for nothing more than to party."

Celeste huffed. "If he listened to half of what I said, he would know that is only seventy-five percent true."

"Your father informed me of your wanton behavior toward men."

Celeste blew smoke in his direction. "What you call 'wanton behavior' I call the fancy to follow a whim wherever it may take me."

Mr. Stanley cleared his throat and shifted in his seat. "He says you will lie with almost anyone." He stood; he seemed taller sitting. He took the few strides to get to her chair, placing a cold hand on her shoulder.

Celeste tensed uncomfortably from the sensation.

"He explained you do not give a care for station or

looks either. That all you need is encouragement." He moved his clammy hand down her arm. "What if I were to encourage you?"

Celeste gently, calmly extinguished her cigar on her plate.

"Then, perhaps you could *encourage* me to write a favorable recommendation to your father." His other had brushed back a lock of her hair from her neck.

"Gerald!" Celeste screamed causing Mr. Stanley to take a step back.

Her faithful servant came in without delay. "How can I be of service, ma'am?"

"Bring me father's Winchester, would you?" she told him. "Now."

Gerald nodded and left the room as quickly as he entered it.

Celeste pushed herself up from her seat and turned to look Mr. Stanley dead in the eyes. They were the same height.

"What do you mean by 'Winchester'?" he asked in a heightened voice, taking another step back.

"My father, oddly enough, is obsessed with the American Wild West," Celeste told him. "He loves to hear stories about the lawlessness of it, so a few years ago, he decided to buy a few of those famous rifles."

Gerald returned and handed her the gun.

"Thank you, Gerald," she said.

Mr. Stanley gave a nervous little laugh. "You don't actually know how to use that, do you?"

"Funny thing about being the daughter of a man who sees women as only a means of reproduction," she replied pulling back the hammer and working the lever of the gun before raising it, "he wanted a son."

Mr. Staley put his hands up. "Now, there is no need to resort to violence," he said.

"You, sir, have insulted my every possible sense, and then you have the audacity, the gall, to think I— seriously, you thought that I would," she paused a moment to take a calming breath. "I would sooner set myself on fire than consensually touch you."

Mr. Stanley smiled nervously. "I will be writing about this to your father."

"You have ten seconds to leave my house or I will shoot you in whatever testicle you like the most."

His face reddened. "You are a foul woman!" he proclaimed.

Celeste aimed the rifle a few inches to his right and pulled the trigger.

The man screamed. "You are mad!" he yelled realizing she had missed.

"That was a warning shot," she told him, working the lever again. "Get out of my house."

Mr. Stanley hurriedly gathered his things and made his way to the door with Celeste not far behind.

"You will be hearing from me soon, Miss Willoughby," he said in an angry, shaking voice as he stood by the carriage. "And I am sure I will see you very soon."

Celeste shot at his feet.

The man jumped.

"Are you sure you want to see me again?" she asked.

"You are a danger to society!" he yelled climbing into the carriage.

"Drive!" Celeste told the driver who lost no time in cracking his whip and steering his horses away from the house.

Celeste swung the rifle over her shoulder and watched

the carriage go victoriously.

A few moments later, Margaret and Amanda came around the corner.

"Was that a gunshot we heard?" Margaret asked concerned.

"Are you holding a gun?" Amanda asked almost the same time.

"'Yes' to both questions," Celeste replied smiling at them. "Did you sleep well last night?"

The two blinked at her in confusion.

"What happened?"

"Why were you shooting?"

"Is everything alright?"

"Who was that driving away in the carriage?"

The two of them bombarded her with questions which Celeste chose not to answer.

"Are either of you hungry?" Celeste asked instead. "I am rather famished."

And with that, Celeste walked back into her house, a trail of swirling dust still hanging in the air from Mr. Stanley's hurried departure.

9

manda left soon after lunch, but Celeste all but forced Margaret to stay with her. Doctor Digsby was expected soon to tend to Joseph's wounds and Celeste needed her to be there.

"Last night went well, I think," Celeste said as they sat down for tea.

"I think Mr. Sharpe would have a different opinion on that matter," Margaret replied.

"Well, other than that incident, it did go almost perfectly."

Margaret raised a brow at her. "I have a bruise on my knee the color of a ripe plum and twice the size," she informed her.

"Oh, Margaret, my heart did stop for you when that happened, but I thought Charles smoothed it over very well."

As if them talking of him summoned him, Charles was announced a few minutes later.

Celeste smiled as he walked in. "We were just talking about you," she said, moving to pour him a cup of tea.

"Were you?" he asked, a hint of excitement in his voice.

"Yes, I was just complimenting you on how well you took care of Margaret after her unfortunate incident."

He nodded. "Glad to help whenever I can."

"Have you come to gossip with us as well or are you wishing to catch another glimpse of the handsome doctor when he comes to tend to Joseph?"

Charles rolled his shoulders and cleared his throat. "I came over to invite you to dinner tonight," he told her.

"That would be wonderful," Celeste replied.

"Margaret, you, of course, are more than welcome."

Margaret gave a soft smile and nod of the head. "I would love to, but I did promise my mother I would be home this evening," she said. "She has been rather lonely with my father and brother off at Cambridge."

"I was very happy to hear Marcus was accepted in," Celeste stated. "Your parents must be very proud."

Margaret replied in the affirmative. "My father is rather enjoying showing him around and has already delayed his stay for another week."

Celeste held out her hand for Charles, who was still standing, to take a seat. "Come sit with us, Charles," she ordered him.

He did as he was bid, taking the cup of tea proffered to him.

"The doctor will hopefully be here soon," Celeste said, a twinkle in her eye.

Charles looked disappointed. "Yes, I have heard he is talked well of throughout town. Though I did not realize it was the same doctor everyone had been speaking of until this morning when I made inquiries of him."

"Have you?" Celeste asked. "Well, go on and tell us about him."

Charles cleared his throat. "He is here taking care of

his ailing aunt, Mrs. Bridges."

"I heard she has been ill for several months now," Margaret added softly.

"Yes, I visited her not two months ago. She was dreadfully pale and everything seemed to throw her into the most horrid of coughing fits," Celeste said putting down her tea. "What more can you tell us of her nephew?"

"He has just finished his studies to become a doctor and was looking for a place to reside," Charles continued, not touching his tea.

"How perfect!" Celeste exclaimed grinning at her friend.

Margaret gave a weak smile back.

"Is there anything else you can tell us?" Celeste goaded.

Charles lifted his brows and shook his head. "I believe that is about all I know," he replied.

"You did not hear whether or not he is attached to anyone?" she asked.

Charles sucked his teeth a moment. "I do not recall."

Celeste gave an elegant wave of her hand as if to say, 'it doesn't matter.' "I shall find out later."

Margaret looked at Charles with interest as he sat there almost unmoving next to Celeste while she spoke freely. She watched as he stole secret glances of Celeste, his eyes silently moving about her face.

Margaret knew that look; she understood it.

"I believe Joseph's accident will actually prove useful," Celeste thought out loud.

"You know, you never explained to me how it happened," Charles stated.

"Nor I," Margaret added. "I heard he had been attacked by something?"

Celeste paused, biting her bottom lip in hesitation. "Seems all rather silly now," she responded, trying to brush it off. "It is almost not even worth mentioning."

Both Margaret and Charles raised their brows at her.

"You are not getting off that easily," Charles told her, putting his tea on a side table and turning to look at her.

Celeste looked at the both of them, their faces stern, serious. "Oh, alright!" she said, throwing her hands up in defeat. She took a deep breath and let it out slowly. "He might have been trying to propose last night and before he could, he tripped and fell over one of Sir Edwards's poor peacocks."

"He was trying to propose?" Charles repeated.

"How awful for him!" Margaret said, pressing her hands to her face.

"Yes, and the bird's tail became pinned under him, so in an attempt to free itself, it began to attack Joseph who put up one pitiful fight," Celeste continued.

Charles stood and moved to one of the windows.

Margaret thought he seemed agitated.

"The bird is not much worse for wear though," she added. "He lost a few tail feathers, but other than that he is fine. All three of the birds were returned to Sir Edwards in good health earlier this afternoon."

"That is a small consolation," Charles muttered.

"It is," Celeste agreed.

Not long after this discussion, Doctor Donald Digsby arrived at the house. Celeste, who had been by chance peering out of the window as he was riding up, waved Margaret over to take a look.

"Look how well he rides, Margaret," she whispered as if he could hear them from outside. "He is a very handsome man, is he not?" Celeste fanned her face as they watched him hand his horse's reigns to one of her servants.

"He is rather attractive," Margaret answered in accord, though less enthusiastically.

"Perhaps you both should marry him," Charles whispered to himself.

"He is even more handsome in the daylight," Celeste added as he took off his hat. She lifted a brow. "And he does not seem too loose in the pants if you catch my meaning."

Margaret looked over at her wide eyed. "I am sure I do not."

"Oh, Margaret, the act is not so terrible as you think," Celeste informed her. "All you need to do is close your eyes and think of England! Though, in your case, God."

Charles cleared his throat. "Are the two of you going to be hovering by the window when he is introduced into the room?" he asked.

Celeste gasped. "You are quite right, Charles!" She took Margaret by the hand and brought her back over to the couches. She pinched her friend's cheeks to bring color to them before posing her on the couch, making sure she was angled toward the door. She then handed her a half full cup of tea. "Hold this," she ordered before sitting on a couch positioned perpendicular to the other one.

"Do you not wish to tell me where to sit as well?" Charles asked with a small laugh.

"Do as you like," Celeste told him. "He will not be looking at you when he comes in anyway." She grabbed another tea cup raising it half way to her lips, pausing to listen for footsteps. "Back straight, Margaret," she whispered. "I hear him coming."

Her friend swallowed hard, obeying orders.

"Margaret, must I say how stunning you looked last night?" Celeste said in a tone loud enough for whoever was about to enter to hear. "I have never seen a dress look so well on anyone."

The door was then opened, and the doctor introduced.

The ladies stood and curtsied while Charles bowed stiffly where he stood.

Celeste had been right. The doctor had looked right at Margaret and the effect was immediate. His eyes lit up as soon as he saw her. Margaret blushed and shifted her gaze to the floor.

"Doctor Digsby, how good of you to come and check on our poor Joseph so soon," Celeste said.

The doctor gave a half bow. "It is my duty to do so," he replied. "How is he?"

"I am told he is faring very well," she told him. "I have not seen him yet myself as I thought he should rest."

She led the doctor up a different set of stairs from the night before, with Margaret following behind obeying orders and Charles just wanting to watch the spectacle.

They found Joseph sitting up, being fed by the maid Samantha, whom Celeste entrusted with his care.

"Miss Willoughby," the bandaged man on the bed said stretching out an equally bandaged hand. "You have come."

"Yes, and I have brought the doctor to tend to you again," Celeste answered, gently and uninterestedly patting the back of his outstretched hand.

"You are my angel," he said, his eyes brimming with tears.

Charles coughed back a laugh causing Celeste to shoot him a cross look.

"You are so special to me," Joseph continued. "I did

not get to tell you last night, but you are the most—"

"Yes, yes, very good, Joseph," Celeste interrupted him. "Margaret and Doctor Digsby are going to see to your wounds. But do not fret, I will be elsewhere in the house wishing you a full and quick recovery."

"Do you think you can manage, Miss Hepworth?" Doctor Digsby asked gently.

Margaret blushed and bit her lip but nodded. "I was just surprised by it all last night," she replied softly.

"If you need anything, Doctor, Samantha can get it for you," Celeste added as she took Charles by the arm led him back out the room.

"I bet you think you are clever," Charles said later that evening as they drove in Celeste's carriage to his house.

"Of course, I am clever!" she said with a smile. "My plan is working! He asked her if he could call on her tomorrow!" She gave a satisfied sigh.

"And it could all be for naught," Charles added.

Celeste frowned at him. "There is no need to trample through my garden with your negative thoughts," she told him. "I do not see how it could not work. He is about twice as handsome as John Howard is and significantly more charming too. Can you believe he is also Catholic?" Celeste clapped her hands together in joy. "Can you imagine the luck? If I believed in a thing as ridiculous as fate that is what I would call it." She grinned at him. "Honestly, I almost thought this whole thing would be more difficult."

"Now, you just have to find yourself a husband," Charles replied sarcastically.

Celeste's smile fell. "Ah, yes."

"Seems Joseph is still more than willing."

Celeste scratched the back of her head. "Poor thing. I will obviously have to wait until he has recovered from his injuries before I let him down."

Charles gave half a smile and laughed through his nose. "You really know how to kick a man when he is most vulnerable, do you not?"

She didn't reply, merely giving a small shrug.

"I am sure you will receive another proposal soon enough. If not, it is off to the madhouse for you."

Celeste shifted uncomfortably. Charles's words were meant in jest, to help open up the door to a conversation he had wanted to have with her for a while now, but he saw she felt them keenly.

"Are you alright?" he asked her, noticing her distant look. "You do not believe your father means to make good on his threat, do you? How many times has he made the same threat to you and failed to follow through? Just the other day you seemed unbothered by it."

Celeste pressed her lips together. "There is something I need to relay to you, Charles," she told him in a serious voice.

Charles blinked at her, his heart in his stomach. He was not used to her speaking in such a tone. "What has happened?"

She cleared her throat. "I did not want to tell you this, and I certainly could not tell Margaret, but if I were to relay it to you, I know I can trust you to not tell anyone."

"Why do I feel as if I am not going to like what you are about to say?"

"Oh, I am positive you will not like it. You might even become cross with me." She cleared her throat again and began.

Charles gaped at her in horror when she was done relaying her story about Mr. Stanley's visit.

She, however, gave a triumphant grin. "So, my father can try to scare me all he likes," she continued, "but I will never be taken that easily. Oh," she pressed a hand to her chest, "by the way, I need someone to patch the hole in the floor of the breakfast parlor before father comes home. Do you know of anyone?"

"I should have brought a drink for this ride," Charles muttered burying his face in his hands.

By then they had made it to Charles's estate. Celeste was handed out of the carriage, but Charles hesitated in his seat, trying to process what she had just told him. He finally poked his head out a minute later.

"That really happened this morning?" he asked her.

She nodded. "Yes, truly, it did. Now, get out of the carriage so we can go inside."

He hopped out, frowning in his thoughts as he escorted her inside to the parlor. "So, you are telling me that you shot at the man who potentially holds your future in his hands?"

"He thought he could touch me with his corpse-like hands," she replied shivering. "Ugh. They were unnaturally cold and uncomfortably long and thin, so, of course, I shot at him." She shook her head moving to pour herself a glass of brandy. "If he thinks he has a right to do that to a high-class woman who is not under his care, think of what he does to the women who *are* in his care. That man belongs in one of his cages."

"You could very well end up in one of those cages, Celeste, if you keep going about like that!" Charles said a little heatedly. "When are you going to start taking this issue seriously?"

Celeste blinked at him. "When do I take anything seriously?"

Charles sighed and closed his eyes. "Celeste, your father paid this man to come see you. When does your father ever pay anyone anything? He is the most miserly son of a bitch I know."

"There is no need to insult my grandmother, Charles," she gently scolded while bringing him a glass.

He took a gulp. "You need to consider that your father might be serious this time in his threat."

Celeste shook her head. "It crossed my mind, but I cannot see father going through with it. There is too much at stake."

Charles gave an exasperated sigh and began pacing the room.

"When is the last time you bedded someone?" Celeste asked narrowing her eyes at him.

"What?" Charles said in surprise. "What does that have to do with anything?"

Celeste shook her head. "You have just been awfully tense lately."

Charles frowned at her. "That is because you are the most frustrating woman I have ever known." He looked down into his glass. "Are you truly not worried?" he asked her in a softer tone.

Celeste looked down into her own glass for a moment before taking a sip. "To be honest, the thought of marriage scares me more than being sent away."

"Truly?"

Celeste nodded. "The thought of attaching myself to one person, to be dependent upon one person, to lie with one person, to," she paused and looked at him, "love one person for the rest of my life and trust that they will do the same." She shook her head. "It does not seem possible." She moved to the couch and sat down.

"It is not possible for *you* to do those things?" he asked tentatively.

Celeste smoothed out her dress and shook her head. "No, I believe I could," she replied. "I just do not believe I could find a man who could." She shrugged. "I do not know. It just seems so," she hesitated, "restrictive, or binding." She rubbed her arm as if she were cold.

Charles moved toward her. "We are not all like your father, Celeste," he told her, sitting beside her and taking her hand. "There are good men out there."

Celeste gave a small smile. "We both know I do not deserve *good*, Charles," she told him. "Perhaps, decent at best, but not good."

He creased his brows and regarded her for a moment. "What in the world would ever make you think that?" He placed a hand on her cheek and stroked it with his thumb. "You deserve more than you give yourself credit for, Celeste," he told her, his voice almost a whisper. His hand moved slowly to her chin, gently lifting it so her eyes met his. "You are worth more to m—"

Suddenly the doors to the room burst open, causing both Celeste and Charles to jump from their seats in surprise.

"Cousin!" gleefully shouted a dashingly handsome, blonde man with a wide grin on his face.

"Graham!" Celeste exclaimed happily when she saw who it was. "Charles, you did not tell me Graham was to dine with us tonight!" She moved to him.

"I did not know he was coming," Charles grumbled.

"Celeste," Graham said kissing her fully on the mouth. "You are just as beautiful as when I last saw you. Nay, even more so."

Celeste playfully fanned herself. "How charming you are. You really know what a woman wants to hear."

He winked at her.

"Unannounced, as always, cousin," Charles said clasping Graham's hand.

"I prefer it that way," Graham replied. "The best way to catch people is unawares." He turned back to Celeste. "Just as seeing you here has caught me so."

"Oh?" Celeste asked raising a brow with a coy smile.

"I was hoping to catch you unaware later this evening, hopefully in your night gown."

Celeste laughed and slapped his arm half-heartedly. "You are the worst kind of tease," she said.

He lifted a brow at her, brandishing a charming grin. "I was not teasing."

Charles cleared his throat disapprovingly. "What has brought you here this time, cousin?" he asked breaking Graham's attention on Celeste. "Another gaming debt?"

"Well, someone is a grouch this evening," Graham replied, pouring himself something to drink.

"It is the usual way with you," Charles retorted.

"Let us not quarrel," Celeste broke in.

"Who is quarrelling?" Charles asked holding his hands up. "I am merely stating what tends to be the case with my cousin."

Graham nodded throwing back his drink. "I cannot argue with that," he said, pointing at Charles. "It is usually the case, but not this time. This time, I have come for nothing more than the pleasure of your company."

Charles huffed.

"It is a shame you did not arrive last night," Celeste told him. "I threw a ball and would have loved to have you twirl me on the dance floor."

"Is that so?" Graham said. He stepped toward her, wrapping an arm around her waist and taking her hand in his as he whirled her around the room, all the while singing.

Celeste laughed in delight as he moved her about in exaggerated movements. "Oh, stop," she squealed in pleasure. "I can scarce breathe from laughing!"

He did one more round before letting her go and bowing elegantly.

She laughed and curtsied in return. "You are, without doubt, a lively partner."

He took her hand and kissed it. "And you a lovely one."

She laughed again.

Charles, who had been joylessly watching the whole display, cleared his throat again. "I believe I just heard the dinner bell," he told them. "Perhaps we should move to the dining room."

"Excellent!" Graham exclaimed. "Allow me ten minutes to change." He took Celeste's hand and gave it another kiss in a hyperbolic display of affection causing her to laugh again. "I shall return, my dear," he told her and made his way out of the room.

"He is in an excitable mood," Celeste observed walking over to Charles and taking his arm. "It is quite infectious."

"Surely," Charles replied tonelessly. "Celeste," he started, turning to her. "Before he came in, I was trying to—"

A servant opened the door interrupting Charles once again. "Dinner is ready, sir," he said with a bow.

Charles rubbed the bridge of his nose and cursed under his breath. "Yes, thank you, Edgar," he replied.

"Shall I set another place for your cousin?" the servant

asked.

Charles nodded. "Yes, thank you."

"Very good, sir." The servant bowed and moved back out of the room.

"What were you saying, Charles?" Celeste asked after a moment.

He shook his head. "Nothing," he said forcing a small smile. "Nothing that I cannot tell you another time." He had lost his nerve.

"Come," Celeste said gently. "Escort me to dinner."

Celeste rolled over, a satisfied sigh escaping her mouth. "Thank you for being so kind as to escort me home. It is wonderful seeing you again." She sighed. "Please tell me you are here for an extended stay," she said brushing her hair from her face. "I need more nights like this."

Graham pushed off of the bed and began kissing her neck, causing her to laugh. "I will stay as long as you want me to," he told her, planting a kiss on her lips.

She laughed again. "I have missed your eagerness to please," she told him wrapping her arms around his neck.

He playfully nipped at her nose. "Is no one else so eager?" he asked her.

She sighed again before shaking her head. "Unfortunately, no," she replied. "More often than not I am left having to finish the job myself."

He gasped jokingly. "You poor creature. However do you survive?"

She pressed the back of her hand against her forehead. "Barely, sir. Barely."

He slipped a hand under her back and rolled over so that she was on top of him. "Perhaps you need some saving."

"Perhaps I do," she replied with a playful smile.

He sighed contentedly. "I believe I am in love with you, Celeste."

Celeste groaned and rolled off of him. "Do not spoil the moment," she said.

He laughed. "Is that what love does?" he replied. "Spoil things?"

"It most certainly does!" she exclaimed. "Besides, I do not believe you love me."

"No?" he asked, turning on his side and propping himself up on his elbow so he could look at her.

"I believe you love the end result which is what I have just given you," she continued. "And, in the heat of the moment, it inspires something akin to love, but, after the moment has passed, the feeling will fade."

He laughed. "You are a very cynical woman."

"Not cynical," she corrected, "realistic."

"Those two often go hand-in-hand, you know?" he told her.

She yawned.

"What about my cousin?" he asked hesitantly after a moment.

"Charles? What about him?"

"Is he not eager to please?"

She rolled over onto her stomach and held herself up on her elbows. "Charles was always wonderful," she told him.

"Was?" Graham arched a brow at her.

She rubbed her lips together for a moment. "We no longer partake in such activities."

"He is a fool."

She laughed. "What makes you think it was he who

chose to stop?"

He creased his brow at her. "You did then?"

Celeste took in a deep breath and let it out slowly. "I did."

He gave her a skeptical look. "Why?"

She tilted her head, causing her hair to cascade onto the pillow. "That is a story for another time," she replied.

"Humph," he said pushing himself into a seated position. "Where do you keep those cigars?"

She pointed to a little table with a drawer by the door. "In there."

He got out of the bed, his pale skin just visible in the glow of candlelight. "Are you in love with him, then?" he asked as he opened the drawer and pulled a cigar out.

"With whom?" she asked, sitting up.

"With my cousin."

Celeste opened her mouth to reply, unsure of what to say, when suddenly the door to her room flew open.

She screamed as the figure of a bandaged man stood in the doorway.

"Miss Willoughby," the figure moaned.

"Joseph, what are you doing here?" she yelled wrapping the sheets around her naked body while motioning for an equally naked Graham to hide.

Joseph approached, his arms outstretched. He was clad in a white night gown and what little of him that stuck out from it was wrapped in bandages, giving him the appearance of a mummy.

"I have missed you," Joseph cried. "I must speak with you."

"Joseph, this is very inappropriate," Celeste said in a scolding tone.

He fell at the side of the bed reaching for her. "I love

you," he proclaimed. "I love you!"

Celeste heard Graham chuckle from behind her partition.

"I want to make you my wife," Joseph continued, his words slightly slurred.

"Are you drunk?" Celeste asked him, sliding over to the other side of the bed to get away from his reach.

"I have had some whiskey with what the doctor gave me," he replied. "But that is not what has brought about these feelings I have. I feel what I feel for you in my heart."

Graham stifled another laugh.

"That is very good, Joseph," Celeste told him, reaching for the bell to get the attention of one of the servants. "But you still should not be in my room during this hour. It is not proper."

"No! No, you are right," he said struggling to get up. "I would never want to do anything to ruin your reputation."

Samantha came hobbling in a few moments later, breathing heavily. "Oh, miss, I left 'im for two seconds to fetch another blanket and he was jus' gone!" she said, taking Joseph under the arm. "I do 'pologize, ma'am."

"Marry me, my love," Joseph said as Samantha dragged him away. "Marry me!"

"I'm so sorry, ma'am," Samantha apologized again sheepishly as they walked back out the door.

When the door was shut, Graham came out from behind the partition chuckling, still naked. "Seems I am not the only one in whom you inspire strong feelings," he told her, grinning.

"Yes," she replied dryly. "It is certainly my burden to bear." She sighed. "Poor Joseph. He is a sweet young man, but he is not for me."

Graham caressed her face and kissed her. "I think I

should go," he told her. "Unless you need someone to protect you from whatever that was."

Celeste laughed. "He is truly harmless. He just looks a little rough right now."

"I shall call on you again," he told her as he started to get dressed.

"And I shall look forward to it," she replied, sliding back into bed.

He bowed. "Until then, my fair lady," he said grinning at her.

"Until then, my good knight," she replied dramatically.

Graham shot her a wink as he opened the balcony door and climbed down to the ground below.

10

Celeste's skeptical view on marriage was solidified by her father's philandering while her mother still lived. Celeste was rather close to her mother, Elizabeth, who, in her view, was an angel. She had never heard a cross word leave her lips and had the most patient disposition. She was, however, of a sickly constitution and was often in bed with a new illness.

Celeste would spend hours at her mother's bedside reading to her or speaking to her mother in French. When her mother was well enough, she was brought into the music room to listen in on Celeste's harp lessons.

There was barely a moment Celeste did not spend with her mother if she could. She would go for rides with Charles, whom she had known her entire life, and, at her mother's request would host small tea parties for some of the other young ladies, including Margaret, in the neighborhood, but her mother was her whole world.

They shared everything together; hopes and dreams were whispered to each other, and tales of romance imagined between them.

Her mother would always tell a tale of young lovers

triumphing over the greatest odds to be together, forsaking all others, and living for no one but each other. This had been Celeste's earliest view on love. She had felt there was no other way to love than that, and she believed that marriage inspired those tender feelings in everyone; it was how she viewed her parents' marriage. Her father was always sweet and attentive, ready and willing to pay for the best care for her mother.

Celeste had been proud of his actions. She had thought her father was the perfect example of a husband, but she soon learned her folly.

Despite what their relationship turned into, Celeste had at one time been close to her father. He had doted on her, taught her how to ride, shoot, fence and other things that would be considered 'inappropriate,' but that all changed when Celeste was fourteen.

Her mother had just contracted the disease that would ultimately claim her life. She had spent a restless night coughing and Celeste, who had stayed up with her, had left her bedside in the middle of the night to refill the water pitcher.

The moon had been eerily bright that evening, and the winter chill was just starting to creep its way through the walls. She remembered wishing she had put on slippers because the floor was so cold.

She had to pass her father's room to get to the back stairs to the kitchen and it was as she approached his door, she heard a noise she was unsure of. It sounded like a low moaning followed by gasping or sighs.

At first, she had thought her father might have been unwell, so she opened the door to check on him. But, instead of finding her father ill in bed, she found him wrapped in the embrace of one of their maids. Their shadows danced on the walls in the flickering light of a candle as their bodies clashed against each other.

Celeste had stood there unmoving, her breath coming in short horror-filled gasps until the weight of what was happening before her finally broke through the fog of confusion. Anger coursed through her body, white, hot anger she could not contain. She screamed, breaking the dead of the night as she hurled the pitcher she had been carrying across the room, causing it to smash against the wall, shattering into a million pieces.

The act had terrified both her father and the maid who fumbled to cover themselves, falling over the matted sheets and each other.

But it was too late.

The damage had already been done.

For a brief moment, Celeste had caught her father's eye and they stood silently staring at one another. Hatred in one's eyes, shame in the other's.

From that day on, Celeste's views on love and marriage, much like the pitcher she threw, were shattered. Millions of broken pieces scattered about, unable to be pieced back together. And, from that day on, Celeste's feelings toward her father had changed.

She no longer viewed him as the loving husband she had once thought him to be. In fact, the incident had brought about earlier moments in her life where she had caught her father in similar circumstances. Stealing glances from maids, disappearing with other women at parties, strange noises she often heard coming from his room when she thought him alone.

They all made sense.

The love he had for her mother had been a lie.

Their marriage was a lie.

Love itself was a lie.

And she would not fall for it.

Resentment was all she had left for the man who had betrayed her mother's feelings. Resentment was all she had left for the man whose lies had destroyed something she had thought was beyond beautiful.

From that night, Celeste refused to be alone with her father, denying the gifts he tried to give her to win her back and stopping all of the lessons they once enjoyed together. It was during this time she grew closer to Margaret who had always been an attentive, close-lipped listener.

Despite the solace she found in her friend's company and the gentle urgings of forgiveness her friend spoke of, Celeste's resentment for her father only grew. With her eyes now opened to who her father really was, Celeste remained vigilant as she watched her father gallivanting behind her mother's back. These feelings worsened when her mother passed away less than two years later, crushing Celeste's reserve and breaking her heart even more.

After that, her life's goal seemed to be to do everything in her power her father would disapprove of, to hurt him the way he had hurt her and her mother, to disappoint him as he had disappointed her. And that is exactly what Celeste had vowed to do.

11

Joseph was soon deemed out of danger the next couple of days and shipped back to his own house, though in significantly lower spirits than when he first arrived. Celeste thought it imperative to break it to him she had no intentions of marrying him before he was seated in the carriage.

It had been a sad scene, but it was done and over, and Celeste felt pretty good about it. She felt even better about having her house back to herself. Adding to her happiness was a letter from her father extending his stay in London another week, giving Celeste more opportunities to entertain. She held a few more gatherings, though small, making sure to invite Margaret and Doctor Digsby.

Unfortunately, the doctor found himself a lot busier than he imagined having just entered the neighborhood, and was unable to attend all but one of the events. Regardless, Celeste had been delighted, seeing her friend much admired by the handsome young man.

Margaret had been shy and reserved at first, but with some encouragement from Celeste, she saw her friend falling easier into conversation. They spoke about books, poetry, and religion. The two of them sat alone, set apart from the rest of the room just so they could talk.

With a little more encouragement and time, Celeste saw her friend well on the way to mending her heart and possibly giving it to someone more deserving.

The following week, Celeste was invited to tea at Amanda Haderly's. It was the first time the young girl had hosted anything, and she was insistent that Celeste attend. Celeste, of course, would not have missed it otherwise, but she assured the young girl that she would be there.

She actually looked forward to it. She had not seen Margaret in several days and Charles had been too busy to answer her calls as of late, so she was relishing the chance to socialize.

There had been Graham, of course, but his visits were limited to nighttime meetups, lasting an hour or two at a time.

She had her horse saddled up, excited the weather was fine for a ride, when the sounds of someone's arrival halted her. She looked up the drive to see her father's carriage approaching two days earlier than expected.

She cursed and without another second's thought, she jumped on her horse and steered it to a different path, but it was too late; he had seen her.

"Celeste!" she heard him shout. "Where are you going? You are to go nowhere until I have spoken with you!"

She saw him leaning out the window, waving his arm in an attempt to get her attention.

"Sorry, father!" she replied, moving her horse away. "I am late. I really must go!"

"You ungrateful child! I said do not move!"

"I cannot hear you in all of this wind!" she said with a wave. "I shall see you later! Hope London was eventful."

She didn't wait for an answer before she leaned into her horse and hurried it off as fast as she could.

She arrived not long after at Miss Haderly's, her hair blown a little out of place and her cheeks flushed.

Amanda greeted her warmly. "You came!"

"Where else would I be, my dear?" she replied taking a seat at the table.

Margaret smiled at her, but the other two women at the table gave her cold, stiff nods in greeting. Celeste smiled at the both of them. Mrs. Thorpe and her sister Miss Cleary.

"How are you, ladies?" Celeste asked. "I have not seen you in some time. You look well."

"You do not seem to have changed, Celeste," Mrs. Thorpe replied, a woman about Celeste's age with a pinched face and mousy brown hair.

"We heard Joseph Sharpe proposed to you," her sister, a plain girl a year or two younger, added.

"Another proposal, another man left in the wind," Mrs. Thorpe continued, in a disapproving tone.

Celeste raised an eyebrow. She wasn't sure how the information about Joseph got out. "I would hardly call it a proposal," she replied, thanking Amanda for the tea she gave her.

"Hmph," Mrs. Thorpe said in reply.

Celeste exchanged glances with Margaret who hid her smile in her tea cup. "How is Robert, by the way?" she asked causing Mrs. Thorpe to choke on her tea. "I have not seen him in ages. I hope he is well."

The woman gave Celeste an angered look. Her husband had, at one point, been one of those men Celeste left in the wind. He was her second proposal, and Mrs. Thorpe, shooting daggers across the table with her eyes, was his second choice.

"He is rather well, thank you," Mrs. Thorpe replied a little tartly.

"Glad to hear it." Celeste nodded. "Amanda, did you come up with this menu by yourself?" she asked, changing the subject.

She nodded. "I have been trying to pay attention to what other people serve at their teas and tried to take a little something from each one."

"These little cakes are delightful," Celeste told her.

Margaret nodded. "They truly are."

"Amanda, where is your mother?" Celeste asked. "Surely, she would not miss your first tea."

Amanda smiled. "She has gone to Brighton for at least a month," she replied. "She does not know I have invited anyone over."

Celeste smiled coyly at the girl. She was proud to have such a fast-learning pupil.

"You are such a sweet girl to invite us, Amanda," Mrs. Thorpe stated, interrupting Celeste's thoughts. "We were very delighted to receive your invitation."

"Is your brother in by chance?" Miss Clearly asked.

"Eric?" Amanda shook her head. "No, I believe he is at the Wilmingtons. He seems quite taken with Sarah."

Miss Cleary deflated a bit. "Oh."

Celeste almost felt bad for her, but the feeling soon passed when her sister spoke again.

"So, when are you ever to marry, Celeste?" Mrs. Thorpe asked. "You are almost thirty, are you not?"

Celeste smiled and blinked at her. "I am five and twenty, Caroline," she replied. "And I guess by now I would have been married for five years had I accepted your husband's proposal."

Amanda, ignorant of the situation looked from one woman to the other; Margaret gaped at Celeste; Miss Cleary's hands flew to her mouth; Mrs. Thorpe's face twitched.

"But," Celeste continued, pausing to allow the tension to linger for just one more second, "his second choice seems to suit him much better than I ever would have." She smiled. "Would you be a dear and pass the sugar, Caroline?"

"Miss Willoughby, had I known of your history with Mrs. Thorpe, I would not have dreamed of inviting them," Amanda said later after the other two women had left.

"Pay them no mind," Celeste told her. "And, please, call me Celeste. We are beyond formalities now."

Amanda beamed. "Celeste," she repeated with a nod.

"Oh, it was a whole debacle almost six years ago," Margaret said. "Poor Mr. Thorpe had been so taken by Celeste. He had thrown this grand party in her honor and not even halfway into the night he gathers everyone around and proposes to her right there with everyone looking at them."

Amanda gasped. "But why would he do such a thing?" she asked. "It is his own fault really. You cannot put a woman on the spot like that in front of all of those people."

"Thank you, Amanda," Celeste said. "It was quite awful. Part of me wanted to say yes just to spare him and then break it off later." She sighed. "But I did not. I gave him a firm no and left the party."

"The poor man was crushed," Margaret continued. "And everyone at the party did not know what to do."

"It had been a very good evening before that

happened," Celeste added.

"So, Mrs. Thorpe is still jealous you refused her husband?" Amanda asked.

"Seems silly, I know," Celeste told her. "Especially since had I accepted him, she could not have married him, so, honestly, she should be thanking me."

Margaret nodded. "He asked Caroline to marry him the following year."

"Which she should consider the greatest favor I could have ever bestowed on anyone," Celeste proclaimed. "I doubt she would ever have been married otherwise."

Amanda giggled while Margaret shot her a disapproving look that Celeste chose to ignore.

There was a knock at the door and a few moments later Stephen Browning was let in.

Amanda's face brightened while Celeste frowned; Margaret looked uncomfortable; Stephen, upon seeing Celeste, looked surprised.

"Mr. Browning," Amanda said calmly after recollecting herself. "You have caught us quite by surprise. We were not expecting you."

Stephen bowed an apology. "Forgive my intrusion. I hope I did not interrupt anything important." He shot a quick glance at Celeste.

"You have only interrupted the most important of discussions," Amanda said with a grin. "Gossip."

"Oh?" Stephen replied with a smile of his own. "Anything I should know?"

Amanda smiled and shifted her gaze. "Well, we certainly cannot discuss it now that *you* are here."

Celeste silently applauded the girl's flirting skills. They were not perfect, but she had come a long way in a very short time.

The four of them made small talk for a few minutes until Amanda suggested to Margaret to open the piano. Margaret hesitated at first, disliking to be put on display, but when Amanda told her she wanted to sing, she acquiesced.

Celeste saw what she was doing. Amanda, who had the voice of an angel, was trying to impress Stephen.

"I did not think to see you here," Stephen said, taking the seat next to Celeste.

"Nor I you," she replied not looking at him. "Especially after the agreement we came to a few weeks ago."

He cleared his throat. "I had not seen you alone since that night," he explained. "And then what do I hear?"

Margaret began her song; Amanda, standing by the piano facing her other two guests, waited for her queue.

"I hear that Graham Pratt is in town," Stephen continued.

"What is your point, Stephen?" she asked, watching as Amanda swelled her breast with air to begin singing.

"You yourself said you would not share my bed with another woman," he hissed. "Why must I share your bed with another man?"

"Oh, do not for one minute think I do not know about you and Marcia Haysworth," she retorted.

Stephen started but collected himself. "That was only for a few weeks," he told her.

"Really?" Celeste replied smiling as Amanda began her song. "*She* told me it was for almost the entire winter, until she left for her aunt's in Kent for Easter."

Stephen cleared his throat again and shifted in his seat. He sighed and turned to look at Celeste. He opened his mouth to speak but she interrupted him.

"Eyes forward, Stephen," she ordered him gently. "She

is putting on this show for you, at least pretend to pay attention."

He hesitated but did as he was told. "I want you to stop seeing him."

"Graham?" Celeste asked. "I will stop seeing him when he leaves next or he tires of me. Whichever one comes first."

Stephen rubbed his mouth to hide a scowl. "We both know he will not tire of you while he is here."

She shot him a glance. "Are you truly jealous, Stephen?" she asked with a hint of laughter in her voice.

Stephen stiffened.

"I thought at first you might be, but did not believe it," she continued. "Now, I know that you are."

"Stop seeing Graham Pratt or I will continue my pursuit of Miss Haderly," he warned her. "She has a voice that inspires wonders in a man."

Celeste put a hand over her mouth to hide a laugh. "Now you are trying to make *me* jealous," she replied. "It was a poor attempt." She let out a small sigh of satisfaction. "I like this side of you, Stephen."

He gave her a sharp look.

"It shows me you are capable of feeling more than lust."

"Do you think me a bottomless pit?"

She bit her bottom lip as she smiled. "No, just a troglodyte."

"You snub me and then insult me," he stated with a nod. "You will not come back to my bed, then?"

"You do not own me, Stephen," she told him matter-of-factly. "No man does." She shrugged. "I guess you could say my father does, but even *he* cannot control me."

"All of this flirting and fucking you do, Celeste, will be

worth nothing when you die alone."

She frowned at him. "Do not be vulgar, Stephen," she told him. "It is unbecoming." She stood and clapped as Amanda and Margaret finished their song. "That was wonderful!" she exclaimed. "Margaret, your skills on the piano are beyond reproach and, Amanda, your voice inspires *wonders*!"

Stephen glared at her.

Amanda, trying her best to control her usual exuberance glided back over to them. "I was a little nervous at the start," she replied.

Stephen stood himself and smiled at her. "No one would have been able to tell," he said. "It was transcendent."

Celeste moved to the window to hide her amusement at Stephen's pathetic attempts to make her jealous.

"Do you think so?" Amanda asked, her excitement slipping out a bit.

"I truly have never heard a voice more angelic than yours," Stephen replied. "Would you honor me with another song?"

The young girl's cheeks flushed, and, for a moment, she was unable to speak merely nodding at his request. Celeste decided she had more work to do as she watched Amanda almost skip back to the piano.

Stephen moved over to the window to join Celeste as Margaret and Amanda decided on the next song.

"Taking her is going to be so easy," he whispered.

Celeste scowled. "Taking her might be, but getting rid of her after will not," she warned him. "She is an attachment waiting to happen, Stephen. It will end in disaster."

"Are you jealous now?" he grinned.

Celeste laughed quietly. "Do not flatter yourself," she replied. "I am merely giving you friendly advice. Amanda will not bed you without expecting a proposal as I told you a few weeks ago."

"Perhaps I will give her one."

Celeste laughed harder. "You will no sooner marry that girl than I will marry Joseph Sharpe."

A servant came through the doors just then, carrying a letter on a silver platter. He brought it to Celeste.

"For you, ma'am," he said presenting it to her.

"Thank you," Celeste replied taking it. She groaned when she saw the seal.

It was from her father. A servant must have told him where she had gone. She opened it tentatively, reading through it quickly.

She sighed and folded it back up. "Seems my father is requesting my immediate return."

"Visit me tonight," Stephen told her after a moment.

She shot him a playful grin. "Perhaps I will," she replied. "Or, perhaps I already have plans."

12

Celeste greeted her father with the façade of warmth, kissing him on both cheeks. "You look well, father," she said moving to take a seat on the couch. She fanned herself, ignoring the stern look her father was shooting at her. "It is very hot outside," she complained. "Gerald, would you bring me some water?"

Gerald bowed obediently and ducked out of the room, glad for the excuse to leave the tension-filled air.

"I received the most curious of letters the other day," Her father finally said, his face not losing its stern constitution.

"Oh?" Celeste asked, unfeeling, as she began to play with the bracelets on her wrist.

"Yes," her father continued. "From Sir Edwards."

Celeste paused momentarily but caught herself. "What could he have written to you about?"

"He invited us to dinner next week."

Celeste shrugged. "Shall we go?" she asked. "He does put out the most luxurious of spreads."

"He then asked me something I did not quite understand," her father said, ignoring her question. "He asked me if I enjoyed his peacocks at my ball last week and apologized for not being able to have made it himself."

"What a strange thing to say," Celeste said after a moment. "Poor Sir Edwards. He is getting rather old."

"Sir Edwards is not even fifty-five," her father replied. "Answer me carefully, Celeste, and do not lie. Did you throw a ball after I specifically told you not to?"

"Yes," she replied without hesitation. "I threw a ball after I specifically told you I would."

Her father threw his hands up in agitation. "My grief with how you have turned out is beyond words!" he exclaimed.

Celeste did not reply, but showed no indication that his words affected her.

"And what is more?" her father continued. "I get a five-page letter from Mr. Stanley listing all of the reasons why you should be sent away immediately."

This time Celeste frowned.

"He says that in an attempt to persuade him to write you a positive review, you offered to sleep with him."

Celeste jumped off the couch in a fury. "That is the most egregious lie I have ever heard!" she shouted back. "That disgusting, snake of a man touched me without permission. Ask Gerald, he was witness to it!"

"Will Gerald also refute Mr. Stanley's claim that you shot at him?"

Celeste paused in her fury to hide a smile. "*That* I did."

Her father ran his fingers through his thin, graying hair. "You—" he pointed a finger at her in anger before balling his hand back into a fist and biting his knuckle. "You are—" He shook his head, unable to form words.

"What?" she said, goading him. "Should you not be proud that your daughter is able to fend herself from unwanted attentions?"

"Six months, my dear," he finally said. "If you are not engaged by December the thirty-first, you will be spending your New Year's Day in the back of a carriage bound for Mr. Stanley's asylum."

"Either way, we will be rid of each other," Celeste said, a hardened look on her face. "Good."

Her father looked taken aback for a moment, but it passed.

"And where is your mistress?" Celeste asked acidly, looking around. "Did she not accept your offer to stay here for a while? Did she tire of you so soon?"

Her father cleared his throat. "She and her brother will be joining us in a few days. They had some business to wrap up first. I came home because I wanted to talk with you before they came and make sure the house is in order."

Celeste didn't reply.

"The count seems like a very good man," he told her. "Very sophisticated."

Celeste rolled her eyes and moved to exit the room. She knew where this was headed.

"Where are you going?" her father asked her.

"Out," was the only reply she gave.

Celeste stood in the clearing in her woods, waiting. She was still fuming at her father, running their conversation over and over in her head, each time getting angrier. She paced for a while, then she sat, but her anger made her restless, so she stood and began to pace again.

Finally, she heard the sounds of hooves approaching her.

“I did not expect to hear from you so soon,” Stephen said as he hopped off his horse.

“I was not sure where you were,” Celeste told him. “I sent identical notes to Miss Haderly’s and one to your estate.”

“I was still at Miss Haderly’s but I left as soon as I received your note.”

“Good,” Celeste said as she moved to him, kissing him hard, her hands fumbling to take off his clothes.

Stephen grabbed her hair at the nape of her neck and pulled her head back, kissing her neck as she undid his pants. The two of them fell to their knees, throwing off jackets and pushing up skirts as they fell into rhythm. Their bodies arched, aching with pleasure.

Their movements were hard and fast; one fueled by their argument earlier in the day; the other fueled by her father’s harsh words. Hate, anger, and the want of release charged their movements until they fell gasping for air in the tall grass.

Celeste brushed back her hair with one hand while pressing the other one over her heart. Stephen rolled over and began kissing her neck and shoulder.

“That was quite athletic,” he finally said pulling her closer.

Celeste laughed. “It certainly was.” She sighed as she sat up. “I should be getting back.”

“What? Now?” Stephen replied. “But I have only had you once.” He sat up and continued kissing her neck, his hand cupping her breast. “You know I cannot let you leave until I have had you at least twice.” He playfully bit her shoulder and she laughed.

“One day,” she started as she turned to him, “I am going to say no to your ‘second time.’”

He laughed as he pulled her back down into the grass. "One day, but not today."

13

A few days later, Celeste invited Margaret over for tea. Her father had taken the carriage to meet the duchess and her brother, and they were not expected back until dinner. She had invited Charles too, as a means to further annoy her father, but, like all of the other invitations as of late, he had not replied.

"Doctor Digsby is not here, is he?" Margaret asked when she entered.

"No, my love," Celeste told her, taking her arm. "It is just the two of us. You will have to be content with just that."

"I am glad," Margaret replied.

Celeste shot her a glance. "Why?" she asked. "I thought you and the doctor get along well."

"We do," Margaret replied. "I have seen so much of him recently, it is nice to just have some time with you."

Celeste grinned at her. "I had invited Charles as well, but he has been snubbing me of late. Have you heard from him?"

"Actually, he called on me the other day."

"Charles called on you?" Celeste asked as she handed her friend to the table. "Whatever for?"

Margaret shook her head. "It was the strangest thing really, but I—" she sighed as she took her seat. "I should not be telling you this."

Celeste lifted a brow as she sat across from her. "Tell me what?"

Margaret wrinkled her nose. "Well, I feel as if Charles might have been telling me this in confidence, though he did not necessarily ask me not to say anything."

Celeste narrowed her eyes at her friend as she poured the tea. "Go on," she encouraged.

Margaret gave another sigh. "He just seems a little put out by you," she replied.

"What on earth for?" Celeste asked, carefully handing her friend a cup of tea.

Margaret shrugged. "He was really only there for a few minutes," she informed her. "He came in very agitated and seemed to leave worse off than he came." She shook her head again and sighed. "Honestly, it was quite surprising. He breezed in and breezed out before I could offer him anything to drink."

"Did he say anything specific?"

Margaret thought for a moment. "Most of what he said was spoken so quickly and he caught me in such surprise that I could barely make out three words out of ten."

Celeste pursed her lips for a moment. "That is rather convenient," she said observing her friend.

Margaret shrugged. "Though he did say something about his cousin Graham. Something about him coming in and you practically falling over him."

"Why does he not tell me things?" Celeste pouted. "Why must he tell you who he knows will tell me. If he is so upset with me, why should he not speak to me about it?"

Margaret did not reply.

"Was he drunk?"

She shook her head. "I do not believe so. He did not appear to be at least."

"I shall have to call on him then," Celeste said with a nod of her head. "He has been acting so out of character lately, I am truly worried about him. He even canceled tea with me last minute a couple of days ago, saying some business emergency had come up." She sighed. "And I wanted him to be here when the duchess and her brother arrived."

"Are they to arrive this evening?" Margaret asked in a heightened voice.

Celeste nodded. "It is the reason I invited you here. I am a selfish, weak creature and I need the support. It is also why I did not invite the doctor. He seems a very nice man and, for your sake, I cannot expose him to the spectacle that is my father."

"Does your father intend for you to marry the count then?" Margaret asked.

"My father intends me to marry anyone who will have me at this point," Celeste grumbled.

"Which is not a short list," Margaret laughed. "How many proposals have you accumulated over the years?"

Celeste grinned. "Joseph made six."

"Six proposals!" Margaret exclaimed. "Six, when most only ever get one and some never receive any at all!"

Celeste sighed contently. "It is a fine collection, I must admit."

Margaret laughed. "And how many more do you think you will receive until you actually accept one?"

"When I find a man who can better me," Celeste replied, "then, and only then, will I make him a wife."

Celeste had not yet told Margaret about her father's threat. She did not want to worry her friend with her well-being. It was usually the way with Celeste. She heard, and took in, and tried to fix everyone's complaints, but never voiced her own issues to anyone.

Except for Charles. Celeste found she could tell him pretty much anything, which is why his absence bothered her so much.

Not long before dinner was ready to be served, Celeste and Margaret were alerted to an arriving carriage.

Celeste had put on a new gown that exposed every curve of her body and was the color of blood. It accented the red of her hair. She did this, of course, to show herself off, to play into her father's game. She pinched her cheeks and bit her lips to bring color to them, waiting for the doors to open.

"Am I presentable?" she asked with a sneer to her friend.

"You look as if you are trying," Margaret told her.

"Trying too hard, or just enough?"

Margaret smiled and shook her head disapprovingly. "You look beautiful enough to make a room full of people stop and stare at you."

"Perfect."

The doors soon opened and her father, followed by the duchess, came through. He made a display of greeting Celeste and Margaret, being overly tender and warm. A few seconds later the room felt as if it were shaking when the largest man either of the two women had ever seen, walked in.

"Dear God, Margaret, it is a bear," Celeste whispered

in terrified surprise.

Margaret crossed herself in disbelief.

The man, who had to bend over so as not to hit his head on the door frame, stood at least seven feet tall; his hands were the size of plates and his body was riddled with muscle, making him appear as if he were about to burst out of his clothes.

"Margaret," Celeste whispered as the two of them stood unmoving at the count's entrance.

"Yes," Margaret replied in just as hushed a voice.

"I believe my father is trying to feed me to this bear."

"Yes," Margaret agreed.

"My dear," Celeste's father said coming over to her. "Allow me to introduce Count Orkoff to you." He held out a hand indicating the giant as if the count could be anyone else in the room.

The count took the two steps he needed to get to her, though he seemed on the other side of the room, and bowed, his head still hovering over her. "It is grr-reat pleasure to meet you," he said in a harsh, though understandable accent. He then gently took her hand in his, dwarfing hers by comparison and brought it to his great lips.

Celeste grabbed onto Margaret with her other hand for support, but the kiss was soft and light and her hand was returned to her in one piece.

For a moment, Celeste could not find her voice. She was still stunned over the size of the man standing before her who, had he not been born into enormous amounts of money, would have most certainly been sold to a freak show. It was not until her father cleared his throat did she regain her composure.

"Count Orkoff," she said, smiling sweetly, "allow me to

introduce my dear friend Margaret Hepworth."

Margaret blushed deeply as the count shifted his gaze and bowed to her.

"It is pleasure, Miss Hepwort," the count said.

Margaret nodded and gave a weak smile. "It is a pleasure, count," she replied in barely an audible whisper.

"I hope your stay in London was enjoyable. Was it your first time?" Celeste asked him.

"No," the count started. "I came when I was small boy, when my sister Natasha was to marry the duke."

"Well, it must have been a completely different experience this time around," Celeste replied. "We always see things differently when we are children, blind to the harsh realities of the world."

"You are trrrue. The experiences varied grreatlly," he agreed with a nod, his R's and L's thick against his tongue.

Celeste burned to ask him how he fit in the carriage on the way here, but knew it would be impertinent. Instead she smiled and addressed the count and the duchess.

"You both must be very tired from your journey," she said. "Let me have the servants show you to your rooms so you might freshen up before we eat."

She was still clinging to Margaret when they left the room. She took a deep breath and put her other hand over her stomach as she let it out slowly.

"I was wholly unprepared for that," she told Margaret, finally letting go of her arm. "Of all the things my father said to describe him, he very much failed to prepare me for this."

"He— he is very tall," Margaret said.

"Tall?" Celeste repeated. "That man uses tree trunks as toothpicks."

"I suppose you are not so keen on playing your father's

game as you were before you met him," Margaret said.

"Oh, no, I am still keen to do so," Celeste replied undeterred. "I just have to readjust my strategy."

"How on earth did he fit in the carriage?" Margaret burst out after a moment of silence.

"Perhaps he was the one pulling it."

Margaret clasped a hand over her mouth to keep from laughing. "You are terrible, Celeste," she said. "There is no need to be mean."

"I was not trying to; it was just the only solution that popped into my head when you asked."

Margaret allowed a small chuckle to escape her lips. "It was still terrible."

The dinner bell was soon rung, and Celeste and Margaret moved to the dining area where the servants were doing their best to raise the dining table.

"That poor man must not ever have enough leg room," Margaret sympathized.

Celeste nodded as she watched Gerald give orders, frustrated it was not working out correctly. The blocks of wood they found to raise the table with were not the same size, making the tables uneven. Celeste stepped in with a suggestion.

"Bring in one of the standing tables from the billiard room, Gerald," she told him. "Father's instructions were last minute, so there is nothing we can do about the unevenness of the tables. I will sit with the count at his table so he does not feel ostracized, but I will need something to lift my seat so I can reach the table. Do you think this would work better?"

Gerald nodded. "I do, ma'am," he replied, relieved.

"Good. We can work on getting the table lifted tomorrow," Celeste said. "Tonight, we will just have to go with the easy fix."

The table was brought in from the billiards room and set up as requested for two. Her father was surprised by the change of plans since it was not what he had ordered, but Celeste explained it away. Count Orkoff had been pleased.

Dinner was served and Celeste tried her best not to fidget in her seat.

"Your father spoke verrry highlly of you," the count told her.

"Did he?" Celeste replied, feigning surprise.

"Yes, he spoke to me of your beauty and wit."

"Do not be too disappointed by what he told you," she replied with a grin. "He only says such things when he is trying to get rid of me."

The count laughed. "No!" he said waving a hand. "No, I see is trrrue. You are beautifull to see and have good humor. That is good in woman."

"Well, thank you," Celeste replied, reaching over and gently touching his arm for a brief moment. "It is very refreshing to hear a man say such things. I have never been one for silence."

"Bah!" the count cried. "That is not my bellief."

"No?" Celeste asked, raising a brow. "Then what *do* you believe?

He chuckled. "I bellieve a sillent woman is dangerous one."

Celeste laughed. "Like your sister?" she asked with a raised brow and a grin. "I do not think I have heard her utter more than a few words at a time. Should I be concerned?"

"Ah, she is quiet one, but has good soull."

"And what about you, count?" Celeste asked lifting her

glass to her lips. "Do you have a good soul?" She took a sip, not breaking eye contact with him.

Count Orkoff blushed slightly. "Perhaps," he told her, "but is not for one to decide about themself."

14

"Is there a reason you have been avoiding me, Charles?" Celeste asked upon bursting into his billiards room the following day.

Charles had been leaning over the table, ready to shoot when she interrupted him. He stood and leaned on the pool stick instead. "Good morning, Celeste. I am well. Thank you for asking. How are you doing?" he replied sardonically.

Celeste's shoulder's dropped in annoyance. "Had you answered any of my invitations this past week and a half we would not have to ask each other such menial questions since we would already know how the other person is."

Charles arched an impatient eyebrow at her.

She huffed. "Fine," she said giving in. "How are you doing today, Charles?" she asked in a sing-song voice.

"I am rather well, thank you, Celeste. How are you?"

She picked up a cue and chalked the tip. "Terrible!" she replied moving to the cue ball and forcing Charles off to the side. "All night I was riddled with dreams of the cyclops from *The Odyssey* trying to hold me captive in his cave. And," she said cueing up her shot, "to make matters worse, he is actually staying at my house right now." She hit the cue ball causing a confusion of movement on the table; three of the balls found their way into pockets.

Charles frowned at her. "That was my shot," he mumbled.

"He seems kind and everything, but he is Russian and I am rather convinced that he would stab me through and through with his—"

"Wait," Charles started, pressing the bridge of his nose with his thumb and forefinger. "What are you talking about?"

"Count Orkoff, the Duchess Natasha's little brother from Russia." She paused to make sure Charles was following.

"Right."

"Turns out, he is not so 'little,'" she continued.

"Okay," Charles replied.

"He is an actual giant."

Charles stared at her.

She shook her head and moved to hit the cue ball again. "Do you not think it uncomfortable my father is bedding the sister of the man he is trying to marry me off to?" she asked as she hit. Another two balls went in.

Charles made a face that matched his feelings. "Yes, I do."

"I wish you were there, Charles," she told him, moving to the cue ball again. "It was a disgusting display my father put on for his guests." She shook her head as she hit again. One more ball fell into a corner pocket.

"This was my game, you know," Charles muttered to himself.

"My father kept calling me 'my dear.' 'My dear' this." She put her hand on her chest in an exaggerated display.

"'My dear' that. Would you not play your harp for us, *my dear*? You play so wonderfully!" She hit the cue ball again this time with too much force, sending the ball flying off the table and crashing through the window to the veranda outside.

Charles rubbed his mouth with his hand, lifting his other one in a helpless attempt to point out the damage she had caused.

"Last night was absolutely sickening," Celeste continued without saying anything about the broken window. She sighed. "Luckily, Margaret had been there to help smooth everything out. At least I have one friend I can always count on."

The room fell into silence.

"Are you angry with me, Charles?" she finally asked almost sheepishly. "I have been worried for days now that you no longer enjoy my company."

Charles regarded her for a moment before shooting her a smile and wrapping her in a friendly, yet, intimate hug.

"No," he replied softly. "I am not angry with you. And there will never be a day I do not enjoy your company."

"Good," she replied burying her face in his chest. "I do not know sometimes where I would be without you. We have been through so much together and a life without you as my friend would be the worst thing I could imagine."

Charles held her tighter, closing his eyes and breathing in her scent. "It is the worst thing I can imagine as well." He kissed the top of her head, brushing his cheek against her soft hair. "Why do you not marry?" Charles asked still holding her.

Celeste shifted her head but did not break away.

"What?" she asked. "You think I should marry the count?"

Charles gave a chuckle. "No, not the count, just in general."

Celeste took a moment in her reply. "I thought we talked about this the other day?" she started. "And why are you saying this to me now? You have always been against marriage before, same as I."

He nodded. "Because then, at least, you will be able to distance yourself from your father. You will be free of him."

Celeste sighed. "Yes, but I will have traded one evil for another," she grumbled.

He frowned. "How do you mean?"

"I would be trading one prison for another, except in the new prison, the warden is allowed to touch me whenever he wants."

He finally took a step back from her. "Certainly, I would expect you to marry someone you love or at least highly regard."

She strolled over to a chair and took a seat. "I do not believe in *love*, Charles. Not since I was fourteen. You of all people should know that."

He bowed his head slightly. "Sometimes, whether you believe in something or not, it is still real."

She looked at him curiously. "That was rather poetic," she said. "Where has this come from?"

He moved closer to her. "Celeste," he started. "You are, without doubt, my best friend. It might sound strange, me being a man, and you being a woman, but it is true."

She grinned. "I behave enough like a man for it not to be so strange."

He gave a small laugh. "You and I go back to our swaddling clothes; we have known each other almost since the day we were born."

"All of those times we would sword fight with our sticks and all of those times I would win."

"All of those times you *cheated*."

"All of those times I made you cry."

Charles frowned and rubbed his arm, remembering. "You hit too hard."

She laughed. "You and your mother were always there for me and my mother," she said a little more solemnly. "I do not know if I have ever properly thanked you. I do not know if I ever could. You are owed more gratitude from me than I could ever show in a lifetime."

He crouched down in front of her and took one of her hands. "You have thanked me more than enough over the years."

She arched a brow at him and shot him a coquettish smile.

He rubbed his lips together. "Not in *that* way," he told her. "I mean it. You have done more for me than I can even recall."

They fell into silence for a moment, her hand still in his.

"Celeste," he almost whispered, his voice shaking slightly, emotion swelling his chest.

"Yes, Charles?" she replied just as softly.

"There is something I have been meaning to tell you for some time now." He swallowed hard and cleared his throat. "And, perhaps, this is long overdue but I—"

"There you are!" Graham said bursting into the room as he had a habit of doing.

Charles stood slowly, inwardly cursing.

Graham pointed at the scene. "What is going on here?" he asked. "Have I interrupted something?"

Celeste smiled at him and shook her head. “Charles was just consoling me,” she replied.

Graham narrowed his eyes and lifted his chin. “Why should you need consoling? Are you ill?”

She shook her head again. “I am just a pitiable creature in need of kind words from a friend.”

“Ah!” Graham replied going over to her. “You are the most beautiful of women, full of life, humor, and an appetite for adventure.” He pulled her out of the chair causing her to squeal and laugh. “Wit flows through you, making you a fountain of wisdom and snide remarks.”

She laughed as he kissed her on the lips.

“There!” he exclaimed. “Has that done the trick? Are you consoled?”

“Completely,” she replied, smiling.

“Good!” He gave her another kiss. “Now, shall we have a game of billiards then?” He turned to the table and began organizing the balls. “Where is the cue ball?” he asked after a moment.

Charles motioned with his head to the broken window. “Outside.”

Celeste pressed her lips together. “That was my fault,” she replied. “I was rather angry when I first came.”

“You threw it?”

She shook her head. “No, I hit it. I just hit it too hard.”

He laughed. “I shall retrieve it for us. Then, we can smoke our cigars and drink too much brandy as we play.”

“I would love to, just like old times, but I must go,” Celeste replied. “I am expected for tea and then I am to show the count around the grounds.” She gave them both kisses on the cheek. “Thank you both for saying what I needed to hear. Perhaps, I will be able to sneak out later tonight.” She gave a wink and was gone.

Charles watched her go, regretting again what he could not say.

15

"You lleft so sudden after brrreakfast," the count said as they strolled the grounds. "We had no," he paused to think of the correct word, "cllue where you went."

Celeste shot him a grin, her neck straining as she looked up at him. "A lady is allowed her secrets, count," she replied.

"You have them?" he asked, smiling back at her.

"What lady does not?"

"Willl you telll me one?"

Celeste laughed. "It would not be a secret then."

"It could be *our* secrrret," he told her.

Celeste put her hands behind her back as she walked, pretending to look pensive. "I once broke an expensive vase my father received as a gift from the Lady Pembroke. I told my father that my pet Great Dane had run into the stand causing it to fall over." She gave a small smile. "In reality, I had been running around the room with my friend Charles. He was chasing me because I had been teasing him about his new hat. I had snatched it from him and was waving it above my head as we ran about the room. I then knocked over the vase causing it to shatter into thousands of pieces." She held a hand to her lips to hide a smile. "You should have seen my father's face. It was almost purple, he was so angry." She then lost her smile when she realized the gift was probably given to him after an illustrious affair. Lady Pembroke, if she remembered correctly, was a renowned flirt.

The count chuckled. "How young?"

"I think I was only ten at the time. And, you know, he still talks about that vase, blaming my poor dog."

He laughed again. "But, surelly, you have other secrrrets."

"Other secrets worth listening to, you mean?" she asked, arching an eyebrow at the count. "Ones about stolen kisses and clandestine embraces?"

"Do you have?"

She smiled as they passed the tree where she gave Charles her innocence. "Perhaps, I do," she replied slyly, her gaze lingering on it. "Perhaps, I have a vault full of secrets, none which you are privy to." She shot the count a smile.

"You are devillish, I can telll," the count said sounding pleased.

"But I never will!" Celeste proclaimed, turning back to the house. "I suspect Margaret and Doctor Digsby to be here soon, shall we return?"

The count offered his arm which Celeste took so as not to offend him, but she felt like a small child clinging to her father.

As Celeste predicted, Margaret and the doctor were there and had been for a few minutes before she and the count returned. The doctor, at first, had seemed surprised at the count's unusual size, but he had regained his composure more quickly than Margaret and Celeste had. After the initial shock had passed, he seemed to regard him as a curiosity.

Celeste could tell that medical questions burned behind his eyes, but propriety forbade him to ask them.

The duchess and Mr. Willoughby later joined them, her cheeks flushed, and a few curls on her head out of place.

The sight was not lost on Celeste and her stomach churned with the knowledge of where they had come from, but she smiled when the duchess approached her.

"Might I hear you play the harp again?" she asked softly, her accent much less pronounced than her brother's. "It brought me such pleasure last night."

Celeste could not refuse a direct request from the duchess, so she, as gleefully as she could, sat behind her harp and played a few tunes all the while sending small smiles in the count's direction.

Margaret noticed the exchanges and, once her friend was done playing, pulled her aside for a private conversation about them. Doctor Digsby took this as a chance to talk to the count, tentatively trying to bring up the questions he burned to ask.

"Are you purposefully flirting with the count?" Margaret whispered to Celeste once they were alone.

"Does one un-purposefully flirt?" Celeste asked in response.

"Oh, Celeste, do not play with people's emotions so."

"Did I not make it clear those were my intentions all along?" Celeste asked. "Did I not tell you I intended to play my father's little game?"

"Yes, but now I see it happening and can see that the count already seems taken by you. Do you not think it wrong? Must you punish him as well as your father?"

"Do not fret, Margaret," she replied patting her friend on the hand. "He will be gone in a few weeks and all of this flirting will be for naught. I am merely trying to give my father what he wants, or a small notion of it."

"And what is that?" Margaret asked suspiciously.

"Hope," Celeste grinned. "Hope that he might finally see me married." Her eyes went wide. "To a count, none the less." She arched a brow at her friend playfully.

Margaret gave her one of her cross looks. "You are trying to get a proposal from this man so you might add it to your collection?"

"Now, Margaret," Celeste said pressing a hand to her chest, feigning offense. "What must you think of me to do something so cruel?"

"You must stop treating people's feelings as a game," her friend replied sternly. "A broken heart is nothing to laugh at."

Celeste sighed and took on a more serious approach. "You are right, Margaret. I promise, I will try my best to do better, but you know it is my nature, and I can no sooner change my nature than I can change the color of the sky." She bit her lip. "Plus," she paused, a smile spreading across her lips again.

Margaret frowned. "Plus, you cannot give up an opportunity to torment your father?"

She kissed her friend on the forehead. "Plus, I cannot give up an opportunity to torment my father," she repeated. "But, after this, I promise, truly promise, I will make more of an effort to change. I might even say, 'yes.'"

Margaret couldn't help but smile at her friend.

"Forget all of that, though. Tell me about the good doctor," she said looking over at the handsome, tall man now dwarfed in comparison next to the giant count.

"How do the two of you fare?"

Margaret blushed. "We get along well as I have said before. There is nothing new to report."

"But do you *like* him?" Celeste asked. "He is too handsome not to at least pique some interest, and he is smarter than any other man in the neighborhood. There cannot be anything you do not like about him."

Margaret gave a weak smile. "We do have rather intelligent conversations and he does not seem to condescend to me about certain subjects because I am a woman."

Celeste looked at her friend with a brow raised. "What 'certain' subjects?"

Margaret blushed deeper. "Nothing of that nature!" she said in a loud whisper. "He is a perfect gentleman. What I meant was, he does not talk to me as though I am a child incapable of comprehending what he is talking about."

"Oh," Celeste said sounding a little disappointed. "Well, I am at least glad he is not a total ass like most men seem to be."

Margaret looked at her friend wide eyed and smiling. "You are quite harsh."

Celeste gave a wave of her hand. "Honesty and harshness often go hand-in-hand."

"Then it is settled!" her father exclaimed, clapping his hands together and causing the whole room to look his way. "Celeste, my dear girl, we shall throw a ball!" He walked over to her with arms stretched out. "I, of course, will leave all of the planning up to you," he told her, taking her hand and leading her back to where everyone else was situated.

Celeste gave her friend a look of bewilderment. "A ball, father?" she asked. "But you hate such festivities."

"Nonsense!" he said. "There is much to be enjoyed when they are done properly."

"I have not gone to a ball since before my husband died almost two years ago," the duchess said. "I would be honored if you threw one."

Celeste curtsied, giving the duchess a small smile, though her stomach churned with anger. "It will be my pleasure," she lied.

Celeste paced her bedroom.

It was now around midnight and she was still fuming with anger at her father. Not once had he ever thrown a ball for her or her mother and, now, all *she* has to do is smile and speak softly to him and he does exactly what she wants.

She huffed.

But she was resolved do it. She could not deny herself the pleasure of entertaining, especially at her father's expense. She would throw a grand ball, but, not as grand as the one she threw for Margaret. No, the duchess did not deserve that.

She nodded at her decision.

There was a scratching noise coming from her balcony and she turned to find Graham climbing over the railing.

"Finally," she said going over to him.

"Apologies," he started. "I had some trouble with—"

"Just get in bed," she ordered.

Graham laughed but did not hesitate as he began peeling off his clothes. "And what has started this fire under your dress?" he asked with a grin.

"I asked for your company in my letter," she replied

pulling her night gown over her head, "not your conversation." She pushed him onto the bed and kissed him. "Now, what was that move you wanted to show me?"

Celeste sat on the floor against her bed, blowing an unsuccessful smoke ring, her sheet draped over her naked body. "That was certainly different," she said after a moment.

"I think I strained my back," Graham groaned, stretching. He was still lying on the bed. "Ah. Definitely pulled something."

"Where did you learn that from?" she asked looking over at him.

"A friend of mine went to India and brought me back this book for a souvenir. It is an interesting read with some very descriptive pictures."

"You can read Hindi?"

He laughed. "It's mostly pictures, so reading is not entirely necessary."

She held up the cigar for him to take.

"Thank you," he said taking it from her.

"Well, I would not mind looking through that book when you are done," she said with a satisfied sigh.

He laughed harder. "I do not believe I will ever be done with that book."

She chuckled.

"Charles tells me your friend Margaret wants to become a nun," Graham said, taking another drag of the cigar.

Celeste nodded. "Hopefully not for too much longer," she replied. "We have a deal that if I can get her to fall in love by the end of the year, she will stay."

"What would make her want to do such a thing anyway?" Graham asked.

Celeste shook her head. "She has been left broken hearted after a worthless man left her for another woman," she explained.

"So, she thought joining a convent would help her?" he questioned skeptically.

Celeste turned to look at him. "How could it, right?" she agreed. "At any rate, she is well on her way to forgetting those plans." She took the cigar from him and puffed on it a bit. "I have matched her up with a handsome young doctor who is very taken with her." She handed him the cigar again and leaned back against the bed when a wave of melancholy came over her. She sighed a little woefully.

Graham frowned when he heard it. "What is wrong? What are you thinking?"

Celeste crossed her arms over her bare chest. "I am thinking I would like to run away."

Graham sat up. "Are you serious?" he asked.

She shrugged. "Sometimes," she replied. "Other times, I come to my senses soon after the thought has passed."

"How often to do you have these 'sometimes'?"

"Every now and then since my mother passed away."

He gave her the cigar back.

She took it and stood, the sheet slowly sliding off of her body as she walked to the corner of her room and pulled a bottle out of a drawer. She snubbed the cigar and left it.

"Are you hiding alcohol now?" he asked, lifting a brow.

She took a swig and smiled, handing the bottle to him. "I only put it there the other day," she replied sitting on the bed next to him. She wrapped herself in a blanket. "I almost did once."

"Huh?" he said taking a drink.

"Run away."

"Really?"

She nodded as she took her pillow and laid it in his lap. She then laid her head on the pillow. "It was maybe six months after my mother died and my father had been having this one woman over. She was the visiting sister of some neighbor, I cannot remember, but I just could no longer stand seeing the two of them together, giggling and flirting. So, I took my horse from the stable and rode it as fast as I could through my tears." She sighed. "I think I only made it ten or fifteen miles before I got off my horse and collapsed into sobs." She huffed. "How very girlish of me."

"Did you just return home then?" he asked, stroking her hair.

She shook her head, creasing her brows. "I sat in this field for hours, my horse grazing lazily about me, when Charles found me. I do not know *how* he found me. I suppose someone passing by saw me and told him, but there he was. I refused to go back to my house, so I stayed at his for a month until my father ordered me back. But that feeling never left. That need to get away is still there."

"Then why do you not follow that feeling?" Graham asked. "What is keeping you and me from running away together tonight?"

Celeste laughed and rolled onto her side. "I cannot run away now," she told him. "I have a deal with Margaret and I must see it through."

"Is it really Margaret you are holding out for or is it someone else?" he asked looking down at her.

She rolled back over and looked up at him, confused. "How do you mean?"

He shook his head. “Never mind,” he replied smiling softly. “Perhaps, I imagined it.”

“Imagined what?”

“I should be going,” he told her, gently lifting her head from his lap.

She sat up. “I am having a small gathering in a few days,” she told him. “You and Charles must come. Margaret and Miss Haderly will be there as well.”

He nodded. “I will keep my schedule open,” he replied getting dressed. “Come over for tea tomorrow, or later today actually. Charles has been terribly cross with me lately. We could use a buffer.”

Celeste laughed. “I will. Should I bring a few others to help?”

“It might liven up the house, so, please do!” He gave her his usual kiss on the lips when he was ready to go. “Until we meet again fair lady.”

“Good night, brave knight,” she said in mock reply.

16

"And where do you think you are going?" Andrew Willoughby asked as Celeste was about to slip out of the door.

"I was invited to tea at Charles's. Margaret and Doctor Digsby are going to be there as well."

"Did you invite Count Orkoff?" he asked, lifting a brow.

"Am I not allowed to venture out of the house without him?"

"He is our guest."

"He is *your* guest," she whispered. "I should not have to decline offers to visit with friends because he was not personally invited, nor should I have to press his company upon my friends every time I go out."

Her father gave her a cross look. "There is no avoiding it now," he replied. "I have already ordered the carriage and sent him out ten minutes ago."

"How did you even know?" she asked, containing a scoff.

He held up a letter in his hand. "It seems Charles's cousin Graham is in town."

Celeste reddened with anger.

"He sent an interesting letter reminding you of your promise to come today."

Celeste walked over to him and snatched the letter from his hands.

"Seems my threats of the madhouse have not stopped you from whoring."

She slapped him across the face. "How *dare* you read my messages," she hissed.

The blow shocked her father who took a step back before anger filled his face.

"And how dare you threaten me for doing the same thing you have been doing your entire life. If anyone around here is 'whoring' it is you." Celeste shook with fury. "You tell me I have until the end of the year to find a husband, yet, tell me, father, why would I ever want to promise myself to one man when that man is just as unlikely to promise himself to me?" she asked, glaring accusingly. "Like you vowed to do to mother, yet, never, *never* kept! Why would I ever want to put myself through that kind of pain?"

Her father swallowed hard before bowing his head. "I am not proud of everything I have done in my life," he retorted. "The way I treated your mother is one of those things I truly regret."

Celeste huffed and shook her head. "Yes, regret. As your actions have proved every day." She turned to move away but stopped. "You have no right to tell me what I am doing is wrong."

Celeste rushed out the door and stood on the steps of the house for a few moments recollecting herself. Her hand stung horribly from the slap she gave her father, and her body shook with a mixture of anger and something close to heartache. She took deep calming breaths, letting them out slowly, shakily as she tried to calm herself.

After a minute or two, she rubbed her face and walked out to the awaiting carriage where the count was already uncomfortably cramped inside.

She gave him a charming smile. "Are you ready for a ride?"

Celeste tried to make as pleasant conversation as she could on the way to Charles's, but the argument she had with her father was still foremost in her mind. She pointed at a few of the sights along the way, but was not able to put on the façade of happiness as she intended.

Fortunately, the ride was not long enough for the count to notice, or for him to gain the courage to ask her about it.

To her pleasure though, Graham and Charles had been waiting for her arrival outside. Graham lifted a glass in greeting as she stepped out of the carriage. That same glass fell to the ground, shattering, as the count emerged like a large animal from an entirely too small cage.

Celeste held in her amusement at their surprise and gave them both a kiss on the cheek. "I told the truth, did I not?" she whispered to a wide-eyed Charles. She took a step back to introduce the count to the other men.

The count stooped, for his movement could hardly be called a bow, and smiled at the other men. "I am plleased to meet you both," he replied. "Celeste has told me good things."

The other men gave stiff bows in response, still in shock.

"Yes," Charles replied, gaining his composure first. "The pleasure is all mine to have a count as a guest in my house."

"Shall we enter?" Graham said after clearing his throat. "And, please, mind the glass. My hand was wet and it slipped right out of my hands."

Charles offered Celeste his arm which she took. "You might have warned me he was coming," he whispered.

"I could not," she replied. "Father snuck him into the carriage just before I left."

"That man could not sneak anywhere," he stated.

Celeste gave a hushed chuckle before furrowing her brows. "Where are all of your paintings?" she asked noticing that several places on the wall were blank.

"I have gotten rid of them," Charles answered hesitantly. "I never liked them and hope to redecorate with something a little livelier."

Celeste lifted an eyebrow, shooting him a sideways glance, but said nothing in response.

"You have llovelly home," the count said once they were seated.

Charles nodded. "Thank you, sir, it has been in my family for nearly two hundred years."

"Verrry imprrressive," the count added, wrapping his fingers around his tea cup.

Charles and Graham both watched in interest as the large man delicately sipped from his cup. They seemed relieved when he placed it gently back on the saucer as if they believed he might swallow the drink whole.

"I thought Margaret and the doctor were joining us?" Celeste said after a moment.

"Margaret complained of a headache and the doctor's aunt is not doing well today," Charles replied.

"Is grrreat shame," the count replied. "For I have gift for us to enjoy."

Everyone looked at him in surprise.

The count pulled a large glass bottle from his coat pocket and placed it with a heavy thud on the table, causing all of the china and silverware to jump slightly.

"Where were you hiding that?" Charles whispered, confused.

"This is vwodka!" he exclaimed excitedly.

"Ha! Excellent," Graham replied with a smile, putting his tea cup down.

"Wodka?" Celeste repeated curiously.

"Vodka, my dear!" Graham said rubbing his hands together in delight and reaching for the bottle. "May I?" he asked, looking at the count.

"Yes! Try! Try!" the count replied happily. "We willl have good time!"

Graham pulled out the cork and smelled the bottle. "Wooo!" he said. "This is honey vodka."

"This man knows!" the count said, pointing at Graham.

"Shall we save tea for another time, then?" Charles asked, standing to retrieve four glasses.

Celeste sipped her tea thoughtfully. "I am not sure I have ever tried vodka before, though I think I have heard of it."

Graham poured them all glasses. "Be prepared. This is nothing like your port." He handed her one.

She lifted the glass to her lips and took a sip, the liquid burning as it moved down her throat. She shuddered, but was not repelled to take another taste. "It is not entirely unpleasant," she replied. "In fact, I think it improves upon further sips."

Charles took a large swig and erupted into coughs, making the others laugh.

The count threw his glass back without a second thought. "Ah!" he exclaimed. "Now, party has begun!"

The four of them finished the bottle, starting another one. They talked and laughed at each other as the evening wore on. The count sitting on a cushion on the floor in an effort to keep his legs straight, was sipping on the third bottle of vodka. Where and how he stored the bottles on his person was still a mystery.

"I am sorry I do not have a more suitable chair for you, count," Charles said.

The count waved a hand. "Not your fault. Only my castle has suitable furniture. They were made especiallly for me." He pointed a sausage-like finger at himself.

"You live in a castle?" Celeste asked as she laid propped up on the sofa, one leg dangling off.

"Dah!" the count responded. "Has been in my familly for over five hundrrred years. We fought many battles to keep it."

Celeste held back a yawn. "I am incredibly exhausted," she exclaimed trying to sit up. "And have definitely had enough to drink."

"Vodka certainly does the trick, does it not?" Graham asked.

The count eyed Celeste for a moment. "Perhaps, we return. We have missed supper."

Charles looked at the count staring at Celeste and got an uneasy feeling. All night the count had been keeping her glass full, watching her carefully. Something did not sit well with him.

"Graham and I will join you," he blurted, realizing what the count was trying to pull.

Everyone looked at him.

Celeste sat up slowly and smiled at him. "Why?" she asked eyeing him skeptically.

Charles looked from her to the count and then back.

"It is a fine evening," he replied. "I think a good airing would do us all some good." He shot his cousin a glance. "What say you, Graham?"

Graham saw the intensity of his cousin's gaze and nodded. "I agree," he finally said after a brief hesitation. "We can take the phaeton. That will give you a little more room, count."

"There is no need," the count insisted. "Mr. Willoughby's carriage does fine."

"No, no," Charles said waving a hand in dismissal. "We should all go together. Why stop the party now?" He stood from his seat, taking a moment to steady himself, and rang the bell. "I will order it ready and we will be gone in no time."

For three out of the four in the group, the phaeton ride was pleasant. They continued to laugh and joke while the fourth kept silent, looking sullen. Charles took note of it. He knew he had disrupted the count's plans, but he did not care; his only concern was Celeste's well-being.

When they arrived at the house, Mr. Willoughby greeted them with unusual kindness, going so far as to offer them refreshments, but they were declined.

"I am off to bed," Celeste said. "Have Samantha bring me up some water, would you?" She swayed slightly as she made her way up the stairs.

The count moved to help her, but Charles got there first. He took Celeste's arm and wrapped it around his.

"Seems I cannot be rid of you," she whispered smiling.

"No, you cannot," he replied just as quietly, his cheeks slightly flushed.

"Very well," she replied. "I am glad for it since I feel I might fall if you let me go."

Charles escorted her to her room and waited until

Samantha came with her water before leaving. He then went back down the stairs. His cousin, Mr. Willoughby, and the count were sharing a drink and making awkward small talk.

"Charles, my good man!" Mr. Willoughby said clasping the young man's hand. "How are you?"

"I am well," Charles replied in a strained voice. "And you?"

"I am well myself. Cannot complain. How is your mother? I know she must miss your father exceedingly. He was a respectable man."

Charles tensed and nodded. "I think you would be surprised by her ability to overcome her feelings of loss. She is doing quite well without him."

"Is she?" Mr. Willoughby asked, confused by Charles's vague speech.

"Perhaps it is a story for another time, sir. Unfortunately, I cannot stay long," he told him. "We merely came to escort the count and Celeste home."

Mr. Willoughby nodded. "That was very good of you. Very neighborly."

"Yes," Charles said without feeling. "Come, Graham, it is getting late."

Graham opened his mouth in protest, but, upon seeing the same intensity in his eyes as before, acquiesced. He threw back the rest of his drink, bowed to the host, and wished the count a good night.

A minute later they were in the carriage. Halfway down the drive, however, Charles stopped.

"What are you doing?" Graham asked as Charles began to climb out.

"I am going to spend the night with Celeste."

Graham frowned. "I thought you two were no longer—"

"She is drunk," Charles said in a harsh voice. "I would never press myself upon her ever, but certainly not in that state."

"Then what are you doing?"

"Did you not notice the looks the count was giving her this evening?" Charles asked. "How he forced drink after drink down her throat? And then his excitement to go home after she stated she was in fact drunk?"

Graham thought for a moment. "No."

Charles huffed and shook his head. "I do not trust him. So, I am going to keep vigil over her."

Graham blinked at him. "You love her, Charles," he said. "Do you not?"

Charles avoided his eye. "She is important to me, yes."

"No, I mean *in love* with her," Graham clarified. "Are you in love with her?"

"I will be home early in the morning," Charles replied, ignoring his question. "Do not drink all of my alcohol while I am gone."

"I make no promises," Graham replied, moving to take the reins.

Charles nodded and slipped through the woods. He ran parallel to the house for a few yards before heading back out to the gardens and around the back of the house. He then climbed the familiar balcony to Celeste's room. He had not done it in over a year, but had done it so often before he still remembered where the best holds were. Though he had climbed up and over easily, his heart was pounding, and his hands were shaking. Memories of nights wrapped in each other's arms coursed through him, making his heart beat faster. He stood on the balcony looking at the French doors for a minute before advancing, but before he reached them,

Celeste flung them open.

They looked at each other in surprise for a moment, their eyes twinkling in the pale moonlight. Charles smiled and let out a ragged breath, advancing slowly. He stopped when he was right in front of her and gazed down into her eyes. His heart caught in his throat as he looked at her, captivated by her beauty. She smiled softly, silently at him as he gently reached out and cupped her cheek in his hand, stroking it with his thumb. The impulse to kiss her, to wrap her in his arms enveloped him when Celeste wretched the contents of her stomach all over the front of trousers. He froze, unsure of what to do, the magic of the moment gone.

Celeste coughed and spat, crouched over. After a half a minute, she looked up at him. "What are you doing here?" she asked breathlessly.

"I came to look after you in your inebriated state," he replied, clearing his throat removing his jacket.

"You have never done so before." She groaned and pressed her hand to her stomach.

He shrugged. "Well, I am here now."

She nodded as she heaved again, holding onto Charles for support.

He helped her back into the room and sat her on the bed before walking over to the main door and locking it.

Celeste fell back onto the bed. "I have not had this much to drink in a very long time," she replied.

Charles didn't reply.

"I apologize if I ruined your pants."

He laughed. "It was well worth it." He paused for a moment. "Would you mind if I took them off?"

"Is that what you really came for?" she asked, smiling as she tried to stay awake. "To bed me?"

“Is that what you believe I would do?” he retorted.

She shook her head. “Not for a second.”

“I would never touch you without your permission.”

She smiled and nodded. “I know. Come, lie with me.”

He took his soiled pants off and wrapped himself in a blanket. He then grabbed her nightgown that was still hanging on her dressing partition.

He pulled her up and she groaned. He gently undressed her and put her dressing gown on.

“Why are you being so nice?” she asked as he helped her under her covers.

“We are friends, are we not?”

She smiled sleepily. “You will stay with me through the night?”

He sat next to her on the bed, above the covers. “I will,” he whispered. He watched her as she slept for a few minutes and began dozing off himself when the sound of the door handle jingling woke him. He sat still for a moment watching the handle. After several seconds, he heard a gruff whisper from the other side of the door and then silence.

He laid his head back against the headboard and gave a sigh of relief.

He had been right about the count.

After the anger and surprise of the moment passed, he slid down further on the bed, resting his head on the pillow. He turned on his side, just able to make the silhouette of Celeste in the moonlight, her breath lightly rising and falling, and he smiled, his heart full of what he could not tell her.

After watching her sleep a little longer, Charles finally closed his eyes and joined her.

17

The days flew by as if nothing had happened. Celeste and her father didn't bring up their argument; Celeste and Charles did not bring up that night. Nothing had happened, as he said, but still he had woken up the next morning with her arm draped over him and her head resting on his shoulder. It had raised his spirits and made his heart swell, but still, he did not talk to her about it.

The only one to talk about that day was Graham. He had grilled Charles when he returned about his feelings for Celeste, unrelenting.

"Do you love her, Charles?" he asked more than once. "If you do, why would you allow me to go over there night after night?"

Charles closed his eyes and took a deep breath. "I do not want to talk about this with you, Graham."

"Well you obviously do not want to tell her about it either," Graham retorted. "Why would you not have told me? I would never have gone over there had I known."

Charles gritted his teeth. "Celeste is not mine to control, Graham. If she willingly gave herself to you, I cannot stop her."

"That is not what I am saying, cousin," Graham replied sternly. "I am saying I would not have done so had I known you are in love with her."

"Are you so sure that I am?"

Graham regarded his cousin for a moment. "Yes," he finally replied. "I am very sure that you are. I am only stupefied that I did not catch on before. I actually thought that maybe she—" He shook his head. "I am truly sorry, cousin. I am almost ashamed."

Charles rubbed his face, tired both physically and emotionally.

"Why do you not tell her?"

"To what purpose?" Charles shot back. "I have nothing to give her."

Graham chuckled, a confused look on his face. "Nothing to give her?" he repeated. "What are you talking about, Charles? You are onc of the richest bachelors in the county. What is there not to give?"

Charles shook his head and rubbed his face with his hands. "I have nothing, Graham," he told him softly.

Graham blinked at him. "Forgive me. I have not the pleasure of understanding you."

Charles sighed. "My father left my poor mother and me in horrendous debt. Gambling; bad investments; mistresses with illegitimate children; several mortgages on the house, some with overdue payments." Charles rubbed the back of his neck. "My mother is not in Bath on holiday; she is there to solicit help from her sister's husband who is a judge because if we do not receive help soon, we are very likely to lose everything. Including the house."

Graham looked at him concerned. "I— I had no idea," he said, bewildered.

"I had not wanted to tell you." He rubbed his lips

together. "I have already started selling off things we can do without. Three of the guest rooms are completely empty. Almost all of the art is gone. The music room no longer boasts a piano. Half of the furniture in the main parlor was sold off and has been replaced with things from storage. And I am in the process of selling a quarter of my land. Next, I will have to start letting some of the servants go." He shook his head. "I cannot bring Celeste into such an unstable home, not when I want to give her so much more."

"But she is to inherit her father's estate and all of the businesses that he owns, all of his prosperous investments," Graham told him. "Would that not benefit you?"

Charles looked at him in earnest. "And have her find out what a poor state I am in and think the only reason I wanted to marry her is so I could save face?" He shook his head again. "No, she has had her share of fortune hunters, and I will not be one of them."

Graham shrugged. "Then what is the point?" he replied heatedly. "What is the point of harboring these feelings?"

Charles didn't reply.

"Are you to just love her from a distance? Stand by as other men wheedle their way into her life? Do nothing as *those* men try their luck with her?" Graham shook his head. "Celeste deserves better than that." He paused a moment. "Tell her how you feel. Tell her the obvious torment you have been going through. Tell her about your unfortunate circumstances first if you want to. This is Celeste we are talking about. She knows you. She knows you are no fortune hunter."

"I have tried!" he exclaimed, throwing his hands up. "Lord knows I have tried, but every time I do—" He stopped himself, shaking his head. "It would not matter anyway."

"Why would it not?" Graham asked.

"You do not understand. She does not believe in love, Graham," he informed him. "She will turn me down like all of the other men, and then I will have lost her for good." He rubbed his face again. "I would just be another rejected proposal in her collection. I could never face that reality."

"Why did the two of you stop being intimate?" Graham asked after a moment's pause. "What were her reasonings?"

He shook his head and shrugged. "I honestly do not know. She just said one day it would be best if we kept our relationship within the bounds of friendship."

"But she did not say why?"

He shook his head again. "No," he replied. "And since then I have realized that she was purely the only good thing in my life. I knew I always loved her, but I did not realize I could not live without her until then."

Graham sighed. "And this is the reason you have been uncivil toward me since I have arrived."

"Have I truly been so terrible?"

Graham raised a brow at his cousin. "Your looks were so lethal, and your attitude so sharp I thought you were plotting my death."

"Forgive me," Charles said trying to smile. "I should have told you my feelings. I just—," he paused and sighed, "I just did not know how to go about telling you. I know you are fond of her too."

Graham gave a small laugh. "Being fond of someone is not the same thing as being in love with them," he replied. "I am *fond* of you, but— you get my point."

Charles nodded.

Graham gently squeezed his shoulder. "I will refrain from seeing her from now on," he assured him.

"You will not tell her of our conversation, will you?" Charles asked, his voice heightened.

Graham shook his head. "You may depend on me, cousin," he said giving his shoulder another squeeze. After a moment, he sniffed the air and frowned. "What is that awful smell?"

"Ah," Charles said stepping back. "Celeste threw up on me last night and I have not had the chance to change since you have been interrogating me from the moment I arrived."

Graham finally noticed Charles's pants and gagged. "Oh," he remarked, covering his mouth with a hand. "Please go and do that before I add a stain of my own."

Charles chuckled and left the room.

While Charles's feelings for Celeste remained hidden, the count was taking on a more direct approach. Every day the count would solicit her for long walks about the grounds or for rides in one of her father's phaetons. He talked often of his castle and high status in Russia, and how every year he was invited to stay with the Czar for two weeks.

Celeste listened attentively, laying on her charms, encouraging the count's attentions. She even went so far as to say how she would love to visit Russia and see his grand castle.

When she visited with Margaret, however, it was another story.

"He is utterly boring!" Celeste complained one day, having slipped out of her house unnoticed. "All he talks about is his stupid castle, and how much it snows during the winter." She shivered. "I would rather drown at sea."

Margaret shook her head. "Then why encourage him?"

"You know why!" Celeste told her. "To teach my father a lesson; that he can no more force *my* hand than I can force *his*. Though, to be honest, I do believe I cannot control myself sometimes. The impulse to flirt often oversteps my better judgment." She sighed. "The count and my father's pet will be gone soon anyway. After the ball, she will return home and he will," she paused, "climb the beanstalk from which he came."

Margaret let out a burst of laughter before catching herself. "Stop it!" she told her friend. "He can no more control his height than you can control yours. Do not make fun of him for it."

Celeste grinned at her friend. "You are too good," she told her. "You want nothing but justice for everyone."

They were soon interrupted by the arrival of Doctor Digsby. He bowed at them both as he was led in.

"Oh, Doctor," Margaret said, blushing as usual. "I was not expecting you."

"Forgive me, I gave no notice," he replied. "I was on my way to St. Anne's church and thought you might like to accompany me."

Celeste turned her head to hide a smile.

"You have told me before it is one of your favorite places."

Margaret nodded. "Yes, it is," she replied softly.

"The invitation, of course, is extended to you, Miss Willoughby, if you would like to join us."

She glanced at her friend, who seemed to request her attendance with her eyes. "You know, I have not been to St. Anne's in years," she replied. "I would love to join you.

Thank you."

"I have brought some refreshments, but perhaps it is not enough for three people," the doctor told them.

Celeste grinned at her friend. *On his way to St. Anne's indeed*, she thought.

"I shall have more prepared for us," Margaret replied.

"Forgive me, I am a terrible host it would seem," the doctor said looking rather uneasy at his mistake.

"Not at all. It is no trouble," Margaret told him.

The three of them set off in the doctor's small, open carriage, which he drove himself. The sight of it made Celeste smile even more, convincing her more than ever that the doctor was not just on his way to St. Anne's, but had planned all along to stop and ask Margaret to join him.

Celeste liked the doctor more and more for her friend. It was obvious he liked her, as any man with sense should, in her opinion, but he also made an effort to include Celeste in conversation. He was truly a gentleman in every respect which is everything her good, kind friend deserved, but Celeste was concerned that Margaret, though she blushed frequently in his presence, was not reciprocating his attentions at the same level she was receiving them.

Noticing this as their little day trip went on, Celeste took several opportunities to commend the doctor for taking care of his poor aunt. She said she had even heard he was attending the poor for little or no cost at all.

"Is that true?" Margaret asked, her voice piqued with a hint of excitement and admiration.

It was the doctor's turn to blush. "It is true," he replied sheepishly. "I have been making my rounds through the poorer parts of town and providing assistance to the sick."

"And you take no payment?" Margaret questioned.

He shook his head. "They sometimes give me little trinkets or offer me what little they can provide, but I tell them I believe it is my Christian duty, so require no payment."

That had seemed to do the trick.

Margaret beamed at the doctor in admiration. "That is very good of you!" she exclaimed. "The poor are often ignored by those of your profession since they cannot pay."

He nodded. "It is true," he agreed. "I have witnessed it first hand with colleagues of mine and it stirs inside me feelings of disgust and shame."

"I wonder why you would not have mentioned this to me before!" Margaret stated, turning a little more in her seat.

Doctor Digsby bowed his head slightly, and blushed more deeply. "It was not that I was keeping it from you," he replied.

"Oh, do not blame the doctor," Celeste added, joining in. "He is all that is good and modest! To tell you of his good doings would be bragging and he is not a man for bragging."

"Thank you, Miss Willoughby," he replied with a small nod.

"Well, the next time you go, I shall like to go as well," Margaret said.

"Really?" Dr. Digsby asked, trying to contain his exuberance.

Margaret nodded.

Celeste, satisfied with the outcome of her comment, held back from the other two as they gushed over the injustices of the world and the lack of Christian response to those in need, and she watched triumphantly as her plan came into fruition.

"I often bring bread and cheese to the poor," Margaret informed the doctor as they walked the ground of St. Anne's church. "Celeste has helped on several occasions as well. Then, during Christmas I orchestrate a charity where I go to several of the genteel families and ask for alms. I then distribute them along with salted hams or bacon donated."

"I am glad to hear you do not just talk of injustices the impoverished suffer, but act by helping them," the doctor replied. "All too often you hear people speak of how the poor are treated unfairly yet do nothing to change it."

"How true!" Margaret replied, impassioned.

Celeste watched them both with a smile, happy at how things were turning out. After a few minutes, Celeste claimed to be tired and she wanted to rest. Doctor Digsby offered her his arm but she politely declined.

"I am going to find a bench and enjoy the delightful breeze," she replied. "Please, do not stop walking on my account. I shall be fine. I am never lonely when I am in my own company." She smiled, noticing Margaret was more at ease.

As her friend and the doctor continued the tour of the church, Celeste wandered outside taking in the fresh air of the early summer day. Though the last few days had been hot, the day was pleasant and filled with the sweet smell of summer flowers.

She had, of course, not been tired after all. No, she was just allowing her friend and, perhaps, her new lover to enjoy their own company without a third person to worry about. The doctor had been especially polite engaging her in conversation, but she knew he had wanted to spend time alone with Margaret.

She started to make her way through the cemetery littered with headstones of all shapes and sizes, varying in height. She walked through some of the rows and read them, wondering who they were and how they lived their lives. She was deep in thought about one woman she decided was a seductress killed by a jilted lover, when she heard her name being called.

She turned to see a slightly rotund, middle-aged looking man in expensive clothes walking her way.

She forced a smile. "Sir Edwards," she said, giving him her hand to kiss. "How are you?"

"My dear, lovely girl," he replied, smiling broadly. "I am well. Better now that I have run into you. What a happy coincidence."

She gave him an elegant nod of the head.

"What brings you here, my pet?"

"I have come with Margaret Hepworth and Doctor Digsby, but I broke away and found myself here."

"Ah! This is certainly a lovely place," he remarked. "My late wife grew up in this church and is buried just over there." He pointed in the distance.

"I never knew that," Celeste replied. "Lady Adelaide was a very sweet woman, full of spunk if I recall correctly."

"She was a pistol to be sure!" he proclaimed with a laugh. "Would you walk with me for a while, my dear?" He held out his arm for her to take, which she did with a smile.

"Do you come visit your wife's grave often?" Celeste asked him after they moved further down the rows.

"I come once a month," he told her. "She was an angel. I did not deserve her."

"And how is your son doing? He must be at least sixteen now?"

"He was seventeen in May," he replied with a nod. "He is a good lad, though I wish he paid more attention to his studies."

"What young man does?" Celeste said smilingly.

"You are quite right." He gave a nod and cleared his throat. "I am glad I have met you here, though, Miss Willoughby."

"Oh?" Celeste replied. "How so?"

"It saved me the trouble of a trip to your house."

Celeste raised an eyebrow at him. "And?"

"And," he cleared his throat and straightened his shoulders, "I am hosting a gathering of sorts in the next few days and I was wondering if you would mind being in attendance."

"A ball?" Celeste asked.

Sir Edwards shook his head. "No, just a small gathering of friends where we will be able to shed off the pretense we wear while out in society."

Celeste smiled. "It sounds like my kind of party," she told him. "What day is it to be?"

"I have settled on this coming Tuesday," he told her. "Do you think you will be available? I am going to test out my new camera."

She gave small nod. "I am sure I shall be. It will certainly be a change from what I have been doing. And I do love getting my picture taken."

"Oh, delightful!" he exclaimed. "Photography is a new hobby of mine."

Celeste smiled and nodded.

"How do you find the count and his sister?" he asked her after a brief pause.

Celeste wanted to say they have overstayed their welcome and she was anxious to have the house back to herself, but she didn't. Instead, she did the only proper thing to do in that situation; she lied.

"They are both wonderful house guests," she forcefully remarked.

"I heard the count is a bit of an oddity," he continued cautiously.

She smiled. "Well, he *is* Russian, Sir Edwards. I am not sure what you would expect."

He chuckled. "Yes, there is that of course, but I heard he had some sort of deformation."

Celeste let out a laugh. "My, rumors are a dangerous thing, are they not?" she asked.

"He is not deformed then?"

She laughed. "No, he is not one for hiding in bell towers and ringing the bells if you get my meaning, but he is rather tall," she told him. "Unusually tall."

"Ah," Sir Edwards said. "I was hoping, for your sake, he was not."

Celeste looked at him, confused. "Why is that?"

"The word of the town is he shall whisk you away to his castle."

She patted the man's arm. "Fear not, Sir Edwards," she reassured them. "Your favorite flirt is not so easily whisked away. You know how people just talk to hear the sound of their own voice. There is barely any truth in what they say on a good day."

He squeezed her hand. "Good, good. I am even more glad then."

"Did you receive my gift for letting me borrow your lovely birds?"

He nodded. "A very fine bottle of port. I shall save it

until you come and enjoy it with me."

She nodded.

"I heard one of my birds caused quite a disturbance."

"Oh, hardly," Celeste replied. "The poor thing got caught under Joseph Sharpe's feet, but I think they both came out rather unharmed."

Celeste waved as Margaret and Doctor Digsby came into view.

"There is my party," she said. "Thank you for allowing me the use of your arm, Sir Edwards. It has certainly been a pleasure as always." She moved away from him, curtseying slightly.

He bowed to her. "I shall send you a formal invitation to my gathering soon," he told her. "Feel free to bring a friend. Maybe even the count. I would love to make his acquaintance."

"Perhaps I shall, or perhaps I shall come by my lonesome," she said, giving him a wink.

He laughed. "You are a saucy little minx."

She laughed as well and moved toward her friends who still seemed to be in a mutually fervent discussion.

"Celeste, there you are!" Margaret exclaimed. "We thought we had lost you."

"Did you not see me wave?" she asked, taking the other arm the doctor offered her.

"I am afraid we were too deep in our conversation about religious persecution though we are supposed to have free reign over what we believe," Doctor Digsby claimed.

"Yes, well, man only knows one true religion and that is hypocrisy," Celeste stated with a nod.

"How true you are, Miss Willoughby. I could not agree more," he said steering them toward the carriage.

18

Celeste toyed with the idea of whether to invite the count to Sir Edwards's small gathering or not. Part of her wanted to continue the attachment she already saw growing inside of him for her; he would be gone in less than a week anyway. But the other part of her relished the idea of going alone.

Her invitation came early one morning, and she was quick to take it, read it, and burn it lest her father catch wind and invite the count on her behalf anyway. It had not mattered anyhow. Her father, the duchess, and the count had made plans to map out the best hunting areas.

It turned out the duchess was fond of hunting and the count even more so.

Celeste, who never cared for such a grim activity, easily excused herself from the party. But as she was about to slip out the door, Graham entered.

She smiled at him. "Well, I have not seen you in ages," she told him.

"It has only been a little over week," he replied with a shrug. "Were you on your way out?"

She nodded. "I was but I am allowed to bring a guest, so you can join me." She took his arm and guided him back out the door.

"Where to?"

"Sir Edwards is having a small gathering. He says he wants to try out his new camera."

"Oh?" Graham replied lifting a brow. "I have not had my picture taken in years."

They chatted lightly in the carriage on the way there. She was her usual flirty self, but he was a little more distant than usual, not reacting to her jokes as much as he usually would.

She lifted a brow at him. "Is there something wrong?" she asked him.

He shook his head. "I am just in a pensive mood, I suppose."

She pursed her lips. "You are not turning into your cousin, are you? These pensive moods are not catching, are they?"

He chuckled. "Perhaps they are."

"Well, stay away from me then," she told him. "Life is too short to always be brooding."

They arrived at Sir Edwards's house soon after this. They made their way in where Celeste was greeted with great enthusiasm.

"My dear, I am so glad you have come!" Sir Edwards exclaimed giving her a kiss on her cheek. He then turned to Graham with a skeptical eye. "Mr. Pratt, is it?" he asked less pleased.

Graham bowed. "It has been a few years, Sir Edwards."

"Was the count unable to make it?" Sir Edwards questioned, disappointment apparent in his voice.

"He had made other plans," Celeste answered.

"Pity. Oh, well," Sir Edwards said. "Mr. Pratt is an acceptable replacement, I suppose."

Celeste and Graham exchange glances, both noticing Sir Edwards was not wearing a jacket and his shirt was partially unbuttoned.

Graham made a gesture indicating Sir Edwards had already been drinking and she nodded smiling.

"Are we the first to arrive?" Celeste asked.

"We are all in the back," he told her as they followed him. "That is where the best light is."

A servant came and handed them both drinks.

Graham frowned at the liquid. "Absinthe," he whispered. "What kind of party is Sir Edwards throwing?"

"I do not react well to absinthe," Celeste replied.

They both placed their glasses on a table as they passed by.

"Now," Sir Edwards began as they reached French doors leading to a large veranda outside, "do not be shy. I realize this might be your first time to such an event, but I can assure you, you will fully enjoy yourselves."

Again, Celeste and Graham exchanged glances.

"I am not one prone to shyness, Sir Edwards," Celeste replied hesitantly, "but what do you mean 'such an event'?"

He clapped his hands together and rubbed them. "Just wait, my dear, I will show you."

He opened the doors to the veranda and Celeste jumped as a naked woman ran by, giggling. She grabbed Graham's arm as an equally naked man chased after the woman.

"Come! Come!" Sir Edwards enticed.

Mechanically, Graham and Celeste walked through the doors, their eyes wide as they were greeted with the sight of other naked people. One couple in the corner was openly kissing each other, their hands caressingly moving about their bodies.

Celeste took a few patchy breaths. "Graham," she whispered.

"Yes?" he said with just as much surprise in his voice.

"What in the hell is this?"

Graham swallowed hard. "I believe this is an orgy."

"I am quite frightened," she said. "I am not sure I can move."

"My dear girl, do not fret!" Sir Edwards said coming over to her. "There is no shame here!" He had already begun to take off his shirt, exposing his hairy chest further.

Celeste's grip on Graham's arm tightened. "Sir Edwards," she started. "I do not know what kind of woman you take me for, but this is not it. Why on earth would you invite me to such a thing?"

He looked at her confused, the absinthe having kicked in long ago. "I thought you and I could finally lie together. You have long been leading me down that path."

"I have done *no* such thing!" Celeste exclaimed. "If you took my harmless flirtations as an invitation to— to," she looked around her, "to this than you are daft!"

Everyone in the room had stopped to look at them, though their hands still traveled over their prospective partner's body.

Graham tried to clear his throat. "I, uh, I think we should go," he said not taking his eyes off of the scene.

"What?" Sir Edwards said. "Why would you want to leave? I thought we were to have some fun! I have not yet had a chance to use my camera."

Celeste shook her head and took a few steps backwards. "Enjoy your gathering, Sir Edwards. I am sure they are a lovely time," she told him shakily. "But they are not for me."

Celeste and Graham quickened their pace as everyone continued to stare at them in the midst of their groping. When they stepped over the landing through the French doors, they turned and ran out to the front. Neither of them spoke until the carriage was back on the main road, their hearts pounding in their chests.

Once the carriage broke out into a trot, Celeste and Graham looked at each other and burst into laughter.

"As long as I live, I will never forget the sight of Mrs. Horton holding Mr. Vance's manhood in her hands," Celeste said with a shudder. "What on earth? I cannot get over what just happened."

"It was rather," he paused, "eye opening." He shifted uncomfortably in his seat, crossing and uncrossing his legs, then crossing them again.

Celeste lifted an eyebrow at him. "What is wrong?" she asked skeptically.

He shook his head. "Nothing, I am just trying to—"

"Dear God, tell me you were not turned on by that scene!" Celeste laughed, seeing Graham's reason for his constant shifting.

He cleared his throat. "I am not saying it was the most attractive scene, but as a man, the thought of such an act can cause such a reaction."

Celeste laughed. "Incredible," she said. "Incredible that something like that can inspire even a breadth of desire in you."

"This does not necessarily imply 'desire,'" he replied defensively.

"I, for one, am sure I will not be lying with anyone any time soon."

Graham gave a solemn smile.

"Does that spoil your plans for later?" she asked laughingly.

He shook his head. "To be honest, it was part of the reason I called on you today. Not to solicit any sexual favors, but to inform you of my plans to leave, and, therefore, let you know we can no longer meet."

Celeste's smile fell from her face. "You are leaving?" she asked. "Where will you go?"

"I have plans to go back to Oxford and finish my degree," he told her. "I only have a year left."

"That is wonderful news!" Celeste exclaimed. "I know Charles must be rather proud of you. When are you leaving?"

"Tomorrow morning."

"Tomorrow?" Celeste repeated, shocked. "Have you been planning your escape this long?"

He shook his head. "It was a last-minute decision," he replied softly, smiling almost sadly.

Celeste didn't reply right away. "Surely, term does not start for another month. Why are you to leave so soon?"

"I must return now," he replied. "My mother's brother, Uncle William, expects it of me. He wrote me before I came here demanding if I did not return by the beginning of August, he will disinherit me." He shrugged. "We both know I cannot afford that."

She nodded. "And will you not visit me tonight before you leave?"

He cleared this throat and gave a weak smile. "I thought you no longer could stomach the idea after what we witnessed today?"

She gave a small laugh. "I will try if it means another go with you. You can call it a parting gift."

He looked at her earnestly. "I should not be asking you

this," he said hesitantly, giving a small laugh. "I promised I would not."

"What?"

"That one night we spent together, you said you sometimes thought about running away," he said. "Do you want to run away now? Together." He leaned over and took her hands in his. "Say the word and we can be gone in an instant."

"And what about your inheritance?" she laughed.

"I would not need one if you told me you loved me."

Celeste swallowed. "You are being serious." She looked at him solemnly. "Oh, Graham, I have treasured many moments with you, laughing, talking, among other things, but what you ask for is too much."

Graham bowed his head, but continued holding Celeste's hands.

"I did not realize what we had was anything more than," she paused for a moment thinking, "physical."

He nodded, giving her hands a slight squeeze. "Nor did I, until I realized I will no longer see you."

She looked at him. "Certainly, we will meet later as friends," she told him.

He shook his head. "Perhaps, but it will be different." He laughed. "Forgive me. How lugubrious I sound. You must not take my words too seriously. They are said in the heat of the moment, on a whim, perhaps."

She nodded.

They drove the rest of the way back to the house in silence.

Graham helped her out of the carriage and brought both her hands to his lips. "I hope to see you next during a happier occasion." He took a step back and bowed. "Take care of Charles for me," he said as he made his way to the stable for his horse.

"Graham," she said calling after him.

He turned back around, looking hopeful.

"What did you mean you promised?" she asked.

He blinked at her.

"When you asked me to run away with you, you said you should not ask me, that you had promised you would not," Celeste said. "What did you mean?"

He gave her a soft smile. "I hope one day you find out," was all he said in reply.

19

Invitations were soon sent out for the duchess's ball. Celeste was disgruntled at first since the festivities were pushed back another couple of weeks, which meant the count and his sister were staying longer.

Until that time though, Celeste hosted a number of teas, inviting Margaret, Amanda, Doctor Digsby, and Charles; she even invited Stephen on a few occasions, who lingered after everyone else had gone.

At first, Amanda had been petrified by the count, her poor small frame shivering in his shadow, but warmed to him just like everyone else, except for Charles. Charles harbored great suspicions toward the count whom he did not trust after the incident with the vodka. He thought the man deviant and honor-less, but he was the only one.

To everyone else, the count was charming and a novelty. When the apples in Mr. Willougby's orchard were ready to be picked, he easily hoisted Amanda up on his shoulders, who squealed in delight. From there she was able to pick the best of the apples.

They all laughed at the spectacle, except, of course, Charles.

"Are you not at all amused?" Stephen asked him, seeing his stern face.

"Seems ridiculous," Charles replied.

"That is the point!" Celeste proclaimed.

"Does not seem right to use a man in such a way. Using his deformity as a means of entertainment."

"I say, Pratt," Stephen started, "you certainly are getting rather grumpy in your old age."

Celeste suppressed a giggle when she saw Charles was affected by what Stephen said. "Come now, Charles," she said, squeezing his arm. "The count is not being exploited in any way. He offered his services willingly. And why should he not use his God-given gift to help others?"

Charles gave a 'harumph' in response.

And, so, the days flew by.

Celeste sought comfort in the arms of Stephen; Margaret continued to be pursued by the doctor; Amanda was delighted about the prospects of another ball; the count began keeping a closer eye on Celeste; and Charles continued to suppress his feelings, becoming more cantankerous by the day.

Then, the day for the duchess's ball finally arrived. Everyone was abuzz, knowing how Celeste can throw amazing parties. The guests came, and the wine flowed freely as the music played.

Celeste, unable to let her contempt for the duchess fully melt away, did not present her to everyone the way she did with Amanda and Margaret. Instead, the duchess was merely led into the room on her father's arm.

She was a stunning woman, Celeste had to admit. She couldn't have been more than forty and still drew the eye of every man there, old and young alike. Though she never truly smiled, you could see her emotions dancing in her eyes. She was the very definition of mysterious and she awed the guests as she moved among them.

But, no one awed the guests more than the count who stood at least a foot taller than anyone. His booming voice and laughter could be heard across the room, and he was, of course, easily spotted amongst the crowd.

When the dance floor was opened, the honored guests along with their partners started everyone off. The duchess moved gracefully with Mr. Willoughby as her partner, and the count, surprisingly, moved almost just as well with Celeste as his.

She felt awkward at first, since her head came just below his chest. She was unsure of where to look since either direction seemed to make her feel just as awkward, but she quickly learned to work through it. When the song ended everyone clapped and the floor opened for everyone. Young girls moved in quickly to claim the count as their next partner, some stepping on Celeste's foot to get to him. She quickly backed away to the safety of the wall.

"That was rather entertaining," Stephen said, finding her. He gave a small chuckle. "Seems you were almost trampled."

"*Almost*? My foot feels rather differently," she replied, frowning.

"Perhaps, you would like a partner whom you can actually look in the eye?" he asked offering his hand.

"Depends, what does that partner want in return?" she replied raising a brow, her lip curled into a coy smile.

"Now, what must you think of me?" Stephen answered, feigning offense.

Celeste took his hand smiling. "I think you are a man

who knows what he wants and how to get it."

The night was significantly more successful than the last ball, in the sense that no one was attacked by a disturbed bird, but it certainly lacked something else. It took Celeste half of the evening to realize that Charles was not there. She had searched for him, and even asked a few other guests if they had seen him, but he was nowhere to be found.

Margaret told her she *had* seen him and spoken to him at the beginning of the night, but he mentioned he was feeling unwell and returned home early.

"I remember greeting him earlier, but then he was gone," Celeste told her. "He did not seem unwell then." She frowned. "I wonder what could be wrong?"

"Are you speaking of Mr. Pratt?" the doctor asked, handing Margaret the drink he went to get for her.

Celeste nodded. "Yes, have you seen him?"

"He received a letter about an hour or so ago," the doctor replied. "I saw him pale as he read it. I asked him what the matter was and he claimed he had a sudden headache. I offered him my assistance, but he refused it."

Margaret nodded. "Yes, he left soon after that."

Celeste looked concerned. "I wonder if I should not go to him and see what the matter is."

"And leave all of your guests?" Margaret replied.

"Well, if something is wrong with him, I want to know about it," she told them. "If my father asks, tell him you think you saw me heading to the gardens."

Margaret nodded. "Are you sure you do not want us to go with you?"

She shook her head. "No, it would be much easier to get out on horseback than by carriage. I should not be gone long."

Within minutes, Celeste had her horse hitched and she rode as fast as she could to Charles's house. What she saw when she got there was confusing. Several men were coming in and out of the house with furniture, pictures, statues, and even some large, silver candelabras. She slowed her horse down to a trot and watched as they piled everything on to different carts.

She slid off of her horse and stood there, confused, unsure of what she was seeing.

"Celeste?" Charles's voice came in the dark.

She turned and saw the worn-out figure of her friend standing in his doorway.

"What are you doing here?" he asked.

Celeste slowly walked over to him. "Doctor Digsby said you looked ill," she replied, turning her head to see the carts being towed away.

"You came all this way because you thought I had taken ill?" he asked, his voice softened.

"What is going on here? Why are all of those men taking your things?" She turned to him, her brows creased.

Charles swallowed hard. "Perhaps you should come in," he told her.

Celeste walked into a bare front hall. A marbled room that once housed expensive art and a grand statue that greeted you as you first walked in was now empty. She blinked almost unseeing. "I do not understand," she said hesitantly, her voice gently echoing off of the now barren walls. "Did these men rob you?"

He continued down the hall and pushed open the doors to the parlor.

The room, once lavishly furnished, boasted a single side table and a small couch. Celeste entered, surprised by how loud her steps were against the empty floors.

"They took your curtains too?" she whispered looking out into the night sky.

"They were Japanese silk of the finest quality," Charles mumbled. "Kind of silly for curtains if you ask me."

She turned and looked at him. "They were the creditors then, were they not?"

Charles bowed his head. "They were supposed to come tomorrow afternoon, but circumstances changed, and they came this evening. My servant Edgar sent me a letter while I was at your party."

"Oh, Charles," she whispered. "How bad are you in?"

He cleared his throat. "Father left my mother and me three failing factories, and over a hundred thousand pounds in debt."

Celeste fell to the floor and pressed a hand over her mouth. "A hundred thousand pounds."

He nodded, sitting next to her on the cold floor. "I am in the process of trying to sell two of the factories, but they will not cover everything. They are worthless as is."

"How did this happen?"

Charles smiled weakly. "Father had gambling debts amongst several failed investments. Not to mention several mistresses we are just finding out about. Two of them with children he fathered who want a thousand pounds a year to keep quiet about the whole thing."

"But, your father always seemed so," she hesitated, thinking of the right word, "straightforward."

He sighed. "Yes, it surely was an awful thing to have sprung on us as well. A year after he was dead and buried, we discover all of this."

"How long has this been going on?"

"I received the first letter perhaps three months ago," he said joining her on the floor.

"And you did not tell me?" she asked gently. "I know you would not receive help from anyone, but you could have at least shared your burden."

He nodded. "I did not *want* to burden you," he replied sheepishly. "I know you have your own troubles."

"My problems are nothing in comparison to this!"

There was a brief silence.

"Is this why Graham left?" she asked.

He shook his head. "My cousin had his own reasons for leaving."

"Did he know?"

"I told him just before."

Celeste reached out and took Charles's hand. "No more secrets, Charles," she said squeezing his hand. "We promised each other once we would never keep anything from one another. When did we stop doing that?"

Charles sniffed and smiled, but didn't reply.

She gave his hand another squeeze and stood. "I should go. Can I convince you to come back with me?"

He shook his head and stood as well. "No, I am going to see what else, if anything, I can get rid of to help pay this debt."

"Have they given you a timeline?"

He nodded. "I have until next year to pay off what I can, or it will be debtors' prison for me."

Celeste wrapped him in a hug. "We will not let that happen," she told him.

He smiled. "My next move is to sell the house or put it up for lease."

"I have plenty of room in mine," she told him. "Father will not even notice."

Charles laughed and planted a kiss on her forehead.

"Will you be alright tonight?"

He nodded. "Return to your guests," he told her gently. "I will survive the night."

Celeste gave him a weak smile, then opened her mouth as if to say something, but thought better of it. After a moment, she gave his arm a light squeeze and left.

Charles sighed as he watched her go.

Another missed opportunity walked out the door.

As it turned out, Celeste had been missed almost as soon as she had left. Her father was furious when he caught sight of her again.

Her hair was falling out of place, her cheeks were flushed, and her dress was wrinkled. He grabbed her by the arm and dragged her out into a hallway when he saw her.

"Where in God's name have you been?" he asked in a harsh whisper. "What were you doing and *who* were you doing it with?"

She wrenched her arm free. "I was not doing anything, father," she replied just as harshly. "I rode off to Charles's because I was concerned when he left in such a hurry. All we did was talk."

"You look as though you did more than talk."

She shook her head. "I do not have to prove anything to you."

"The count has been asking about you all night," her father hissed. "This is your party. You cannot just leave in the middle of it."

"No, this is *your* party. A party where you can show-boat your new toy," she retorted. She made her way to the stairs.

"Where are you going?" he asked angrily.

"To make myself more presentable," she replied mordantly. "I would not want to embarrass you or anything, father."

She sat in front of her vanity for several minutes, staring at herself, yet unseeing. She closed her eyes and a single tear rolled down her face. She wiped it away quickly before anyone else in the room she was alone in could see.

She blinked away the other tears, dabbing at her eyes to keep them from falling. She then pinched her cheeks, cleared her throat and went back down to rejoin her guests.

Margaret was the first one to find her. "I heard you had returned," she said. "Is Charles alright?"

Celeste nodded. "Yes, it is just a headache. I found him lying on his sofa with a cool cloth on the back of his neck."

"It is nothing serious?" Margaret asked, concerned.

Celeste squeezed her friend's arm. "He will live."

"Ah, I have found you!" came the count's booming voice. "Come walk with me." It was not a question and Celeste had the strong urge to say no, but she smiled and took his outstretched arm.

"Is this a private party or might we ask Margaret and Doctor Digsby to join us?" Celeste asked.

"Yes, have her and doctor join," he said. "I just need air and I llike doctor's conversation."

Relieved, Celeste encouraged the other two on a walk hurriedly moving them outside along the lit path.

The count took in a deep breath of fresh air and let it out noisily. "Ah! Is beautiful night, no?"

"The air has certainly cooled since this morning," Margaret replied. "I was glad for it. This summer has been unusually hot, has it not?"

"It will be autumn before we know it," Doctor Digsby replied. "It is my favorite season."

"Mine as well," Margaret told him.

Celeste smiled to herself at this. She was glad they were getting along so well.

"Will you still be here, count, for autumn?" Margaret asked. "It is the loveliest thing to see here. The different colored trees lining the fog covered hills as the sun is just beginning to rise. I have never seen anything more beautiful."

"That is reason I want to talk to you alll," he replied, sounding pleased.

Celeste turned her head slowly to look at him. She had a feeling she was not going to like what he was going to say.

"My sister and I llike it here in countrrry," he continued.

Celeste felt her stomach churn.

"We have much enjoyed the people and the sights, so Natasha has decided to purchase house. And I shalll stay at lleast untill that purchase is finallized."

"Well then, you might see the autumn sun rising over the hills after all," the doctor said cheerfully.

Celeste felt annoyed.

"We should all go to the hills early one morning to see," Margaret added. "There is nothing more beautiful than nature."

The count nodded. "I llike it. We should go," he agreed.

"Do you not have tenants, count, back home in Russia?" Celeste asked after a few moments. "I thought in one of our conversations you mentioned the difficulties of being a landlord. What will become of them with you gallivanting all across Europe?" There was a playfulness in her tone, but her words were an attempt to remind him he had business elsewhere.

The count laughed. "My younger brrrother is taking care of duties whille I am gone," he explained.

"Oh?" Celeste continued. "A younger brother? Is there a rivalry there? Perhaps he is trying to usurp your title."

The count laughed harder. "He might trrry, but he is onlly twellve. Not much he can do."

"Ah, yes, I suppose not," Celeste replied.

"And when we have house, we will throw balll," he told them.

Celeste was starting to tire of balls and gatherings, but a thought crossed her mind that could possibly help Charles.

20

"You want me to rent or sell my house to the duchess?" Charles asked skeptically. "I thought you wanted them far away not just a few miles down the road."

"Ugh, I do!" Celeste proclaimed sitting on the only couch in the room. "Lord knows I do, but I want to see you saved so much more."

"And where am I to go?" he prodded sheepishly.

"Do you not have other properties in the area?" she responded. "There was that little cottage on the way to St. Anne's. I always thought it was more your style anyway."

He gave a small laugh. "I have already sold it."

"Oh," Celeste said letting her shoulders drop. "What about the farmhouse?"

He shook his head. "My father actually sold that before he died. He told us it was because it was of no use to him, but my mother and I figured out it was because of his debts."

"Could you not rent something smaller?"

"I have heard Sir Edwards plans to rent out one of his properties."

Celeste shivered. "I would not if I were you."

He lifted a brow. "Why?"

"Trust me, you do not want to know. He might invite you to one of his 'gatherings.'"

Charles lifted a brow at her.

She then rubbed her hands together. "I could ask my father to—"

"No!" Charles said immediately. "I want no help from that man, Celeste."

"Well, you cannot live on the streets!" she exclaimed. "What do you propose to do? Will you go and rent some ramshackle little house on the poorer side of town and live in squalor?"

"Would that bother you so much if I did?"

"How can you ask me that, Charles?" she responded harshly. "Of course, it would bother me because I care. I would not be here trying to figure out a solution for you if I did not care."

"Are those the only solutions you can come up with?" he asked softly, meeting her eye.

She looked at him for a moment. "The only ones I can think you might agree to," she replied looking away.

He nodded and sighed. "I will see about putting my house up for rent," he told her turning to the window.

"This is not your fault, Charles," Celeste reassured him. "What has happened is the cause of your father's carelessness."

He nodded. "Yes, and he left it for me and my mother to deal with."

She went over to him and placed a hand on his shoulder. "If there was anything else within my power for me to do, I would do it."

"I know," he replied, placing his hand over hers.

"I will talk to the duchess about coming to view the place," she told him. "Do not let this eat you up inside. We will get through this."

He squeezed her hand but didn't reply.

"Now, I have to go. I stopped by on my way to Margaret's for tea," she said taking her hand back. "I will call on you soon."

He turned to watch her go.

"You could marry me," he said softly once he was alone. "That would save me in more ways than one."

"Celeste, you are rather late!" Amanda said when she finally sat down. "We thought you had decided not to come after all."

"Forgive me, my dears," Celeste replied. "I stopped to check on Charles."

"Is he doing any better?" Margaret asked handing her a tea cup.

"He is on the mend," she replied. "How is the doctor?"

Amanda smiled. "Yes, tell us how everything goes with him. He is the most handsome of men."

Margaret blushed. "He is well," she replied hesitantly. "My mother adores him. She thinks he is a true gentleman."

"Yes, yes, we *all* think that about him," Celeste told her. "But we want to know what *you* think about him."

Amanda nodded. "He seems to like you very much."

Margaret looked down into her cup. "As I have told you before, I rather enjoy our time together, but that does not necessarily mean I am in love with him."

Amanda looked disappointed.

Celeste reached over and patted her friend's hand.

"Do not fret," she told her. "Sometimes love takes us by surprise. One day it was not there and the next day the man you have known your entire life turns out to be the one you cannot live without."

Margaret creased her brows. "That seems rather specific," she said.

Celeste cleared her throat and shook her head. "Just an example." She gave a wave of her hand. "Anyway, what I am trying to say is, give the doctor a chance. He is genuinely a wonderful man. Truly, he is one of the sweetest specimens I have ever encountered."

Amanda giggled.

"Specimens?" Margaret repeated with a smirk. "The way you talk about men sometimes makes them seem more like creatures in a zoo than people."

"That is because that is what they are," Celeste replied with a grin. "Creatures, animals in a zoo." She nodded her head. "Nothing can convince me otherwise." She looked at Amanda. "Just wait and see."

"What about you and the count?" Amanda asked. "He seems to like you rather well too. Perhaps, he will ask you to be his countess!" The young girl's eyes sparkled.

"Perhaps he will," Celeste replied indifferently. "And, perhaps, I will say no."

"Would you?" Amanda asked incredulously. "You would give up the chance of being called Countess Celeste?"

Celeste cringed. "Most certainly," she replied. "It does not even sound well together." She shook her head. "No, I would most definitely give that chance up."

"Margaret Digsby sounds well though, do you not think?" Amanda asked looking at a blushing Margaret.

"It certainly sounds better than Countess Celeste,"

Celeste replied. "But what of you Amanda? Did you make any knew conquests at this last ball?"

She sighed. "I danced with one of the Wilmington boys; the doctor was also kind enough to ask me; Mr. Pratt was my first partner though."

"He is not the best dancer," Celeste told her.

The young girl shook her head. "He is not, but I like Mr. Pratt. He is handsome and well spoken. I would have asked him for another dance, but I was told he left early due to a headache."

Celeste nodded. "Yes, he has been rather unwell."

"Pity," she shrugged. "Anyway, I was then asked by Mr. Sharpe whose face is almost completely healed."

"Did Joseph make it?" Celeste asked. "I had not noticed."

"The count even asked me to dance as well," Amanda continued.

"It seems you were never without a partner," Celeste said in congratulations.

Amanda nodded. "I danced twice with Mr. Browning, too," she replied with a blush. "He is still so charming though I do not believe he sees me the same way."

"Well, he would be a fool not to," Celeste told her. "Though I must warn you against Stephen."

"Are the two of you not friends?" she asked in a confused tone.

"We are, yes, but so are you," Celeste replied. "So, I believe it my duty to tell you he is a bit of a philanderer."

"Oh," Amanda asked, sounding a little disappointed.

"If that does not bother you, I will not stand in the way, but I do not want you to get your hopes up if he were to start paying an increasing amount of attention to you."

Amanda frowned.

"I do not doubt your guiles as a beautiful, spirited, young woman, but it is important to know what one is up against," Celeste continued.

Margaret nodded. "Do not be disheartened, Amanda," she reassured her. "Celeste only has your best interest at heart."

"I could believe nothing else, of course," Amanda finally said after a moment. "Thank you for putting me on my guard."

Celeste nodded. "Now, tell us about your brother and Sarah Wilmington," she said changing the subject. "Do you think he will propose soon?"

Amanda's smile returned. "Oh, I believe he will," she told them. "He has already asked me if I would like to have her as a sister."

"They are in love then?" Margaret asked.

"I know for sure he loves her," Amanda replied. "She is here often, but I cannot discern whether she feels the same."

"Sarah Wilmington is a simple girl, but she is sweet and shy," Celeste said. "Perhaps, it is not in her character to show her emotions."

Margaret nodded. "Your brother is a nice young man. Sarah would be lucky to have him."

Amanda sighed. "I just hope my time will be coming soon."

Celeste blinked at the young girl. "Your time?" she questioned hesitantly.

Amanda nodded. "To be married."

Celeste cleared her throat and shifted uncomfortably in her seat. "Why would you wish such a thing?" she asked sounding almost offended. She couldn't understand why someone so young and full of life was so ready and willing to give up their freedom to the shackles of conjugality. Disappointment panged in her heart as her hopes of making Amanda a student of industrious flirtations were dashed.

Amanda blanched a moment before she blushed. "The idea of marriage is romantic, is it not?" she asked timidly.

Celeste exchanged a small glance with Margaret. "That, Amanda, is the whole issue," she cautioned her. "Marriage as an idea is romantic, but the reality, you must know, is certainly different."

"Celeste," Margaret intervened gently. "I do believe we all have a different idea on what marriage is and what we want out of it. Amanda's experience on what marriage might be is surely not the same as yours."

"Well, of course, I understand that," Celeste clarified trying to calm her disappointment. "I certainly do not wish you to change your ideas on what you *wish* out of a marriage, Amanda. I just hope you are not brash in whom you decide to marry. Decisions as important and lasting as marriage should be considered without romantic notions."

"Should I not love the man I wish to marry?" Amanda queried, sounding a little hurt and confused.

Celeste tried to smile at her. "I do believe you are misunderstanding what I am trying to tell you," she said. "Of course, you should love the man you are to marry. But love is not something that develops out of thin air. It should never just be based on a single look from across the room or tender words spoken in your ear. Love is a journey. And journeys take time. The feelings you might have for someone now might not last a season, therefore, it is important to wait, to hold out and see if what you truly feel is real."

Margaret regarded her friend a little wide eyed having never heard her talk in such a way before.

"It takes more than just a short acquaintance to truly understand a person," Celeste explained.

"Is that not part of the romanticism of marriage?" Amanda gently argued. "The opportunity to continue to discover new things about your partner?"

Celeste let out a sigh. "In some ways, but I believe one must have a fair grasp of their potential partner's character before they fully invest into something like the idea of marriage." She gave small nod. "For example, it is important to understand and know how their future spouse handles disappointment. Do they become angry? Violent? Cry? Or do they learn from their negative experiences?"

"I believe I am coming to understand what you are trying to say," Margaret added in. "You wish Amanda would not only depend on her heart when choosing a partner, but her head as well. To wait to get to know someone, spend as much time as possible with them before she decides on something so important."

Celeste nodded. "Yes, and it might even justify limiting your time with that person to see how you feel without them," she continued. "Do you even miss them when they are not around or are the feelings you have only fleeting, present only when the person who inspires them is near?"

"Is this from experience, Celeste?" Margaret asked cautiously, curiously.

Celeste flashed a smile. "Just an observation, or, perhaps, the single woman's view on how attachments *should* be made," she replied sounding almost abashed at having run away with her feelings. She soon shook off her embarrassment, however, and smiled broadly. "I just hope, Amanda, you make a decision based off of what *you* want and not what society would have for you."

"I will take your advice into consideration," Amanda replied. "It is more than I have ever received on the subject before."

Celeste nodded into her tea cup. "It is more than anyone ever really says on it."

Margaret looked at her friend as she sipped from her cup. If Celeste had been anyone else, then Margaret would have viewed her speech as highly opinionated, perhaps a little quirky. But Margaret knew Celeste. And hidden within her declamation was a window into a pain and suffering Margaret never realized Celeste felt.

21

"Father, might I have a word?" Celeste asked one morning, finding him alone in his study.

He raised a skeptical brow. "What is it?"

"When I came of age and inherited some of my income, did I not also come into some property?" she asked.

"What is this about?" he questioned with heightened concern.

"I was just reading some of the documents on it and I noticed that I came into a few properties outside of town," she continued with a shrug.

Her father nodded. "That is right," he replied cautiously.

"I made inquiries on them and two of them bring in rent while the other one remains vacant. And has been so for almost two years."

He put down his pen and looked at her with more interest. "Is that so?"

She nodded. "Yes, and I would like to find a tenant for it," she told him. "It is a cute little property. There is no reason it should continue to be uninhabited. If it were, it would fall into disrepair, would it not?"

"Why these questions all of a sudden?"

Celeste smiled. "Do you not want me to take a more active role in things?" she asked lifting a brow. "Once you are gone, there will be no one here left to do it for me, so I must learn to do such things myself."

He took a deep breath and let it out slowly. "If you were married, your husband would take care of such things for you."

Celeste paused a moment, taken aback. "I am ashamed of such a comment, father," she retorted sternly, yet softly. "I cannot always have a man to do everything for me. One must learn to do things for oneself. It is my property to deal with and I should be able to do with it as I please— within legal means, of course."

"You know then?" her father asked.

"Know what?"

"Charles has put his house up for sale."

"For sale? When? I thought he would just rent it out."

Her father picked up the paper he had been reading and handed it to her.

She took it and read the few lines stating the late Tudor-style house was on the market. She closed her eyes and sighed.

"I assume this is reason for the sudden interest in *your* properties."

Celeste looked at her father without a response.

"I told you he was good for nothing, did I not?" he asked with a raised brow.

She glared at him. "This," she said raising the paper and throwing it back on the desk, "had nothing to do with him. It was his father who lied to us all, who put on this façade of good behavior. Racking up gaming debts and collecting mistresses." She snorted. "Sounds familiar, does it not? I wonder what terrible secrets I will discover about you after you are dead."

He stood from his desk. "You ungrateful child!" He wagged a finger at her. "I forbid you from letting your property to him."

"There is nothing you can do about it," she told him defiantly. "I spoke to our lawyer yesterday and he says it is within my rights to do as I please."

Her father let out a frustrated scream. "Why even consult me if you have already figured it out?"

"Just for the pleasure of your company."

"You are nothing but a headache."

"Yes, well, now you cannot blame me later for not having told you about it."

She skirted away before her father could say anything else to her and deciding Margaret would make far better company than anyone else in the house, she had her horse saddled up and she left, smiling triumphantly the whole way.

When she arrived at Margaret's family's humble estate, she gracefully slid off her horse and tied its reigns to a post out front. One of the Hepworth's few servants answered the door and introduced her into the parlor where Mr. and Mrs. Hepworth were exuberating the vision of conjugal bliss.

One was grunting as he read, while the other silently sewed on a sofa, taking only a moment or two to occasionally look up and stare out the window. They both stood however and greeted Celeste with genuine civility.

"Miss Willoughby," Mr. Hepworth said with a bow, "I have not seen you in weeks. How are you?"

Celeste smiled warmly. "I am well, Mr. Hepworth. How was Cambridge? Is Marcus faring well?"

"Cambridge was just capitol!" he proclaimed. "Wonderful town. Marcus should do well there."

"I am glad to hear it," Celeste replied.

"Dear," Mrs. Hepworth began, "would you go and see if Mary has prepared tea?"

"Huh?" Mr. Hepworth lazily replied. "Oh, yes, tea. I shall be back in a moment, my dear."

Mrs. Hepworth smiled at Celeste. "It is good to see you, as always."

Celeste replied similarly.

"I am not sure Margaret has told you, but we are soon to Ireland."

"Are you?" Celeste asked. "I had no idea. Are you visiting your sister?"

Mrs. Hepworth nodded with a chuckle. "Margaret, who inspired the trip, wanting to see its rolling hills, beautiful churches and convents, decided she no longer had the desire to go."

Celeste gave a look of surprise as a smile spread across her face. "How strange. That is not like Margaret at all."

Mrs. Hepworth nodded. "I agree and if it were not for a certain doctor, I would think something might be wrong with her."

Celeste smirked and lifted a brow. "Mrs. Hepworth, you could not begin to understand what joy this information has brought me."

"I very much could, for your joy could not surmount mine," she replied. "I was afraid poor Margaret would never get over John Howard."

Celeste groaned. "Oh, do not even say his name," she said. "Fortunately, all of that is in the past."

"Yes, but do not say anything of the kind to her father," her mother cautioned. "I do wish him to design his own opinion of Doctor Digsby."

"You have my word, nothing of this conversation will ever reach his ears on my account, but you cannot fear your husband will think ill of him, can you?"

Mrs. Hepworth smiled coyly. "I do not believe anyone could think ill of that man."

Celeste gave a small laugh. "I am very much of the same opinion. Is Margaret in her room?" she finally asked.

"Oh, dear me, I should have told you when you first arrived," Mrs. Hepworth said. "I was just too excited about my news to think of anything else. Margaret is out tending to the needy with the doctor."

Celeste's heart swelled for her friend.

"You are still welcome to tea, of course," Mrs. Hepworth told her.

"I am very glad to hear it," Celeste replied. "I have gone far too long without hearing one of your husband's inspiring anecdotes."

The next couple of weeks flew by. The duchess, after Celeste had given her a tour, decided to buy Charles's house, and Charles, after some coaxing moved into Celeste's townhouse downtown.

Seeing that his sister was well settled in her new house, the count made preparations to return to Russia. It had been settled that he would be leaving within the week, and, as of right now, alone.

Celeste's father appeared anxious at what he called the count's 'sudden departure' while she herself took the news better. She was beginning to tire of feigning anything but indifference toward the oaf who was starting to stand and sit too close to her.

With him gone, she would be freer to move about on her own and was freer to meet Stephen for afternoon dalliances. She had been getting a little antsy and annoyed that, even with a house of their own, the duchess and the count still both frequented her abode, dampening her plans.

When the day came for his actual departure, Celeste found the man to be waiting for her early in the morning. She groaned, knowing what his appearance could have meant, but put on her best smile and greeted him graciously.

"Count Orkoff," she said, holding out her hand, which disappeared in his own massive paw.

He kissed her hand lightly. "I have come to say goodbye," he told her.

She pressed a hand to her chest. "Thank you for thinking of me. I was afraid I was not going to see you again. I will certainly miss your company."

He smiled at her. "Your words brrring me grrreat joy," he replied. "And you shalll not llong wish for my company."

"Oh?" she said hesitantly, raising a questioning brow.

"I am to rrreturn in a month or two."

"So soon?" Celeste asked trying to sound more cheerful than she felt.

The count nodded. "You willl be gllad to see me?"

"Oh, of course, you are always welcome, count," she said quickly.

His smile deepened. "Then I willl not prrrolong our agony by llingering." He bowed and kissed her hand again. "I shalll come as soon as my business back home is finished."

Celeste pressed a hand to her temple as she watched him duck out of the door and into the hall. "Ugh," she groaned. "I must stop pretending to be so nice." She sighed and thought she might as well take the time to visit Stephen. Chances were, he was still in bed.

22

Celeste enjoyed several quiet weeks on her own. Some days were spent with Margaret, but she was often venturing off with the doctor and not available. Celeste had been invited on a few excursions, but she did not want to intervene. She had the feeling a proposal from the Doctor was well on its way and did not want to spoil whatever plans the doctor might have.

She had invited Amanda to tea a few times, but she was soon off to London for a few weeks, leaving Celeste a lot of time to think and/or spend in Stephen's bed. But, more and more, she felt there was something missing, something she had been denying herself.

A letter came from Graham, telling her of his studies and how he missed her, and though it made her smile, it did not strike within her more than the sentimental feelings one has for a friend. She, of course, wrote back, but not right away.

Charles was another one of her friends she hardly saw anymore. Now being in town, he was more than three times further away. Instead of a being only three or four miles from her, he was more than ten. And though she had made the trip a few times, he was either out dealing with his lawyer or otherwise unavailable.

Her father, who was never good company anyway, always seemed to be with the duchess at her new house. This did not bother her at all, however. Part of her wished he would just move in there with her, but knew he wouldn't.

Lost as to what to do with herself during her time alone, she took to reading and taking long walks. Often enough, she came to that tree, the one surrounded by the tall hedges, where she first gave herself to Charles. She had avoided that area for a while, but grew a new attachment to it. Even with the fall weather bringing cooler breezes, Celeste had not been deterred from her favorite place of reverie.

Oddly enough, she was rather content. This surprised her, as she used to long for gatherings, parties, and company almost every day, but now all she wished for was solitude. So, when only a month and a half after he departed passed, she was rather irritated to receive a telegram from the count saying he would be returning in less than a week.

Annoyed, she found solace the way she usually did, the only way she knew how, in the arms of a man.

Stephen brushed her hair off of his chest and rubbed his face. "So, the great beast of Russia is coming back, is he?" he asked.

Celeste rolled over on to her back. "Yes!" she groaned. "To propose, no doubt."

He chuckled. "He obviously does not know your reputation."

"You mean the one about my propensity to refuse offers of marriage?" she asked with a smirk.

"That, and the fact you are no longer a virgin."

She shrugged. "Some men do not seem to care."

"I would," he told her.

She propped herself up on her elbow. "Do you plan on marrying any time soon?" she asked with a skeptical brow raised.

He put his hands behind his head and shrugged. "I am not sure," he replied. "I suppose at some point I need someone to produce an heir for me."

Celeste gave an eye roll. "What a wonderful view you must have on wives. They serve no more purpose than producing children."

He laughed. "There is also the occasional use for pleasure."

"Ugh," Celeste said raising herself up.

"Where are you going?" he asked her as she pulled the sheets back and swung her legs over the side of the bed.

"Home," Celeste informed him, standing.

"But I am not done with you," he told her sternly.

Celeste turned and raised an eyebrow at him, giving a small laugh. "Yes, but I am done with you," she retorted. "We cannot always have everything we want."

Stephen reached over and grabbed her by the arm. "Do not dare talk to me like that, you slut!"

Celeste flushed with surprise and fear flashed across her face for a moment before it was replaced with anger. "Let go, Stephen," she growled at him. "You are hurting me."

"I ordered you back in bed," he told her, his grip tightening.

"No one *orders* me to do *anything*," she hissed. "Let go

or you will regret it."

Stephen pulled her closer as he sat up, a cruel smile on his face. "I will let you go when I am done."

Without another word, Celeste punched Stephen in the face. Blood gushed from his nose and a howl of pain and surprise escaped from his mouth. He released Celeste to cover his face.

"What did you do?" he yelled at her, his voice muffled by his hands.

"I told you to let go, did I not?" she replied, unaffected by the sight and retrieving her clothes.

"You bitch," he cried. "You could have broken my nose!"

"Then I would have done you a great justice. Perhaps, I might have straightened it out for you."

Stephen gave a whine when he saw all of the blood on his sheets.

"Well, Stephen," she began, pausing a moment on her way to the door, "this was fun while it lasted, but you can consider this our last time together. I will no longer require your," she cleared her throat, "small services. Honestly, it was never much of a service anyway. It was always over before it started, and I was always left having to take care of myself."

"Get out!" Stephen bellowed at her.

She gave a small curtsey, her smile growing as she turned and walked out the door, but as soon as she exited his house her stomach dropped and her skin prickled with fear. What would Stephen have done if she had not defended herself?

She shuddered at the thought, her stomach churning with anxiety, but she quickly brushed it off, putting on a brave face and putting the dark event where she stored all the others. In the back of her mind.

23

The count returned to his sister's house and Celeste was relieved he did not immediately come to visit her. But, in the event he might be making plans to see her, she made sure she was always out of the house.

She was even delighted to be invited to a small gathering at the Wilmingtons' where Amanda's brother announced his engagement to Sarah Wilmington. It was a touching scene. The young lovers seemed to glow as everyone gave them their sincerest congratulations.

Even Charles was there trying to smile and enjoy himself.

"It is a change to come together for such a happy occasion," Celeste said as she stood by him.

He blushed when he saw her. "Yes," he cleared his throat, "yes, it is."

"I have not seen you in almost a month," she stated. "I was actually surprised when I saw you here."

He bowed his head. "I have been rather busy with the sale of the house and straightening out my father's, now my, debt," he informed her with a hint of bitterness.

She nodded. "I do not expect to see you every day at

tea," she explained. "I understand you are busy; I am just trying to tell you I miss your company."

He gave a small smile.

"So, do you think the sale of the house will help you break even on everything?" she asked after a brief silence.

"That is what I am hoping to find out soon," he replied. He took a glass of champagne from a servant's tray as they walked by. "It seems like every other day a new debt is uncovered." He sipped from his glass.

Celeste squeezed his arm. "Is the house in town treating you well?"

He nodded. "Yes, thank you," he told her taking another sip.

"I suppose we will just have to find you a rich heiress for you to live off of," she said with a sly smile. "If my father had not already claimed her, I would suggest the duchess."

"Is that what you think I must resort to?" he asked dryly. "Fortune hunting? How low you must think I have sunk."

Celeste gaped at him. "Charles, I apologize. I, by no means, was implying anything of the sort," she replied, defending herself. "What I said was purely in jest."

"Forgive me," he said gently. "I have been overly sensitive lately."

Celeste sighed. "Well, I know something that might cheer you up," she said.

"Really?" he asked draining his glass.

"I will no longer be sharing a bed with Stephen Browning," she told him. "I am looking for a new conquest."

He looked at her. "That does bring me a small amount of joy."

"Yes, well," she rubbed her arm where Stephen had

left bruises, "I decided I did not like his treatment of me."

Charles frowned. "Are those from him?" he asked pointing to her arm.

"Yes," she replied, "but you should see the bruise I gave him in return." She smiled.

Charles rubbed his mouth with his hand. "I cannot believe he did that to you," he replied getting heated. "I swear, the next time I see him I am going to wring his neck."

"Charles, please do not make a big deal of it," she told him. "It is all over now. He will not touch me in any way ever again."

He gave an exasperated sigh. "I wish you would have listened to me earlier and just stayed away from him," he said. "I cannot always be there to protect you."

Celeste gave him a confused look. "I am not yours to protect."

Charles opened his mouth to reply, but decided against it. He merely gave a small nod.

"Oh, look!" Celeste exclaimed. "Is that not Miss Dawson?" She pointed to a pretty, fair-haired young woman across the room. "She was a favorite of yours at one point, was she not?"

"We spent a few months together before her father sent her away to her aunt's in Edinburgh. But it was essentially over before that."

Celeste gave a small gasp. "Oh, I believe she has spotted you and is coming this way," she said. "She is a pretty little thing, is she not?" She grabbed champagne as another servant went by. "I forget why you stopped seeing her."

"Charles Pratt," came the very high-pitched voice of Miss Dawson.

Celeste choked on her champagne and coughed. "Excuse me," she said regaining composure. She had forgotten how mouse-like her voice had been.

"Miss Willoughby," Miss Dawson said, her voice almost shrill. "Are you alright?"

Celeste put a hand to her mouth and nodded, closing her eyes for a moment to keep herself from laughing. "I am fine. It is good to see you, Miss Dawson. You have not changed."

"Nor you. Still beautiful and the life of the party, I hear," Miss Dawson replied. She shot a glance at Charles, a hint that Celeste took.

"You are too kind," she replied. "If you will excuse me, I believe my friend Margaret is calling for me." She turned to Charles. "We will talk later," she told him giving him a grin.

She crossed the room to Margaret who was in a one-sided conversation with Sarah Wilmington who was fervently describing her wedding plans and what she had planned for married life.

Margaret, who was not one for drinking large quantities of alcohol, was draining her champagne glass and reaching for another one. She nodded as Sarah talked, unable to get a word in otherwise.

"Sarah, how radiant you look," Celeste said, stepping in and saving her friend.

Sarah smiled brilliantly. "Thank you, Miss Willoughby," she replied. "I am truly happy. Eric is such a wonderful, kind man."

Celeste nodded. "Yes, and very handsome, I applaud you. Though I am sorry your soon-to-be sister-in-law could not make it to this gathering."

"Oh, Eric wanted to wait to propose until after his

sister returned from London, but she was not sure when that would be, so she gave him her blessing to do so without her," Sarah told her.

"That was very kind of her," Celeste replied.

"I shall finally have a sister!" Sarah exclaimed. "I am the happiest of women."

"And so deserving as well," Celeste told her, putting her arm through Margaret's. "I have always said that kind people deserve the best."

Margaret lifted a brow at her friend.

"And you are one of those people," she added.

"Miss Willoughby, I wish you would marry," Sarah told her. "You are as kind as any of us."

Celeste gave a small laugh. "Oh, my dear girl," she replied reaching out and gently squeezing her hand, "you are so sweet. Would you mind if I stole Margaret from you? There is something of importance I must discuss with her."

"Oh, yes, please," Sarah said.

"Thank you and congratulations again," Celeste told her. "I will pray for the happiest of marriages for you."

Celeste and Margaret moved away to a less crowded area, excusing themselves as they pushed their way through the large number of guests.

Margaret breathed a sigh of relief. "You came just in time," she said shaking her head. "Sarah is a very sweet girl, but I thought I would bore myself to tears talking anymore about what color she wants her curtains to be in the house they are getting or how she will make the best wife."

"I saw you trying to drink yourself to an early grave and thought you needed rescuing," Celeste replied. "I am sorry the doctor is not here. He at least would have made this a little more bearable for you."

"Donald was going to come, but his aunt's health has been up and down the last few days."

Celeste raised a brow at her friend. "Donald?" she repeated. "We are using Christian names now?" She grinned at her friend who, of course, blushed.

"He asked that I called him by his given name, and I complied," Margaret told her. "We are good friends now; I do not think it presumptuous to do so."

Celeste smiled at her friend. "No, it is not. I am happy for you, Margaret," she said rubbing her friend's arm. "You seem a lot happier these days."

Margaret nodded. "Yes, but do not think it is because I *love* the doctor. I truly only see him as a great friend."

"Is that not how it should be?" Celeste continued. "Should you not marry someone you see as a great friend?"

Margaret glanced to the other side of the room where Charles was talking to Miss Dawson. "Is that what you truly believe?" she asked.

Celeste nodded. "Well, I certainly would not want you to marry someone you could not stand," she replied. "No, the person you marry should be someone you can tell anything to. Who shares the same passions, dreams, and interests. Granted, you should have separate interests; you do not want to *always* be with each other, but for the most part, the person you marry should be someone who completes you as a person; who fills in the missing gaps in your character. And is that not what friends do?"

"Do you not marry because you do not believe you have found that person?" Margaret asked, shooting another glance at Charles.

"I do not marry because," she paused as if she wasn't

quite sure of the answer, "because my father has ruined the concept of what marriage is supposed to be for me."

Margaret sighed. "Come, let us go and get some fresh air. It is rather stuffy in here."

Celeste nodded, shooting her own glance at Charles and Miss Dawson who seemed to be whispering in his ear. She quickly turned away, taking in a deep breath as she turned and followed her friend.

24

The next day Charles appeared for a visit, looking rather ruffled and agitated. His cheeks were red, his usually tidy hair looked unkempt, and dust covered his boots and pants. Celeste ordered a warm drink for him.

"Did you walk all the way here in this wind, Charles?" she asked, concerned.

He nodded.

"You walked ten miles?" she said incredulously. "What on earth for? Do you not still have a horse? Is there not a coach you could have hired?"

"My horse needs new shoes," he replied. "And I am trying to economize, and a coach is an expense I could do without."

She took him by the hand and led him to a sofa. "Well, come sit by the fire," she ordered. "It is dreadfully cold for this time of the year."

His drink came which he took gladly. He held it for a few minutes, warming his hands.

"I heard the count was back," he said.

"Yes, and thank God I have not seen him yet," she replied.

He nodded and sipped his drink.

"By the way," Celeste started, "how did yesterday go with Miss Dawson?" She grinned at him. "She seemed rather happy to see you again."

Charles avoided making eye contact. "She was," he agreed.

"Well?" Celeste goaded. "How *happy* were you to see her?"

He shook his head. "She offered herself to me, but I," he took a deep breath and let it out slowly, "I was not interested."

Celeste blinked at him. "Not interested? Miss Dawson is beautiful, granted her voice is lacking in— well, it can certainly kill the mood that is for sure, but I cannot imagine you passing her up just for that. One does not necessarily need to speak in order to do the act."

Charles huffed.

"Is everything alright with you?" she asked, eyeing him skeptically. "It just seems that the last few times you have tried to bed someone, or were given the opportunity to do so, you have," she paused to think of an easier way to put it, "fallen short."

Charles blushed. "Yes," he replied a little haughtily. "I know." He ran his fingers through his hair, his agitation growing. He took a deep breath and let it out in a huff. "I have never felt so frustrated in my life."

Celeste failed to stifle a laugh.

He glared at her. "Does my pain amuse you, then?"

"Well, of course, it does!" she replied laughing again.

He let out a haunted sigh and sunk further into his seat, looking defeated. He drummed his fingers on his leg and stood from his seat a few seconds later, pacing the room.

Celeste blinked at him, her brows slightly furrowed. "Did I offend you?"

He shook his head. "It is something you would normally say at any other time. I expected it. We are often unguarded with one another."

Celeste opened her mouth to speak, but was at a loss as to what to say, so she closed it, watching as Charles walked from one end of the room to the other in an agitated manner. "Can I get you something else to calm you down?"

"No, no," he told her, shaking his head. "I just want to," he rubbed his hand over his mouth before holding his hand out, "not talk about it." He closed his hand and let if fall to his side.

Celeste nodded slowly, confused by his strange behavior. He had never been one to shy away from talking about his sexual escapades or being laughed at because of their failures. They had spent several hours laughing at each other for just that.

"If that is what you wish," she told him softly.

"What I wish," he whispered, laughing through his nose.

Celeste sat in silence for several moments watching him, her own anxiety growing. "Something is obviously bothering you, Charles," she finally said. "Would you not tell me what it is?"

He stopped pacing to look at her for a moment, his gaze soft, yet, intense. She was so beautiful, sitting there, her face twisted in concern. For him. And, for a moment everything stopped, time, life, his heart. There was nothing else for him but what he had right in front of him.

He took a shaky breath. "Celeste, I cannot begin to tell you what is wrong," he finally said stepping toward her. "I can only tell you what I believe is right."

He reached down and took Celeste's hand just as the door to the parlor opened and her father stepped in. Charles immediately dropped her hand and stepped away.

"My child, I have some wonderful news!" he exclaimed almost floating into the room. He stopped when he saw Charles. "Ah," he said, his smile fading. "I see *you* are here, Mr. Pratt."

Charles gave a stiff bow. "Sir."

"I guess there is no harm in you hearing the good news as well," Mr. Willoughby told him, his smile returning to his face. "I have just met with the most illustrious visitor." He moved to the other side of the room to pour himself a drink, his grin only widening.

Celeste sighed, indifferent to the excitement her father portrayed. "And who might this visitor have been, father?" she asked more out of duty than curiosity. "Was it some lawyer telling you some great uncle you never heard of died and left you his entire fortune?" She shot Charles a grin who mustered only a small smile in return.

"Better," her father told her giving a small laugh as he sipped from his glass and eyed Charles triumphantly.

"Do you expect me to guess who this person was or are you going to spare us the grueling agony of not knowing?" Celeste finally asked trying to keep her annoyance at bay.

Her father's mood was unaffected as he turned to her, his smile brightening his eyes. "It was the count," he finally told them, laughing as he raised his glass to his lips.

"Count Orkoff?" Celeste asked trying not to laugh. "He is not illustrious. What could he want?"

"You, my dear."

Celeste uttered a small, "Ugh."

Charles colored and moved to the window.

"He asked me today for your hand in marriage," her father continued, almost wiggling with delight. "And I have given him my blessing."

"Have you?" Celeste said almost breathless.

"Indeed, I have," her father replied, draining his glass and placing it on a table. He went over to his daughter and took her hands. "Just think, my child, you will be a countess."

"In Russia," Celeste added blandly.

"You will have such wealth and prestige."

She glanced over her shoulder at Charles who was still facing out the window. "Yes, I suppose I would. In *Russia*."

Her father kissed her forehead. "I am beyond ecstatic."

Celeste narrowed her eyes at her father.

"Are you not moved, my dear?" he asked. "The count went all the way back to Russia just to get the ring. I have seen it! A giant ruby worn by his grandmother." He rubbed his hands together. "Are you not excited?"

"Oh, certainly, father," she replied not trying to hide her sarcasm. "All I have ever wanted was to leave my family and friends to move to a country whose language is one I know not a word of."

She heard Charles move behind her.

"And what do you think of this news, Mr. Pratt?" Mr. Willoughby asked him not trying to mask the satisfaction in his voice.

Charles turned to him sharply. "It is wonderful news," he responded a little coldly. "I congratulate you both." He bowed deeply and made his way to the door.

"Charles," Celeste called after him, standing from the sofa. "Where are you going?"

"There is somewhere else I have to be," he told her, not meeting her eyes.

"But you only just got here," she argued. "You cannot be in a hurry to leave so soon. You must stay."

Charles shifted his gaze from the floor to Mr. Willoughby and then to Celeste; his face contorted in an emotion Celeste could only describe as angry despair.

He shook his head solemnly. "Forgive me, but I cannot," he said softly, sounding defeated.

"Well, let me lend you one of my carriages, please," she said softly. "You do not need to be walking all over the country by yourself in this nasty weather."

He gave a weak smile. "I thank you for your concern, but I must decline."

"Will I at least see you soon? Will you not come to tea in the next day or so?"

He gave her another bow. "We shall see."

She watched him go with anxiety.

"How does next month sound for a wedding?" her father continued unaffected by what had just passed.

"What?" Celeste asked, not paying attention.

"A late November wedding?"

"Oh, father, honestly," Celeste said turning to him. "I have no intentions of marrying the count and moving to Russia. Do not be ridiculous."

He father's smile dropped. "Excuse me?" he said coming closer. "You have no intentions?" His eyes blazed. "You would be a fool to refuse such a man, to refuse yourself such an opportunity."

Celeste shrugged and moved to pour herself something to drink. "Then I guess I am a fool because I shall refuse him as I have done everyone else."

Her father took in a shaky breath. "You would deny yourself the prestige?" he asked incredulously. "I do not understand you child. You are the most difficult challenge of my life!"

"I do not expect you to understand, father," she replied, unaffected.

"It will be November soon, child," he told her. "Do you think you can find anyone else who will have you by the end of the year?"

Celeste turned to him. "Are you still on that?" she asked, trying to remain indifferent.

"Mark my words, Celeste," he said in a harsh whisper. "If you refuse the count, I will make good on my promise to have you taken away."

Celeste threw back her drink and placed the glass on a table. "I love a good challenge," she told him haughtily before exiting the room.

She could hear her father's curses follow her into the hall.

Celeste did not have to wait long until her challenge was before her. The next morning, the count himself arrived just after breakfast. He was dressed in dark reds and furs, a smile brightening his face.

"I was wondering if you woulld honor me with your company," he said offering her one of his colossal hands.

Celeste smiled and grabbed a shawl, hoping to get this whole thing over with quickly.

"How was your trip to Russia?" she asked trying to break the silence. "Whatever business you had seemed to have taken a lot less time than you thought."

He nodded. “Is trrrue,” he agreed, “but not because my business was alll taken care of there. I am here sooner than anticipated because I had business here.”

“It must be rather odious to always have business somewhere,” Celeste told him. “I for one abhor traveling. I would much prefer to stay where I am.” She glanced over at him, hoping this little speech would deter him from his mission, but he either was not listening or did not understand her meaning.

He gave another nod. “Yes,” he replied. “It can be rrrather tiresome.”

She gave a small cough, at a loss for words.

“Are you cold?” he asked, sounding concerned.

She shook her head. “No, I am fine, thank you. The air has a slight chill to it, but there is no wind. I think the weather rather pleasant today.”

They walked on a little further in silence.

“Would you llike to rrrest?” the count asked as they passed a bench.

Celeste sighed, knowing this is where he intended to do it. “Yes, thank you,” she replied taking a seat.

The count stood before her and cleared his throat. “Miss Willloughby,” he started, “Celeste, I did not come to Engll and with intention of finding wife, but, perhaps, that is best time to find what you rrreallly desire.”

Celeste gave a small nod, appreciating his speech.

“When I met you, I thought I would meet just another rrrich brrrat as I have met before,” he continued. “But you are diff-rrrent. You have certain command over your-sellf. Something I grrreatly admire.” He cleared his throat again, appearing nervous. “I bellieve you are special and willl brrring diff-rrrent kind of rrrichness to my llife.”

He pulled out a little box from his pocket and knelt

before her.

"Willl you do me grrreat honor and marry me?" he asked shakily opening the small box in his hand.

Celeste pressed a hand to her chest in surprise. Her father had not been joking about the size of the ruby. The ring was certainly beautiful, breathtaking even, and without thinking, she reached out as if to touch it, but, recollecting herself, she stopped.

Instead she folded her hands on her lap. "Your words have truly touched me," she said softly. "And I am honored beyond words that you consider me worthy enough to be your wife, but," she paused for a moment, taking a deep breath, "I must refuse your offer. I know I would not bring you the happiness you truly seek. I do, however, hope we can still remain friends."

The count blinked at her for a moment, processing what she had said. "I do not underrrstand," he replied, slowly, his accent seeming to grow thicker with his confusion.

"I apologize for any misunderstanding there might have been, Count Orkoff," Celeste said gently. "But I just cannot accept your proposal."

"You no want to marry me?" he asked, his voice rising a little.

Celeste pressed her lips together for a moment. "No, I do not want to marry you," she finally answered.

Count Orkoff stood, his face red. "But you encourrrage me!" he exclaimed. "You fllirt with me!"

Celeste smoothed out her skirt trying not to be affected by his outburst. "Yes, well, I am a flirt. That is what I do," she replied calmly. "I flirt."

"I have *ne*-ver been insullted like you insullt me." He wagged his finger at her accusingly.

Celeste blinked at him, her neck straining from looking up. "Well, if this is how you are to behave at the slightest disappointment, I daresay I dodged a bullet by refusing you."

The count seethed and paced the ground in front of her, his face becoming redder every second. "I offer good home, good llife, and you rrrefuse!" He threw his hands in the air in agitation, going on and on about what Celeste could have had. His ranting and raving grew more heated by the moment, accusing her of trickery and cruelty while Celeste sat on the bench trying not to yawn.

"I have trrreated you with rrrespect and you gave me llies in rrreturn!" he claimed, pounding his fist into his palm. "You have done me injustice! You have rrruined my good name and made me fool!"

On and on he went for what seemed like several minutes until he stopped midsentence. His face turned almost purple and he bent over slightly, his eyes wide as he grasped at his chest.

Celeste looked at him with startled confusion, quite scared by the expression on his face. "Count? What is it?" she asked timidly.

He staggered a few steps toward her causing her to jump from the bench in alarm, stumbling to avoid him.

"Cyka," the count croaked as he fell to his knees and then on his face.

Celeste stood frozen for a few minutes, terrified at what had just transpired. "Count Orkoff?" she called out when he hadn't moved for several seconds.

He did not respond.

She took a few steps closer. "Are you unwell?"

Again, no response.

She timidly tapped on his shoulder with her foot.

"Count? Should I have the doctor sent for?"

When he again did not stir or move, the realization that he was dead finally hit her.

"Well..." Celeste let out in a long sigh, "father is sure to have an apoplexy now."

It took six men to lift the count on a cart and wheel his body to the undertaker. Celeste had the awful task of informing the duchess, who was happily having furniture rearranged in her new drawing room with Celeste's father close by. Both of them beamed at her, expecting good news, but when she hesitated, they knew something had happened. The sister was distraught when Celeste finally told her; her father was suspicious.

"What did you say to him, Celeste?" he asked when he returned from the duchess's room, the duchess being properly sedated by the doctor.

"Me?" she asked offended. "You cannot honestly think that anything I said could have caused this."

"You refused him, did you not?"

"And what if I did?" she retorted. "He would not have been the first man I refused, and all of those poor, wretched souls are still alive."

Her father's face grew red.

"Perhaps, this time I accepted him, and he could not take the excitement." She shrugged. "Could that not be just as reasonable of an explanation?"

There was a clearing of a throat and Doctor Digsby walked in.

"Ah, doctor," Mr. Willoughby said. "How is the duchess?"

"I have given her a light sedative so she can rest," he

replied. "She seemed rather inconsolable."

Celeste and her father both nodded.

"I have asked her if she might allow me to examine her brother's body for cause of death," he told them. "I was hoping she would not mind, but she does not want him cut open." As dignified as he was as a gentleman, the doctor in him did not hide his disappointment very well.

Celeste pressed her lips together to hide a smile. "Do you have any theories as to what could have happened, doctor?" she asked after she composed herself.

"I was told you were there when it happened. Could you describe to me in detail what occurred?" he responded.

Her father raised a brow at her. "Yes, can you?"

Celeste cleared her throat and twisted her hands anxiously. "Yes," she cleared her throat again, conscious of her father's glares. "He had just proposed to me and was explaining the wonderful life we would have together in his castle. He was rather excited, nervous, of course, as such an important situation would make anyone. He was pacing and talking very fervently when, all of a sudden, he just stopped and grabbed his chest. His face then turned purple and he fell to the ground."

The doctor nodded.

"And what was your answer to him?" her father asked. "What was your response to his proposal?"

"Really, father, I doubt that matters right now," Celeste said in a scolding tone. "A man has lost his life."

Her father narrowed his eyes at her.

"It was my theory this might have happened," Doctor Digsby said. "I have read a great deal about gigantism since I met him, and it appears a great number of those with his condition suffer from heart problems. I would venture to say he died from a heart attack." He shook his head. "I am afraid there is nothing you could have done to save him."

Celeste raised a triumphant brow at her father.

Her father gave a 'humph' in reply.

"It is a shame," the doctor said. "He was rather young, was he not?"

"The duchess said he was only just thirty-six years of age," Mr. Willoughby replied. He shook his head. "Though they lived far apart for the better of twenty years they were rather close. She had told me before they would often write to one another. She will miss him greatly."

The doctor made his apologies and then gave Mr. Willoughby directions for using the sedative if needed. Mr. Willoughby thanked him.

"See, father?" Celeste said after the doctor left, "I am not to blame for the count's death. Doctor Digsby believes it would have happened sooner or later anyway."

Her father narrowed his eyes at her. "I am not so convinced," he told her. "I know your favorite game is to twirl a man around your finger just to watch him come undone later."

Celeste lifted her brows. "That is a rather harsh view of me you have," she replied.

"Humph," he grunted. "Just enjoy your last two months of freedom before I send you away."

She glared at him. "Why not save yourself the trouble and send me away now?" she asked bitterly.

He shook his head. "I said the end of the year and I meant it," he replied.

Celeste didn't reply.

"Now, go home and stay out of trouble," her father commanded.

Celeste huffed but left, a sinking feeling growing in the pit of her stomach.

25

The duchess soon left for Russia with her brother's body; Celeste's father tagging along as well for emotional support. Celeste herself remained mildly tormented by what happened to the count. She woke more than once having dreamt the scene of that day.

She sighed as she finished relaying her guilt to Margaret one afternoon.

"You believe your refusal of him killed him?" Margaret asked, stirring her tea.

Celeste shrugged. "Doctor Digsby did say there was nothing I could have done and that people of his size are known to have issues of the heart." She paused, taking a sip of her tea. "But, I suppose my refusal could have expedited the issue." She shook her head. "But who is to say it would not have happened if I accepted his offer? Perhaps, the excitement from that could have caused the same reaction." She put her tea down and sighed. "You were right from the beginning, Margaret. I should not have encouraged him."

Margaret reached out and took her friend's hand. "I do not believe you are to blame, Celeste," her friend told her.

"Donald and I have been discussing it and he has shared with me his research. We are of the same opinion. The count's heart could no longer endure his immense size."

Celeste gave a sigh, this one of relief. "It does make me feel significantly better hearing it from you," she replied. "Your judgment is the only one I truly care about."

Margaret smiled at her. "I have no right to judge anyone," she told her sheepishly. "That right is up to God."

Celeste gave a wave of her hand. "Theoretically, yes, but we as humans tend to believe we have that right. Some are more judgmental than others, I myself being one of them, I cannot deny that, but you, who rarely dishes out any kind of judgment, tend to see things differently. You tend to see people for who they are on the inside without letting what is on the outside influence your opinion."

Margaret gave a small laugh. "I do not believe I deserve such praise."

"I believe you do," Celeste told her proudly. "I also believe you deserve all the happiness in the world. You are too good not to."

"I do not deserve any more happiness than the next person."

"Stop being modest, Margaret," Celeste commanded gently. "You deserve more than anyone else I know, except for Doctor Digsby, who I honestly believe might be your equal."

Margaret blushed. "Please, I do not want to get into that," she replied.

Celeste frowned slightly. "Are you still so unsure about him? Would you honestly still prefer a cold, dank convent over that man who is handsome, warm, and looks as if he would be very accommodating in the bedroom."

Margaret looked abashed.

"Sure, he sometimes smells of garlic due to the poultices he makes for patients, but it is not overpowering. So, what is making you hesitate? What is making you so unsure of him?"

Margaret shook her head. "I am not unsure of *him*. I believe he will make a kind, caring, gentle husband and father, but I do not believe I shall make a good wife."

Celeste looked taken aback. "Margaret, how can you say such a thing?"

Margaret blushed and pursed her lips, shifting her gaze to her lap.

"Have I been wrong in thinking you want to get married and have children?" Celeste asked her.

Margaret shifted uncomfortably in her chair. "I do want those things, but," she paused trying to think of what to say, "but not in—"

"But not with Doctor Digsby?" Celeste interrupted, thinking she was finishing her friend's thought.

Margaret gave a small sigh and shook her head. "I do not know," she replied. "I hold Donald in the highest regard. I just— I just— I do not know what is wrong with me."

Celeste squeezed her friend's hand. "There is not a thing in the world wrong with you, Margaret," she told her matter-of-factly. "It is the most natural thing in the world to show hesitancy when faced with such a decision as marriage. I would think less of you if you did not."

Margaret gave a weak smile. "I know I can always count on you to cheer me up and make me feel good about myself."

The sound of footsteps broke their tête-à-tête and both of them were surprised when Stephen Browning was shown into the room.

Celeste held back a groan while Margaret's face flushed with the uncomfortableness of the scene.

"Stephen," Celeste said in greeting, not getting up from her seat. "Your nose looks well."

He cleared his throat. "Yes," he replied coldly. "It appears it was not broken after all."

"Pity," Celeste replied.

"Forgive me, Miss Hepworth, for my intrusion," Stephen said giving a deep bow to Margaret. "I will only be here for a short duration."

"Short and fast is all you know, Stephen," Celeste replied sipping her tea.

Stephen colored with anger, but kept his cool. "I came to see if you have heard the news," he said, struggling to ignore her comment.

"About?" Celeste asked indifferently.

"About me," he replied with a smug smile.

She shook her head. "No, Stephen, I have not. I do not much care to keep up with old toys."

Margaret looked at Celeste in abashed astonishment.

Stephen's face twitched, and he straightened his back, trying to regain his composure. "I am to be married," he told her tugging on his jacket.

Celeste slowly turned her head to face him. "Well," she said after a moment or two, "I am sure you will make the unfortunate girl very miserable. Who, might I ask, did you trick into this trap?"

Stephen gave her a triumphant smile. "Miss Amanda Haderly, of course," he replied haughtily.

Celeste's face remained blank, but Margaret gave a small gasp.

"Well," Celeste said blandly, "are you not the most

wretched little snake?"

He gave a small chuckle. "I am rather glad you had not heard it from anyone else," he told her. "I wanted to be the one to break it to you."

"And when did this occur?" Celeste asked trying to remain calm. "I thought she was still in London."

His lips curled into an ominous smile. "Yes, and she will not return until tomorrow." He moved about the room.

Margaret shifted uncomfortably again.

"You see, I began to write to her as soon as you left me that afternoon," he explained. "I told her how much I missed her company and how I have tried to resist her charms, but could no longer deny myself the pleasure."

"Ugh," Celeste said in disgust.

"She wrote back with similar feelings, so I rushed to London to visit her, and after a few days of wooing her some more, I proposed."

Celeste rubbed her temple. "Few people disgust me the way you do, Stephen," she told him.

"Yes, well, I guess there is nothing more you can do except to wish me and my future bride all the happiness in the world." He gave a small laugh as he bowed to them both and left.

Celeste, who had kept her cool until the last moment, stood from the table and rubbed her mouth with her hand. "That monster," she growled. "I cannot believe he would do this."

"Do you think he will go through with it?" Margaret asked. "It seems like such a ridiculous thing to do. To marry Amanda just because you slighted him."

Celeste shook her head. "It is exactly something he would do," she replied.

"You do not think he will break it off later?"

"No, he will go through with it. Of that, I am sure."

Margaret shook her head. "I do not understand. It is obvious he does not love Amanda, so why would he trick her into marrying him?"

"Because Amanda is easy prey," Celeste replied. "She believes that if a man shows you any kind of affection, then he must love you. You heard the way she spoke of marriage that day at tea." Celeste pressed a hand to her forehead. "She is too young and naïve for someone like Stephen."

Margaret shook her head worriedly. "Should we not warn her?" she asked. "We cannot just let him ruin the poor girl's life, can we?"

Celeste shook her head again. "No, we cannot," she replied. "Stephen is abusive, demanding, selfish, and a libertine. Amanda deserves none of those things." Celeste groaned. "Poor unsuspecting girl."

"Mr. Browning said she should be returning from London tomorrow," Margaret said. "Should we go together and tell her?"

"No," Celeste replied shaking her head. "This is something I believe I must do on my own. I have gotten the poor girl in this mess, so I should be the one to get her out of it. I am not sure what I should tell her, but I cannot stand back and watch this happen."

Margaret nodded.

"Something tells me the count's death was only the beginning of my troubles," Celeste said softly.

"It cannot be as dire as that?" Margaret suggested. "Surely there is hope?"

Celeste looked at her friend. "Oh, Margaret, I wish there was."

Margaret stood and hugged her friend. "Do not fret, Celeste," she told her. "I am sure everything will turn out just fine."

Celeste gave a soft smile, but there was something else that was bothering her, something she had yet to tell her friend. Despite being able to tell Margaret everything else about her life, Celeste could still not bring herself to tell Margaret she was bound for the asylum come New Year's Day.

26

Celeste waited until two days after Amada arrived home from London to visit her. It was a bitter, cold day and the wind rattled her carriage window as it moved along the road. Celeste shivered as she stepped back out into the gray afternoon.

The day certainly reflected her mood.

She was sorry she was about to break her young friend's heart. There was nothing she wanted to do less than to tell Amanda what an awful creature she had agreed to marry, but it had to be done. If she did not say anything, then she would be letting her friend descend into a bitter marriage. Bitter, like the weather outside.

She was shown into the room where Amanda greeted her warmly, her face lit up with a triumphant smile.

"You have come to congratulate me," Amada said lifting her chin in a haughty gesture Celeste had never seen her make before.

Celeste tilted her head slightly and made an uneasy face. "If it were any other man you attached yourself to, I would," she replied cautiously. "I would throw a ball in your honor, but that is not why I am here."

Amanda's smile faded. "What do you mean?"

Celeste cleared her throat. "Shall we sit?" she began, motioning to the couches.

Amanda hesitated, but after a moment moved to a seat.

Celeste sat beside her and gently took one of her hands. "Amanda," she started, "you are a very sweet girl and I think very highly of you, which is the reason why I am here. If I had not cared for your welfare, then I would not interfere."

"Get to the point, Celeste," Amanda told her in a flat tone.

Celeste blinked in surprise, having never heard Amanda speak in such a way, but she nodded and continued. "Stephen is—"

"I knew that was why you were here," Amanda interrupted her, taking her hand back. "I did not want to believe it, but it must be true. You are jealous!"

"I beg your pardon?" Celeste replied, confused. "Jealous? Heavens no! No!" She put her hands up in defense. "Absolutely not."

"No?" Amanda asked, looking as if she did not believe her.

"I harbor no feelings for Mr. Browning whatsoever. No romantic feelings," Celeste told her strongly. "I merely came to tell you how wrong he is for you."

Amanda stood from the couch with a huff and walked to the other side of the room.

"He is not a nice man. He screams and yells when he does not get his way and I have reason to believe he might even be violent."

Amanda shook her head in disbelief.

"And to top all of that, he is a libertine of the utmost

degree."

"Much like the male version of yourself?" Amanda asked whirling around to look at her, fire in her hazel eyes.

Celeste almost jumped at the sight of her. "Well, I would not go so far as to say that," she replied quietly.

"Stephen told me you would try to break us apart," Amanda said almost in a hiss. "I did not believe him. I told him that you were my friend and would never do anything except wish me happiness, but he was right." She shook her head again. "He told me about the two of you."

Celeste sucked her teeth a bit, sitting frozen. "Did he?"

Amanda nodded furiously. "Yes."

"And what, exactly, did he say?"

"He told me how you seduced him, forcing yourself upon him and then guilting him into continuing a relationship with you, begging him to take you again and again, but he never loved you."

Celeste frowned. "The never loving me thing aside," she started, "that is *not* exactly how everything went."

"Is that so?" Amanda asked sounding more heated. "Then tell me, Celeste, how did it go?"

Celeste narrowed her eyes at the young girl. "Something tells me you would not believe me no matter what I was to say, so I do not see any need to waste my breath."

Amanda nodded. "Yes, well, we all know how you like to meddle in other people's lives," she responded venomously. "Your life is not amusing enough, so you try to interject yourself into everyone else's and use them as your puppets, getting them to do whatever you please."

Celeste was taken aback at such a harsh description of her character.

"Well, I will *not* let you meddle in my life!"

Celeste stood and gave a short curtsey. "Very well, Amanda," she said. "You have made your point very clear. I came with the intention of sparing you a life of misery with a wretched excuse for a man, and you verbally attack me. However true your depictions of my character may be, I wanted nothing more than to help you, someone I *used* to hold in high regard. Now, all I see is a silly girl who is so blinded by her emotions, she refuses the kindly gestures and advice given by someone she once called friend."

Amanda narrowed her eyes at her. "And all I see is a bitter woman who is too old for a second chance at life."

Celeste huffed. "Wait until after you get married," she said turning to the door. "Then you will see whether it is me or you that needs the second chance."

Celeste was seething when she pulled up to Margaret's house. As soon as her carriage stopped, she flew out without waiting for her driver to hand her down. The wind seemed to blow as strong as her fury was raging, and it was a struggle just to get to the door of the house.

She was shown in directly, shivering, but whether it was from anger or cold, she could not tell. The nerve of that little welp, to talk to her in such a way when she was only there to help! How dare she! To call her old! To accuse her of meddling, being bored with her own life!

Celeste was so angry as she replayed the scene over and over in her head that she gave an "ugh!" in frustration as she was shown into the parlor where Margaret was sitting, staring in front of the fire.

Margaret slowly turned to look at Celeste who

immediately flew into a rage, her hands flying about her as she relayed to Margaret what had transpired between her and Amanda earlier.

"Can you believe she threw my goodwill back in my face?" Celeste asked, talking so fast and fervently that Margaret, had she had anything to add, would not have been able to speak. "That scared, flighty, capricious, ignorant of the world of men, little girl had the *audacity* to tell me I was too old for a second chance!" She huffed. "A second chance at what?" she asked rhetorically, throwing her hands in the air. "A second chance at not relinquishing my freedom to some arrogant, self-important, selfish, over dressed, pompous, reptile of a man who would expect me to be subordinate to him in everything that I do, yet, would not for a *second* consider my feelings as he does anything and everything he pleases?!" Celeste shook her head. "That little girl is in for a world of surprise on her wedding night." She took a deep breath and let it out in a small scream of frustration. "I need a drink."

Celeste, after pouring herself a second drink, having drained the first one almost immediately, turned to face Margaret who had remained silent since she first burst her way into the room. She finally saw that her friend had barely moved since she entered; her eyes were red and puffy; her cheeks were tear stained.

"Margaret?" Celeste asked in a soft tone. "Has something happened?"

Margaret cleared her throat and dabbed at her eyes with the handkerchief she had balled up in her hand. "I am sorry for your troubles with Miss Haderly," she replied taking a deep breath. "It will be a sad situation indeed once she realizes how right you were about Mr. Browning." She sniffed. "But there is certainly one point she made that I am inclined to agree with."

Celeste frowned and blinked at her. "And that is?"

"You are a meddler," Margaret said in a shaky voice. "You like to assert yourself in other people's lives, assuming that something you do not understand is an issue you must fix that *only you* can fix, but sometimes what you perceive as broken is not or is so far gone that there is nothing left to put back together." A tear fell down Margaret's cheek which she refused to wipe away. It splattered undisturbed on the back of her hand.

Celeste put her drink down and moved to her friend. "I do not understand, Margaret," she replied almost in a whisper. "What are you talking of? What has happened?"

Margaret gave a small sob. "Donald proposed," she finally gasped, burying her face in her hands.

Celeste froze. "He proposed?" she repeated gently.

Margaret nodded, unable to control her sobbing.

"And you..." Celeste hesitated, "refused him?"

Margaret shook her head furiously. "No!" she exclaimed through her tears.

"So, you are engaged then?" Celeste tried again.

Margaret shook her head again. "No!"

Celeste twisted her hands in confusion. "I do not understand," she finally said after a moment. "You did not refuse him, yet, you are not engaged?"

Margaret nodded taking in a deep breath, wiping away her tears with her handkerchief. "I accepted him at first," she started. "He was so sweet and so sincere in his praise of me that I was so overcome with gratitude." She sniffed. "I could not refuse him." Her chest heaved a few times as if she were to break down into sobs again, but she gained control of herself. "But then, when I returned home and thought about everything, I realized I could not go through with it. So, I returned the next day, this morning, and broke it off."

"Oh, Margaret, I—"

"I care for him, I do! But as much as I regard, esteem, and respect him, I do not *love* him." She shook her head. "And to accept him, I would be lying to myself and to him and he does not deserve that. He deserves a woman who will show him as much love for him as he has for her. And I cannot give it to him." She broke down into tears again.

"Oh, Margaret, I am so sorry," Celeste said, reaching out and rubbing her friend's back.

Margaret recoiled, standing from her seat and moving across the room. "I do not ask for consolation from you," she said a little coldly. "I ask that you leave me be!"

Celeste gaped at her friend. "What?"

"Donald was so hurt when I told him," Margaret said, frowning at her friend. "He was so shocked and confused as to how I could change my mind so quickly. That I could one day bring him all of the joy and happiness in the world he could ever hope for and then take it away the next."

Celeste shifted her gaze to the floor.

"Doctor Digsby is a good man," Margaret went on. "He did not deserve what I did to him." She pressed a hand to her forehead. "You must stop this, Celeste."

Celeste looked up confused. "Stop what?"

"Stop trying to throw these men in my path!" she replied heatedly. "Has it ever occurred to you that I do not want these kinds of attentions? Or maybe this is not what I want after all? That perhaps I want to be left alone?"

Celeste didn't reply.

"Becoming a nun would seem torturous to you, yet, to

me it would mean peace!" Margaret took in a deep breath and wiped away more tears as they fell.

"Margaret, please—"

"No!" Margaret bellowed holding up a hand to stop Celeste from talking. "I broke a man's heart today because you forced me to receive his attentions and encourage them." She covered her mouth with her hand to stop her lips from quivering. "Because *you* wanted me to." Tears of anger were streaming down her face. "I was forced to do to Doctor Digsby what the person I had loved did to me; reject him." She paused to take a shaky breath. "I know you make a game of breaking men's hearts, collecting proposals as you lure one after the other into your trap, but do you have any idea how that feels? Do you even have a heart to break?"

Celeste gave a small gasp at her friend's words. "That is a little harsh, do you not think?" she replied in a dejected whisper.

Margaret rubbed her forehead and closed her eyes, forcing a few more tears to fall. "Please, leave," she whispered. "I want to see you no more."

Celeste stared at her friend in disbelief, her heart sinking in her chest. "You cannot mean it," she said stepping toward her.

Margaret nodded. "I do," she replied. "I most certainly do. I have tolerated your behavior long enough; I will do so no longer. Get out."

The look in Margaret's eyes shattered Celeste's heart and she could feel the tears welling in her own eyes.

"Oh, Margaret, please do not do this," Celeste begged. "I am so sorry. I only wanted to help. I wanted to—"

"I never asked for your help," Margaret replied coldly. "No one asks for your help, Celeste. You just assume you have all of the answers when you are just as broken as the rest of us!"

Celeste's chest heaved, and she struggled to control the crushing wave of emotion threatening to crash down on her. She turned and ran from the room without another word, and without looking back.

She sobbed the entire way home.

27

October drifted into November almost unseen. The days grew bitterly cold, making the evenings even harsher as the autumnal days drew closer to winter. Celeste spent these days alone. Her father still in Russia; Charles seemingly more distant than ever; Amanda preparing her nuptials to Stephen; and Margaret refusing to answer any of her letters.

This, she thought, was how she was going to spend her last days of freedom before her father shipped her off to the asylum. Alone, dejected, and lost in self-pity. Nothing seemed to drag her out of her depression long enough for her to venture out of the house. She no longer enjoyed her long walks, and not even the most intriguing books held her interest long enough for her to care. Even invitations to tea or dinner were promptly refused.

Every day she seemed to relive Margaret's words over and over. She was just as broken. And Margaret was right. Celeste was broken and had been broken for a long time. She had such a bitter view on life, society, marriage, and even love, she barely ever took other people's feelings into consideration.

Her actions were often based on her own selfish wants and desires. Though she did not blame herself for Amanda's mistreatment of her, she did blame herself for the heartbreak she put Margaret and Doctor Digsby through. She wanted to make amends; she wanted to reach out. But, she knew not how.

She had lost one of her dearest friends to her own selfishness. That was her truth.

She wallowed in these thoughts for weeks until a surprise letter from Graham lifted the fog just enough.

It was a small consolation that her friend was doing so well in his studies. Celeste, missing the company of friends and the warmth of another body, decided to pay Graham a visit while he was at his uncle's for Christmas.

The thought brightened the next few days as she prepared for her trip though it did not necessarily fill the void. Wanting, however, to portray to Graham that she was her usual, cheerful self, she kept a smile planted on her face, and when she was shown into the parlor of his uncle's house later that evening, she planted a kiss on his lips as he had done to her countless times before.

Graham looked at her in surprise and confusion as if her mere presence was impossible.

"Celeste," he said, breathlessly, coloring a shade she had never seen him in before. "What are you doing here?"

"I thought I should surprise you for Christmas," she told him gleefully. "And now you, the one who is always giving others surprise visits, have received one."

"Yes, it is quite a surprise," he replied, his face still flushed.

Celeste frowned. "Is something the matter?" she asked cautiously. She looked about the room, but saw no one. "I have never known you to be so standoffish."

Graham avoided her gaze for a moment.

"You wish I had not come?" she asked, her heart sinking.

He shook his head. "No," he replied, giving her a small smile. "That is— I mean, I will always be glad to see you, but, perhaps, I should have told you before in one of my letters."

She blinked at him. "Told me what?"

Just then, the parlor doors opened again and a young, elegant woman was escorted in by a man Celeste knew to be Graham's Uncle William. The reaction, and change in Graham's face was immediate. A smile spread across his lips and his eyes sparkled in a way Celeste had never noticed before.

The young woman detached herself from his uncle and walked over to Graham, her face beaming.

"Ah, Miss Willoughby," Graham's uncle said as gregarious as ever. "I heard we had another visitor! I have not seen you in some years now. How are you?"

Celeste smiled and shifted her gaze a moment. "I am well, Mr. Steele," she replied. "I am glad to see you are still as handsome as ever."

The man laughed. "Ever charming, you are," he said.

Graham cleared his throat to gain the room's attention. "Miss Willoughby," he said, "will you allow me to introduce Fanny Barrett? My fiancé."

The news hit like a ton of bricks, and for several moments all Celeste could do was smile as she registered what Graham had told her. She was polite, of course, heartily congratulating the couple, swallowing her confusion.

"You blame me for not having told you," Graham whispered at dinner, as the other guests chatted loudly amongst each other.

Celeste sighed but smiled. “Of course, I do,” she replied. “I am not unhappy for you,” she quickly added, “but it certainly makes my situation that much more embarrassing knowing what I came here to do.”

He blushed, clearing his throat. “I apologize,” he replied solemnly.

She shook her head. “Why did you not tell me in all of your letters?” she asked him more in a confused tone than an accusing one.

He shrugged. “We have such a strange history, you and I,” he told her. “I just could not form into words what I wanted to say.”

“I do not know how,” Celeste scolded. “She seems like a very lovely person.”

Graham smiled and nodded as he looked across the table at his fiancé. “She has changed my world,” he said. “It was so sudden and unexpected I was not ready for it.”

Celeste gave a small smile. “When did you meet?”

“Almost as soon as I returned to school,” he replied with a small laugh. “She had been walking with one of my friends, her brother, on the school grounds and I knew right away I wanted to be with her.”

“Have the two of you—?”

He shook his head. “We have not,” he confessed with a sheepish smile. “She is the daughter of a vicar. I have not wanted to ruin my chances.”

Celeste arched a suspicious eyebrow at him. “My goodness,” she said trying not to laugh. “I almost do not recognize you.”

He gave a small chuckle.

There was a brief pause between them as they picked at their food, both of them slightly embarrassed and uncomfortable by the day's events.

"I almost said yes to you, you know," Celeste finally said after stomaching a few bites of food.

Graham looked at her.

"The day you asked me to run away with you?" She gave a small smile. "I almost took you up on it."

"What made you say no?"

Celeste looked at Fanny Barrett gently chatting with Graham's aunt. "I knew neither of us really loved each other," she finally replied. "Not the way you love her." She looked back over at him. "I can see it in your eyes. You have never looked at me that way, just as I have never looked at you like that either. Us running away would have been fun, at first, but once we grew tired of the adventure, there would have been nothing left."

"Is that the only reason you said no?" he asked, prodding. "It was not because of something else?"

Celeste looked away. "That was almost four months ago now," she replied. "Who knows what one was thinking then?"

He nodded. "Well, you did us both a favor that day."

"I certainly did *you* a favor," she retorted. "You are quite welcome, by the way."

He laughed. "I heartily thank you," he replied.

"Does Charles know?"

He looked at her and nodded. "I wrote to him as soon as she accepted me, hoping it would give him a push to do the same."

"Why?" Celeste asked hesitantly. "Does Charles have someone in mind for himself?"

Graham's eyes widened and he loudly coughed in confusion causing half of the table to look over at him. He waved a hand to let everyone know he was fine and grabbed for his glass of water.

"Excuse me," he said clearing his throat.

Celeste eyed him suspiciously. "Does he?" she asked again, searching his eyes for the answer.

Graham gave another little cough. "Honestly," he started shaking his head, "You and Charles are both extremely daft, you know that?"

She frowned and lifted a brow at him. "That does not answer my question."

He gave a small laugh. "No, and it is not my business to do so."

Celeste opened her mouth in protest when Mr. Steele asked her a question about how she had been doing since he saw her last, about three or four years ago. "Are you still single?" he asked.

"Yes, sir, I am."

"Smart woman you are!" he exclaimed raising a glass. "I was of the same mind as you! Marriage is such a hassle, though I am glad my nephew has found himself a gem in Miss Barrett."

The young woman blushed. "Thank you, sir," she said smiling and shooting Graham a look.

"I understand you are an accomplished painter, Miss Barrett," Celeste said.

Fanny turned her soft eyes to Celeste. "I believe Graham has been exaggerating my talents again, Miss Willoughby," she said modestly. "I do enjoy painting, but whether or not I am accomplished would depend solely on who the observer is."

Celeste smiled. "Well, I have known Graham long enough to know he is an honest man. Therefore, I trust his opinion and hope to observe your paintings myself."

"Do you paint as well?" Fanny asked.

Celeste shook her head. "Though I love art, I unfortunately can neither paint nor draw. It is a talent I have always envied others."

"But she plays the harp beautifully, if I remember correctly," Mr. Steele interjected. "And luckily, I have had the one in my music room tuned just for this occasion."

"Oh, no, Mr. Steele, I could not," Celeste protested gently.

"Oh, do play for us," Fanny said. "I believe we are similar in a sense. You envy my talent for painting and I envy yours of music."

Celeste smiled. "Then I shall play for you."

"Your uncle is right," Celeste said to Graham the next day as he escorted her to the train station. "You have found yourself a gem."

"You like her then?" he asked excitedly. "I hoped you would."

"There is nothing to dislike from what I saw, though our acquaintance has been of a short duration."

"As I said before, she has changed my life."

"For the better," Celeste added. "I can see it. You seem more grounded, stable. It suits you, Graham."

He gave a small nod. "I wish you would find the same," he finally said after a few moments. "You know I think the world of you, Celeste, and I always will, so I want you to be happy. I want you to have what I have."

Celeste gave a small laugh and patted his hand. "Dear Graham," she said with a sigh, "in some ways it is already too late for me."

He shook his head. "How can you mean?" he asked. "You have more life and energy than girls ten years your junior."

She smiled softly. "Yes, these young girls these days are rather boring, are they not?"

They rode the rest of the way to the station in silence, the clacking of the horses' hooves and the grinding of the wheels filled the carriage as the rest of the world whirred by them. Celeste leaned her head back against the wall and watched it all. Everything blurring in the distance, fleeting moments lost in the greater scheme of things.

When the carriage finally lurched to a stop, Celeste felt tired and beaten. Graham helped her out of the carriage and walked her to the platform where they embraced.

"I did not answer your question last night at dinner," he said as he took a step back to face her.

She creased her brow. "Which one?"

"Whether or not Charles has a woman in mind," he replied.

Celeste felt her heart skip a beat and her breath catch in her throat.

"The truth is," Graham started slowly, "he has."

Celeste shifted her gaze as her skin prickled, and her stomach dropped, a strange uncomfortable feeling. "Is it anyone I might know?" she asked trying to keep her voice level.

"Yes," Graham said with a nod. "And I believe there can be no one else on earth for him."

"And you believe she loves him in return?"

He gave a small chuckle. "Do you not believe him capable of capturing a woman's heart?"

She gave a weak smile and shot him a small glance. "No, you are right. Of course she loves him."

He took Celeste's hand. "But the problem is, he is too scared to propose with his fortune in the situation that it is, he hesitates." He squeezed her hand. "Promise me you will go to him and persuade him to propose to her."

She looked up at him. "I should not," she replied. "I do not want to meddle in someone else's affair. It has cost me too much already."

"Do you not believe he deserves to be happy?"

She gave a nod after a moment. "I do," she said quietly. "And I will. I will convince him that if a woman truly loved him, his financial situation should make no difference."

Graham smiled and gave her hand a kiss. "I knew I could count on you, Celeste," he told her. "I shall see you at my wedding in the spring?"

"Only if you promise me a dance," she replied, trying to smile.

"Then I shall see you there." He gave her a deep bow and one, last lingering look and left.

She boarded the train alone, with a heavy heart and a lump in her throat.

When Celeste returned home later that evening, her father was waiting for her. The duchess was still in Russia sorting through her brother's affairs, but he had returned the same day Celeste had arrived at Graham's uncle's house. She met him in the parlor where he was nursing a whiskey and standing in front of the mantle.

He turned to her, a concerned look on his face.

"Where have you been?" he asked evenly and without anger.

Celeste, overcome with emotion and pain, ran to him, and burying her face in his chest, sobbed.

Confused, yet moved, her father wrapped his arms around her and let her.

28

eleste went to Charles the next day, with only four days left until New Year's Day. She knocked and smoothed out her dress as she waited for him to answer, but no one was there. She felt disheartened as she knocked again in vain. After waiting for what seemed like forever, she left, feeling more dejected than when she arrived.

When she returned back home, she went for a walk around the grounds. It was cold and the air smelled like snow, but it was calm. She pulled her shawl around her and continued down the garden path, her mind blank, buzzing with emotion and emptiness all at once.

When she finally came to the tree surrounded by hedges, she was surprised to see the space was already occupied.

"Charles!" she exclaimed in surprise.

He whirled around, caught off guard.

"What are you doing here?" she asked.

"I came looking for you," he replied. "But they said you were not home."

She gave a small laugh. "I was not, I was out looking for you."

He laughed too.

They stood looking at each other for a few moments without speaking.

Celeste cleared her throat. "I went to see Graham the other day," she told him stepping into the small opening.

"Did you?" He shifted uncomfortably.

"I was surprised to find out he was engaged."

Charles nodded. "Yes, he proposed a week ago I believe."

"She is a lovely woman."

"Yes," he agreed. "I have not met her, but he seems very taken by her in his letters."

"I guess I should be congratulating you soon as well."

He blinked at her. "How so?"

"Graham told me you have your own plans to propose soon," she continued.

"He did?" he asked, his brow furrowed.

She nodded. "He told me you hesitate to do so because you are worried your lack of fortune will come between you."

Charles took a deep breath and let it out slowly. "And what did you say to that?" he asked.

"I believe if you love this woman and she loves you in return, it should not matter what state your fortune is in."

He smiled. "*You* believe that?"

She nodded. "I do," she replied. "I also believe you deserve to be happy, Charles, and that this woman would be a fool not to accept you."

He took a few steps closer to her. "Did he tell you who this woman is I have such apprehensions about proposing to?" he asked still smiling.

She shook her head.

Charles pressed his lips together to keep his smile from taking over. "And you do not have a clue?"

"I do not."

"Oh, Celeste," he said a little laughingly. "You, who has had more than one man throw themselves at your feet professing their love, has not a clue as to the woman I have been tormented by for years?"

Celeste looked up at him, her mouth slightly open and her brows creased in confusion. "Years?"

Charles nodded. "I had been in denial about it, but I know that my love for her has not been a sudden attack of heated passion. It was a gradual, healthy love, built on years of trust, laughter, tears, and friendship."

Celeste pressed a hand to her stomach to quell the sinking feeling she was getting. "It is Margaret," she finally said. "You are in love with Margaret."

Charles gave a small laugh. "What?"

"It all makes sense," Celeste continued. "You have been terse with me for months, before you found your fortune was in ruins, because I put John Howard in her way, because I tried putting other men in her way, but never you." She pressed a hand to her cheek. "Oh, Charles, I am so sorry! I had no idea." Tears welled in her eyes and she turned her head to wipe them away.

Charles gently took hold of her hands. "And you still do not, Celeste," he said looking down at her. He smoothed back a loose lock of her hair. "It is not Margaret whom I love," he whispered shaking his head. "It is you."

Celeste gaped at him, taking a few steps back. "What?"

"I love *you*," he told her breathlessly. "And I cannot bear the thought of living without you. It is *you* I want to marry."

Celeste gave a small laugh in disbelief. "You want to

marry me?" she repeated, shaking her head. "Now I know you cannot be serious. Did you and Graham come up with this together?"

Charles paled. "You do not believe me?"

"No, this is surely one of your jokes and I will not be roped in to give an answer and be made a fool of."

Charles took a ragged breath and shook his head. "Celeste, I have never been more serious in my life. I love you."

"Stop it."

"And I want to marry you."

"I said 'stop.'" Celeste took a shaky breath of her own.

"Then you are resolved not to have me?"

Celeste shifted uncomfortably before she looked at him. "I just do not understand. Are you not— did we not promise not to fall in love? Did you not promise me we would not?"

Charles gave a weak smile and shifted his gaze to the ground. "Can a person not change their mind?" He looked at her, his eyes shimmering with emotion, a look Celeste had seen directed toward her hundreds of times but only now understood. "Were we not still children when we promised each other something so silly?"

Celeste blushed harder than she ever remembered doing so before. "Charles—"

"Please, let me finish," he begged stepping forward and taking her hand again, giving it a light squeeze. "I know this must seem sudden, and for you it might be, but I have been trying to repress these feelings for longer than I can remember because I had been convinced you would not welcome them. But I no longer can pretend what I feel does not exist."

You were my first friend; we were forced upon each

other by our mothers from infancy, and have willingly been in each other's company ever since. We have gotten ourselves into countless mischievous situations and have covered for one another when we were in trouble. We were a team long before we were lovers. You have cried in my arms long before I *held* you in them."

He took a shaky breath. "I want to live and relive all of those moments with you for the rest of my life. I have lived with the torment of losing you, of the possibility of no longer being able to hold you for over a year now and I hope to do so no longer."

Celeste's bottom lip quivered.

"I know the reservations you have about marriage," he explained, "but I am *not* your father. Marry me, please, and I will be yours and yours alone."

Celeste opened her mouth to respond, but instead rubbed her lips together, gathering herself. "And it *is* me you want?"

He looked at her earnestly. "You seriously undervalue yourself so much?"

"With everything you know about me, the societal rules I refuse to conform to, my propensity to meddle in everyone's affairs, my love of fine cigars, all of the—" she paused and looked at him, "all of the men I have been with. Knowing all of this, you still want me for your wife?"

"You forgot to mention your stubbornness, your tendency to show off, your terrible taste for port, and the fact that you snore in your sleep after a night of heavy drinking."

Celeste frowned.

Charles laughed and cupped her face in his hands. "Yes," he said. "Knowing all of that, I still want to marry you."

Celeste felt a shiver run through her body. "You do not want some younger, virginal, pretty little thing?"

He shook his head. "I do not want someone I have to teach," he replied. "I want someone who can teach me."

Celeste finally gave a small laugh. "You are determined then?"

Charles nodded as he bent down to kiss her. Celeste did not resist as she leaned into him, the heat rising in her cheeks and throughout her body. It was the same sensation she would get when they were together, the reason she had stopped their 'nightly visits.' She had been afraid of doing exactly what she had promised she would not do; fall for him.

But, now, her apprehensions seemed silly. Now, she knew she had been wrong to keep him at arms' length.

"Your father, of course, will hate this match," he told her when they pulled away.

She laughed. "I do love defying him," she replied. "But I have not given you an answer."

"I know," he replied. "And you do not need to do so today if you would rather not."

She squirmed a little. "I would not."

He nodded. "Shall I give you until New Year's Eve then?"

She smiled weakly. "My father's deadline for sending me away?" she replied. "Seems like a reasonable amount of time to make such an important decision."

Charles repressed a smile. "I will call on you in four days then." He bowed, gave her hand a kiss, and left.

Celeste watched him disappear behind the hedges before walking unsteadily to the bench that encircled the tree and sat down heavily. She gave a small laugh as she processed what had just happened, a single tear rolling down her cheek.

Not long after Charles had left, snow began to fall slowly and gently. Celeste watched it from under the tree for a few minutes until the frozen air began to seep into her boots. She stood and made her way back to the house, but instead of going in, she ordered the carriage be brought back around.

This was an important decision and it had to be discussed with someone whose opinion she highly regarded.

29

eleste was shown into the modest parlor where Mrs. Hepworth and Mrs. Haderly were discussing the latter's daughter's and son's upcoming nuptials.

They stood and smiled politely when she entered.

"Celeste!" Mrs. Hepworth said, a bright smile on her face. "I have not seen you in ages."

"How was your tour of Ireland?" Celeste asked.

"It was refreshingly beautiful," she replied.

"I am glad to hear it," Celeste said. "Mrs. Haderly, I congratulate you on having two children married soon."

Mrs. Haderly regarded her suspiciously, Amanda having told her about their argument no doubt, but she nodded and thanked her.

"Is Margaret in?" Celeste asked hesitantly.

Mrs. Hepworth nodded. "Yes, she is in her room. She complained of a slight headache."

"Oh," Celeste replied, disappointed.

"She is awake though," Mrs. Hepworth reassured her. "She just sent for tea not five minutes before you arrived."

Celeste thanked her and then made her way up the stairway to her friend's room. She hesitated a moment before knocking, hoping her friend would not throw her out on sight.

"Come in," came the distant voice of Margaret.

Celeste took a deep breath, slowly opening the door. "Good afternoon, Margaret," she said in a quiet voice.

Margaret, who had been staring out her bedroom window, watching as the snow fell, slowly turned. "Celeste," she said in soft surprise, "what are you doing here?" It was not meant nor was it taken offensively.

"I know you ordered me to never come back," she started, "but you also know I have never been one for following orders."

Margaret gave her a soft smile before holding out her hand to her.

Celeste smiled and embraced her friend. "I am so sorry for the pain I caused you and Doctor Digsby," she whispered, sniffing back her tears. "You were right. I never should have interfered."

Margaret shook her head. "You are not the only person who is to blame," she replied. "I allowed, perhaps even encouraged, his attentions. I knew what they could have led to, but still, I did not stop them." She took a step back. "I wanted to love Donald," she explained. "You had been right. He was— well, is, a kind and generous man. He is everything I could ever hope for in a partner, so I wanted my regard for him to grow into something more, but the truth that is now apparent to me is that if I am unable to love a man as handsome and kind as Donald, then I shall never come to love *any* man."

Celeste took her friend's hand. "Oh, my dear Margaret," she said pressing her friend's hand to her chest. "Do not say such things. For if there is hope for me, certainly there can be hope for you as well."

"How do you mean?" Margaret asked, arching a brow.

Celeste bit her lip and smiled sheepishly at her friend. "Perhaps you will laugh at me," she told her, "or completely disbelieve what I am about to tell you, but I am most likely about to accept a proposal of marriage."

Margaret's eyes grew wide. "Seriously?" she asked in surprise. "Did Charles finally ask you?"

Celeste frowned and dropped her friend's hand. "How did you know it was Charles?"

Margaret gave a small laugh. "Any fool could see the both of you love each other," she replied matter-of-factly.

"So, you knew this whole time and never said anything to me?" Celeste asked incredulously.

"It was never my business to say anything," she replied gently. "Not everyone likes to get involved in other peoples' affairs."

Celeste smiled and lowered her eyes. "Right," she said.

"Besides," Margaret continued, "I know you well enough to know you needed to come to the realization that you love Charles on your own. If I had brought it up, you, perhaps, would have fought it harder."

"Perhaps you know me too well," Celeste replied.

"But you said you will most likely accept him," Margaret backtracked. "Does that mean there is a possibility you will not?"

Celeste blushed. "Either option has its own terrifying consequences, do they not?"

"Oh, Celeste," Margaret sighed. "Everything in life has consequences. Every breath we do or do not take, every minute we hesitate, every time you fail to say what you truly feel." She paused to look back out at the falling snow. "Life is full of positive and negative consequences for every action we do or do not make. But it is not about avoiding those consequences, it is about overcoming them." She looked back at Celeste. "Can you risk saying no to the man *you* love because you are scared of the consequences that may or may not happen?"

Celeste moved to the window beside her and looked out. "You have become rather philosophical, Margaret," she said. "But you are right, again."

"So, you will do it?" Margaret asked. "You will marry Charles?"

Celeste faced her friend, a wide grin on her lips. "I shall marry Charles."

They embraced again.

"I am so glad for the both of you," Margaret said letting go and giving a clap of joy. "My dearest friends are finally getting married!"

"Yes, now if we can just find you someone who could make you as equally happy, my life would be complete," Celeste replied.

Margaret's smile faded. "That would be rather pointless," she told her. "As I was saying before, if I could not love Donald, there is not a man in the entire world I am convinced I will ever love."

"Oh, Margaret, I can hardly believe you believe that. You are the romantic one out of the both of us. You are the one that should be getting married and I am the one that should be continuing her refusals."

Margaret shook her head. "My romantic inclinations are just—" she paused thinking about what she was trying to say, "they are just not what most would perceive them to be."

Celeste regarded her friend for a moment. "Why are you always being so cryptic, Margaret?" she asked. "There is no occasion for it."

"I just do not want another situation like what happened with Donald," Margaret explained. "I miss his friendship dearly and would hate to have to hurt someone else in the same way."

"Still I am sure you will find someone. You cannot help who you do or do not love."

"That is what I am trying to tell you, Celeste."

"You are not *trying* to tell me anything, Margaret," Celeste scolded playfully. "You hint on an issue without fully telling me what it is. Your romantic notions aside, why do you feel as if you will never find a man whom you can love?"

Margaret opened her mouth a moment, but closed it, rethinking what she was going to say.

"Come now," Celeste goaded. "It cannot be so horrible. Is it because you are scared to lie with a man?" she asked. "The first time is rather terrifying and rather painful, but after the third or fourth time, it becomes a lot more enjoyable. And if you get a partner who is patient and is selfless enough to take care of your needs, it will even be pleasurable."

"That is not— well, I guess in a way it is it, but that is not really what I am trying to say," Margaret said hesitantly.

Celeste sighed. "Then what are you trying to say? I cannot help if you do not tell me!"

"I do not like men!" Margaret finally exclaimed.

Celeste blinked at her and even gave a small laugh. "Well, no one really *likes* men, Margaret," she reassured her. "They can be such an annoyance."

Margaret shook her head. "No, Celeste," she said softly. "I *like* women."

Celeste shook her head, still not understanding what

her friend was trying to tell her. “Of course, you do,” she replied slowly. “I myself am a woman and I enjoy the company of other women. Mostly just you and myself, of course, since that cannot be avoided.” She gave her friend a playful smile.

Margaret pressed a hand to her forehead. “No, Celeste,” she said giving an exasperated sigh. “What I am trying to say is I want to be with a woman the way you describe being with a man.”

Celeste’s smile faded as her friend’s words finally sank in. She opened her mouth to speak, but closed it again, her brows furrowed in contemplation. For a moment, she looked horrified as she weighed what Margaret had said.

Margaret felt her heartbeat quicken and her stomach drop as she waited for her friend to say something. She struggled to keep her composure as she watched her friend, whom she had never seen so stumped for words, take in the truth. It seemed like hours went by as Margaret stood there watching Celeste open her mouth to speak just to close it again without uttering a word. Like a fish, over and over.

It was gut wrenching waiting for her friend’s judgment. Margaret looked out the window, unseeing as she waited.

Finally, Celeste stopped pacing. “You know, Charles had told me that while he was in Paris, he met a pair of women who were lovers.”

Margaret turned back slowly to face her friend.

Celeste gave a small shrug. “Seemed strange, at the time,” she continued softly. “Perhaps, a little unnatural, in my opinion,”

Margaret shifted her gaze to the floor.

“But who am I to judge on love and intimate relations?”

Celeste continued. “Some would say lying with a man whom you are not wed to is not natural, though I never thought so.”

Margaret looked back up to see Celeste smiling softly at her.

“It was not John you had been pining over, was it?” Celeste asked her.

Margaret blushed. “No,” she almost whispered.

“It was Irene.”

Margaret nodded.

Celeste sighed. “I apologize for verbally abusing her so much in front of you.”

Margaret gave a small smile. “You did not know. You could not have known,” she replied. “But if it is all the same, you did abuse John Howard just as much and you thought he was the one I loved.”

“Yes, well, I still stand by the fact he was extremely boring,” Celeste told her. “Irene, I almost understand. She was the interesting one.”

There was a brief silence between them.

Margaret twisted her hands nervously. “You will not tell anyone, will you?”

Celeste gave an offended sigh and pressed a hand to her chest. “Do you truly think so little of me?” she asked. “Name one secret of yours I have ever told anyone.”

Margaret’s lip quivered. “Then we are still friends?” she asked, her eyes brimming with tears. “You are not disgusted by me?”

Celeste wrapped Margaret in a hug. “We are still friends and I am not disgusted by you, though I may not understand you.”

Margaret let out a sob of relief.

“You have never given me cause to think you are

anything but a kind and gentle person, Margaret," Celeste told her, patting her back gently. "Perhaps, this new information about you might take some time getting used to, but in the past, you have never given me any cause for alarm. Your attentions had never been directed at me, I do not think. Or, I have never noticed. Indeed, I am not sure how I would have reacted. Perhaps, I—" Celeste stopped, realizing she was babbling and not really making any sense.

Margaret pulled away. "Do you believe I would press myself upon you just because you are a woman?"

Celeste thought for a moment. "I suppose not," she replied. "I am attracted to men, but that does not mean I am attracted to *all* men. I would imagine that is how it would work with you."

Margaret nodded.

Celeste frowned. "Well, now that just bruises my vanity, saying I am not attractive enough for you." Celeste shot her a grin.

Margaret laughed. "I think you are beautiful as a woman," she explained. "But you do not stir romantic feelings inside me."

"Very well," Celeste replied with a small nod. "I will accept that."

There was another pause.

"Did Irene feel for you as well?" Celeste asked curiously. "Was she like you?"

Margaret nodded. "At least she said she loved me," she replied.

"Then why would she leave and marry John?"

Margaret cleared her throat and blinked back the tears forming in her eyes. "She knew we could not be together, not with society being how it is."

Celeste gave a wave of the hand. "Oh, hang society!" she said. "What joy has it ever brought anyone? Always judging and accusing what it does not care to know."

"Easier said than done," Margaret said softly. "Had our relationship gotten out, we would have been sent to an institution."

Celeste gave a small laugh. "Maybe we could have been cellmates."

Margaret gave her a confused look. "What?"

"Never mind," she replied brushing it off. "I am curious now though. You did tell me before you never even kissed John, now I believe it, but did you and Irene kiss?"

Margaret blushed a deep crimson.

Celeste's lips curled into a smile. "I believe that is my answer." She frowned after a moment. "There is something I do not understand, however."

"What is that?"

"How you always blushed whenever Doctor Digsby came around or his name was mentioned," Celeste said. "If you did not like him, why were you always blushing?"

"Honestly, you must know by now I am easily embarrassed," Margaret simply replied. "Every time he came around, I knew what you must be thinking, that you wanted us to be together. Every time he looked at me, I knew what *he* must be thinking, that he wanted us to be together. Why should I not blush if the very thought of what everyone must be thinking caused me anxiety?"

"Hm," Celeste said with a nod. "I suppose that makes sense." She sighed. "You are easily tormented. Poor man never had a chance."

Margaret nodded solemnly. "Yes," she replied with a heavy sigh.

"What is it?" Celeste asked her.

"I am truly tormented."

"How do you mean?"

Margaret gave a weak smile. "I know how I feel is a sin. That I do not deserve God's grace but if I were to marry Donald, then I would be pretending to be who I am not, lying every day, and that would also be a sin." She shook her head. "I could not please God no matter what I do because I believe I will always have these feelings." Her lips trembled as tears fell down her face. "I am damned no matter what."

Celeste pulled her friend in for a hug. "Margaret, that speech is rubbish," she stated with conviction. "I have never met with a more devout believer. Even the vicars and priests I have met fall short in their holiness when compared to you." She stepped back and looked her friend in the face. "You have told me several times how forgiving of a god our God is. Why should he look blindly on your requests for forgiveness when those who are only Christians one day a week are given a free pass?"

Margaret wiped away the tears staining her cheeks.

Celeste shook her head. "You are just as worthy, Margaret, and if it was just based on my opinion, you are more worthy."

Margaret cleared her throat. "Thank you, Celeste," she replied gratefully. "I could always count on you to make me feel better about myself."

"You, my dear Margaret," Celeste started, "are all that is good in this world. Do not let anyone else tell you otherwise."

There was a brief pause as Margaret dabbed at her eyes with her handkerchief.

Celeste smiled. "You know, it just occurred to me," she said, breaking the silence, "why you want to become a nun."

Margaret blinked at her. "Why do you say that?"

"You like women and would therefore be surrounded by nothing but women." Celeste shook her head. "Margaret, well, if you are not just some ordinary pervert!" she exclaimed laughing. "And to think I thought so highly of you!"

"Shhhh!" Margaret pleaded trying to calm Celeste down. "Not so loud!"

"I am in utter shock," Celeste continued, fanning herself, bursting into laughter again. "Oh, dear Lord, Margaret."

"That is not why I wanted to join a convent, for your information," Margaret protested. "I truly want to live out my life in His service."

"Yes, but is not the idea of becoming a nun or monk or religious figure to remove yourself from the temptations of life? Not dangle them in front of you?" Celeste chuckled again, covering her mouth with her hand to try and suppress it.

Margaret did not reply, but her face showed concern.

"I am only teasing you, Margaret, as I usually do," Celeste said after a moment, finally regaining composure. "Do you still plan on joining?"

Margaret hesitated. "I do not know," she replied, frowning. "Perhaps you are right and it would only invoke improper feelings."

"You are only human, Margaret," Celeste reminded her. "You are going to have improper feelings regardless. We all do."

Margaret gave her friend a soft smile. "However true that might be, I think I will no longer cosign myself to that lifestyle."

Celeste sighed. "I cannot say I am not glad to hear it, but what will you do then?"

Margaret smiled as a slight, subtle blush colored her cheeks. "Maybe I will go to Paris," she replied coyly.

Celeste laughed. "You cheeky little thing," she teased before frowning slightly. "There is something I do not comprehend, though."

"Hm?"

"If Irene loved you, and had the same romantic notions as you, why did she run off with John Howard specifically? I understand not letting her love for you be known, but how could she marry him? She is beautiful and funny and witty, while he is," she paused, "not."

Margaret gave a half smile. "She wanted children."

"Oh, I suppose that would pose as an issue, would it not?" Celeste said. "But again, she could have had any other man. A smarter man." She gave a pensive look. "Perhaps, that was part of the appeal. If she dallied outside of the marriage, he might not be smart enough to realize. Poor John, but bravo Irene. I hope their children take after her, for their sakes."

Margaret gave her a half-hearted reproachful look.

"Do you not want children?" Celeste asked ignoring the light glare from her friend.

"To be honest," Margaret hesitated, "I do, but not at the risk of losing who I am."

"You mean marrying and living a lie?"

Margaret nodded. "It would not be fair to me, my husband, or the children if I am constantly miserable."

Celeste sighed. "Pity. You would make a wonderful mother."

"I suppose I could always adopt."

Celeste nodded. "There are plenty of children out

there in need of a loving home here or in Paris."

Margaret smiled. "I have been very fortunate to have you as a friend," she told her.

Celeste smiled back. "And I you," she replied. "I was miserable all of those weeks without you."

"I know. So was I."

"Let us never fight ever again," Celeste said taking Margaret's hand.

"I will promise to do so as long as you promise to no longer throw men in my direction," Margaret replied grinning.

"Well, now that I know all of my attempts have been futile, I shall. I promise I will no longer force men upon you."

They gave each other another heartfelt hug.

"I should go," Celeste said breaking away.

"But it is still snowing," Margaret replied, concern in her voice. "You should stay until it has passed."

"I live only a mile away," Celeste told her. "Not to mention, I have not informed my father about my impending engagement to Charles."

Margaret gasped. "Oh, I forgot! They do not like each other."

Celeste shook her head.

"You are not marrying Charles to defy your father, are you?" Margaret asked skeptically.

Celeste laughed. "Did you not say yourself you knew I had loved him?"

"I believe you do," Margaret replied hesitantly. "But I have not heard you say it."

Celeste smiled at her friend. "That is because I have not done so yet. I have felt it in my heart, but I have never spoken the words aloud."

"Then save them!" Margaret replied holding up her hand to stop her. "Let the first time you say it be to Charles himself."

Celeste pressed her lips together to hide a smile. "You are truly the romantic." She turned to leave. "I expect both you and your parents for dinner for New Year's Eve. And," she shot her friend a glance, "I expect to hear more details about you and Irene."

Margaret flushed, as usual, crimson.

"I know you have more to tell," Celeste said, giving her friend a wink as she slipped out the door.

30

The snow, though making the ride a little slower, made it more beautiful. The absence of the wind gave the air a clean, crisp feel and Celeste could not help but open her window as she went along.

Her heart felt light as she thought about the events of the day. She had successfully secured the man she loved, something she had never deemed possible, though she never tried, and she patched up her relationship with Margaret. She still did not understand how Margaret could prefer the physical company of women over men, but it was, as she had told her, not her place to judge her for her sexual inclinations.

Margaret was still Margaret in her mind.

She also laughed at herself when she thought back to the cryptic way Graham had spoken to her about Charles and the woman he wanted to marry. She would have to write him a teasing letter after she broke the news to her father.

When the carriage finally pulled up to the house, she hesitated. The driver, frozen as he probably was, opened the door and held his hand out for her. Had she not noticed him shaking, she probably would not have gotten out right away.

"Oh, lord, Jeremy, I am so sorry," she said finally exiting. "You poor creature. Here I am lost in thought while you stand out here freezing to death."

"Tisn't so bad, ma'am," the driver replied trying to keep his teeth from chattering.

"You do not have to lie to make me feel better, Jeremy," Celeste told him. "Hurry and put the carriage away and then go straight to the kitchen to get warm. Tell Samantha I said to give you a pot of green tea."

Jeremy's eyes lit up. "Never had none of that before. Thank ya, ma'am."

"Thank you, Jeremy."

Celeste approached the door and shivered. She reached out to open it when Gerald beat her to it.

"Miss, your father has been looking for you," he said in a whisper. "He thought something might've gone wrong, you having been gone all day without a word."

"He has always been overdramatic, has he not?" she replied, handing him her coat and gloves.

Gerald opened his mouth to say something, but shut it, instead, giving her a look.

"Yes, well, so have I, but he is where I get it from," she told him archly. "Where is he?"

"In his study."

"Thank you, Gerald," she said. "Oh, and make sure Samantha gives Jeremy some green tea. I know she is stingy with it."

He bowed. "Yes, ma'am."

Celeste made her way up the stairs to her father's study. Her heart simultaneously beating with joy and trepidation as she knocked on the door.

"Come in," came a haggard, almost unrecognizable

voice.

Celeste opened the door and took a few steps in, the warmth of the fire reminding her she had been cold, and she shivered. "You were looking for me, father?" she said hesitantly.

He looked up from something he had been reading. "Celeste," he replied, a hint of surprise in his voice. "You are here."

Celeste blinked and looked about the room, confused. "Did you suppose I would be somewhere else?"

"I thought you— well, the other day when you—" He shook his head. "Were you not out?"

"Yes, I was, but you seem so surprised I returned."

He nodded. "Sometimes I am with how horribly I treat you."

Celeste looked at her father, her mouth partially opened. After a moment, she shook off her surprise at her father's confession and cleared her throat. "I believe we are both to blame for each other's mistreatment," she told him.

He shook his head. "No," he replied softly. "Had I been a better father, a better husband, you would not have turned so against me."

Celeste pulled at her dress sleeves and rubbed her arm, unsure with where this uncomfortable conversation was headed. "There is not much we can do about it now," she said trying her best not to fidget.

Her father nodded, lifting his glass and draining it. "I suppose the past is just that. The past."

Celeste creased her brows. Her father was drunk.

Mr. Willoughby picked up a decanter and tried pouring himself another glass, droplets of liquid splashing onto his desk.

Celeste could only remember seeing her father drunk two other times in her life. One after *his* mother passed away, and the other when *her* mother passed away. She watched as he took another gulp from his glass.

"Is everything alright, father?" she asked cautiously, taking a few steps toward the desk.

He nodded, heavily. "I am just trying to mend my broken heart," he told her.

"Oh," Celeste said quietly, rocking on her toes. "How so?"

He held up a letter. "This," he said. "Do you know what this is?"

"I do not know how I possibly could."

"This is a telegram from the duchess," he informed her. "She has told me, having missed her homeland all these years and having no children with her late husband to tie her to her duchy, she wishes to remain in Russia, indefinitely."

Celeste raised her brows. "But, did she not just buy a house here?"

Her father shook her head. "No, I bought Mr. Pratt's house," he replied, pointing to himself. "It was a gift for her."

Celeste's eyes grew wide. "You bought her a house?" she asked trying to keep her voice level.

Her father opened his mouth to reply but she stopped him.

"Please, allow me a moment to see if I understand you," she started holding up a hand "For my birthday, earlier this year, I asked for a new horse, a younger horse as my poor Winnie is getting too old, and you said no because horses are expensive. So, instead, all you bought me were some new ribbons." She closed her eyes for a moment to gather herself. "And now, come to find out, you bought an entire house, a manor, for some woman who up and leaves three months later." She looked at her father. "Is that right? Have I understood you correctly?"

Her father looked pensive for a moment. "Yes. Yes, that is about right."

"You are unbelievable!" she vociferated, throwing her hands up in the air. "An entire house! With twelve bedrooms, an entire library, three different parlors, a large garden with fountains, a massive ballroom and stables large enough to fit half of the horses in the country!" She took a deep calming breath. "And, all I got were ribbons."

"Does it truly seem that terrible?" her father asked meekly.

"Father, what on earth could possess you to do such a thing?"

He held his hands up and shrugged. "Love," he replied simply.

Celeste sighed and shook her head. "Well, then, I guess your decision was justified. For love is the only reason you need to do anything so foolish!" she proclaimed.

Her father didn't reply.

Celeste shrugged, trying to relieve herself of her annoyance when a thought hit her. "So, what are you to do now? Will this impulse buy break us?"

He shook his head. "Financially, we are fine," he reassured her, waving his hand. "Our ships have done well this year and the railroad investments are bringing in a handsome sum."

A small, triumphant smile curled Celeste's lips and she bit them to keep it under control. "Are you to sell it?" she asked.

He shrugged. "I am not level-headed enough to know

what to do at the moment," he told her honestly, slumping over his desk and taking another long sip from his glass.

After a moment, she laughed. "Might I suggest a solution?"

"Yes, yes, please, say as you wish." He waved his hand lazily.

"Perhaps, you could gift it to me."

Her father's head shot up. "Gift it to you?" he repeated. "What for?"

"As a wedding present."

Her father stared at her, unblinking for several moments before her words sank in. The anguish he had felt a few moments earlier melted away as he stood, his arms spread wide. "My dear girl!" he exclaimed moving to embrace her. "Is it true? You are finally engaged?"

Celeste gave a small "oof!" as her father wrapped her tightly in a hug. "Yes," she said, her voice restrained by his grip.

"You do not know what joy, what happiness this news brings me!" her father exclaimed, pulling away.

Celeste was surprised by the tears falling down her father's face. "Well, to be honest, I have not technically accepted him yet."

Her father frowned. "No?" he replied sounding disappointed. "But you have not refused him?"

"I have not refused him."

"And you will say yes?"

She laughed. "And I will say yes."

"Oh, what joy!" He kissed his daughter's forehead. "But who is this man and why has he not spoken with me first? Should he not have asked me for your hand before he asked you? Is this man a gentleman? Does he come from a good family, have a good name? Tell me, child!"

"Yes, to all of those questions."

"Well, then, who is he?"

Celeste held her head up high. "Charles."

Her father blinked at her. "Charles," he repeated, his eye twitching. "*That* Charles?"

Celeste smiled. "Yes, father, *that* Charles," she told him. "He loves me and he proposed and, seeing as we have been great friends since we were children and have gotten along so well ever since, and there is the fact he defl— well, never mind that— I have never been happier and we will wed."

Her father swallowed and smacked his lips, his mouth dry from all of the brandy. "And how will he take care of you? He has lost all of his money. Are you sure he did not just propose to you for yours?"

Celeste paled and then colored with anger. "Oh, like that Earl who was prone to gambling? You did not seem to take issue with it when he proposed."

"No, but his name came with a title," her father pointed out.

"Well, I do not care," Celeste replied. "You gave me until New Year's Day to become engaged and I have done so. You did not specify as to whom I could not get engaged to."

"New Year's Day?" her father whispered. "Oh, dear Lord, I forgot." Her father began to laugh. He threw his head back and roared with laughter, spit flying from his mouth and his face red with exertion.

"What on earth could you find so funny?" she grumbled.

"You still think I am going to have you sent away?" her father asked her, gasping for air.

Celeste frowned. "Well, not now I am engaged."

Her father laughed a little more. "Oh, dear child," Mr. Willoughby started.

"Is that not what you meant about treating me poorly?" she asked. "You always threatening to have me sent away?"

Her father wiped a tear from his eye. "Partially," he replied. "But I would never have gone through with it."

"You sent the warden of an asylum to meet with me."

Her father chuckled, trying to keep himself under control. "I sent a paid actor to portray the warden of an asylum."

Celeste narrowed her eyes at her father. "I shot at that man."

Her father nodded.

"That man was inappropriate toward me."

"That," her father replied, pointing, "was not in my deal with him. I am glad you chased him off in the way you did."

She stared at him. "Why? What would possess you to do such a thing? To trick me in such a way?"

Her father sighed, taking her hand. "My dear," he said in a somber tone, "I did not know how else to get you to take the issue of marriage seriously. I want you well settled."

"You do not want to just get rid of me?"

"Of course not."

"Then why were you trying to marry me off to the count who lived thousands of miles away?"

Her father shrugged. "That was more of his sister's doing. She thought it was time for him to marry and he expressed interest in you. I thought if I approved as well then the duchess would—"

Celeste groaned. "Do not finish that thought."

"Besides, you seemed to like him. You were always flirting and smiling at him."

"I was doing it to get a rise out of you," she replied.

"It seems that is the reason we do what we do to each other," her father said with a sigh. "I am sorry for it, for my part and for yours. It has been my doing from the start."

Celeste felt a tug on her heart as her father continued to apologize for his past behavior toward her.

"I truly loved your mother, Celeste," her father started. "More than I have ever loved anyone. And my behavior as a husband was—"

"Unforgivable," Celeste finished.

Her father nodded, looking ashamed. "Yes, I hurt her in more ways than one," he confessed with a sigh. "I could never excuse my actions but as a man, there are certain appetites that—"

"Father, we are not going to have this conversation," Celeste said, halting whatever thought her father might have had.

He gave another nod. "I just want to tell you, I am sorry. For everything, but especially what I had done to your mother. I know it pained you greatly."

Celeste hesitantly reached out and took her father's hand in hers, giving it a gentle squeeze and causing him to give a small smile.

"We were close once, you and I," he continued, "but I ruined that by damaging the trust and faith you had in me as a father and a husband." He nodded. "I see that my past actions have formed a negative opinion of me in your eyes, and of marriage. I understand that now. Though I know it will take time, I hope you can forgive me."

Celeste wiped a tear she didn't know had fallen. "Only

if you can forgive me for how horribly I have treated you over the years."

"What have you done that I did not ultimately deserve?"

Celeste opened her mouth to speak, but shook her head. "Perhaps, it is best not to try and recount what we have done."

Her father smiled and pulled her in for another hug. "I have not told you for a very long time, but you are dearer to me than I can express."

"I will do more to make you proud than to cause you pain, father," she said as they pulled away. "I promise."

He took one of her hands and patted it. "Honestly, though I did not show it at the time, I was quite proud of how you handled the Winchester. I believe I asked Gerald on more than one occasion to retell me about it."

Celeste laughed and wiped away another tear.

Her father sighed. "I do not oppose your pending engagement to Charles," her father said after a moment. "At least I no longer have to worry where you will end up when I am dead."

"So, you are not angry with me?"

"Would my being angry stop you?"

Celeste shook her head without hesitation. "It would not."

"Then my anger would be senseless and a waste of breath," he replied. "Besides, though Charles and I have never seen eye to eye on a few issues, he is a good man, and I have known about his affection for you for quite some time."

"It seems everyone except myself knew," Celeste mumbled.

"Shall we toast to your happiness?" her father asked

already pouring the drinks.

Celeste took the drink her father handed to her with a smile.

"May you both live your lives with joy, warmth, and love," her father said raising his glass.

Celeste raised hers likewise.

"And if he ever strays, I will kill him."

31

Celeste, anxious to have her engagement finalized, could not wait for Charles to call on her. So, after the second day, the snow having given way to rain, she made her journey to him. The day was dismal, but it was not a reflection on how she felt as she bounded out of her carriage and knocked on the townhouse door.

Charles opened it a few moments later. "Celeste," he replied, a smile brightening his eyes.

"I have been thinking," Celeste began, pushing her way into the house without formally being invited inside, "if we are to wed, where shall we live? Certainly, I do own a few properties, including this one here, but honestly, I cannot live so closely to my neighbors. People are nosey and like to talk about the most ridiculous things, so living here would not do."

Charles rubbed the back of his neck, a little agitated.

"And we certainly do not want to live with my father the rest of his life. As stubborn as he is, he may never die." She shook her head. "No, I do not believe any of those solutions would work."

Charles, who had lost his smile soon after Celeste

began, gave a small shrug. "I have broken just above even after the sale of my house," he told her. "It could afford us a small place outside of town. I might be able to buy back that cottage my father owned."

Celeste shook her head. "That small little thing?" she asked. "I own hatboxes that are bigger."

Charles nodded, looking defeated.

"I was thinking something larger and more elegant," Celeste continued unable to contain her grin. "Something in the Tudor style?"

Charles's head shot up as Celeste handed him a sealed document. He slowly took it from her, shakily opening it, his eyes scanning the paper.

"But this," he began, "this is the deed to my– or the duchess's house."

Celeste shook her head. "No," she told him. "It is the deed to *our* house." Celeste smiled at him.

"Our?" he repeated. "You are serious?"

She nodded. "Seems my father is the one who bought the house, but after the duchess left, she forfeited it back to him. I have asked for it as a gift and he has given it."

Charles pressed a hand to his mouth as he continued to read. He gave a small laugh as he embraced Celeste, picking her up and twirling her around. He kissed her as he placed her back on the floor.

"For a moment, I thought you were going to refuse me," he told her. "My heart had never been torn to pieces as they had been in those few moments."

"I love you," Celeste said in reply. She covered her mouth with her hands, as if surprised by her words.

Charles gently took her hands in his and kissed them softly. "When shall we wed?" he asked tenderly.

She looked pensive for a moment. "I was thinking,

perhaps, a long engagement," she said pressing her lips together to suppress a smile. "You know, do it the proper way. Five years."

Charles nodded. "Yes, very proper."

"And we shall *not* have relations until the wedding night, of course," Celeste continued.

"Ooo," Charles replied creasing his brows. "Five years *and* abstinence. Seems rather torturous. For you, I mean. I could probably handle it."

Celeste laughed. "Or, we could wed in March, but still abstain."

Charles gave another nod. "The second choice is probably the better of the two, in my opinion," he replied pulling her close. "The sooner the better, but if you wanted to wait another hundred years," he paused, looking down into her eyes.

"Yes?" she said when he didn't continue.

"Well, my hand would certainly become tired waiting so long, but I would try."

Celeste laughed as he kissed her.

"I will not bring much into this marriage," he told her. "Financially, I know I am lacking, but I will show you every day what you mean to me."

Celeste smiled. "You know, this reminds me of that night, when we first held each other. Do you remember?"

"Of course."

"We promised each other we would never marry. We vowed to both be against it until our dying days."

He gave a small chuckle. "I think you are remembering that a little incorrectly," he replied.

She gave him a confused look. "How so?"

"I must confess, I made no promise," he said. "You made the promise for us both."

She frowned, trying to remember. "Are you sure?"

He nodded. "I just remained silent because I knew you were hurting, your mother having just recently passed and your father practically moving that other woman into the house. I thought it was best to just let you speak."

She laughed through her nose. "Smart man," she said. "If that were the case, why did you not marry Lydia Culver when you had the chance? Did you not love her once?"

He shook his head. "No," he replied almost in a whisper. "There has only been you."

Celeste felt the tears well in her eyes as she realized how blind she had truly been. "I love you."

EPILOGUE

Happy was the day when Mr. Willoughby married off his only daughter. It was a day he, and everyone else in the neighborhood, thought would never happen. The occasion stirred so much joy within him, he spent a whole two pounds more on the festivities than he intended.

Everyone seemed to be invited from friends, to neighbors, and even family members Celeste was not aware existed, including one female cousin who kept locking eyes with Margaret.

The bride and groom themselves were elated. They were happy and excited to share such a joyous occasion with those they loved, but were even more excited about getting each other alone. To Charles's chagrin, Celeste had not been joking about abstaining until after the wedding and months' worth of heavy kissing and light caresses was wearing very hard on him. But he was able to thank her later as the anticipation only made the event that much more pleasurable to them both.

As for Margaret, though she remained devout the rest of her life, she did not join a convent. She did, however, find her way to Paris with Celeste's cousin Anne. They lingered there for several months before coming back with a few stories that made Celeste blush for a change. Anne then soon began renting a cottage nearby where Margaret made frequent, long visits.

Amanda had married Stephen and soon learned to regret her decision. She was quickly pregnant and soon discovered that everything Celeste had said about her husband was true. She held on for a few years until their second son was born before she moved out. In a drunken rage, Stephen went after her, but he stumbled down his grand staircase and cracked his head on the marble flooring, and died. At least, that is what everyone chose to believe.

Celeste and Charles, of course, lived in happy contentment. Graham and Fanny were frequent guests as well as Margaret and Anne, whom everyone started to accept as Margaret's dear friend.

Celeste and Margaret remained close for the remainder of their lives pouring into each other their secrets. Charles eventually found out about Margaret, as the two couples often traveled together, but it did not change his view on her either. She was still Celeste's most intimate friend and godmother to their children.

Charles had never told Celeste, but Margaret had been visiting him for months and he visited her in return for encouragement prior to their engagement. He had confided long ago about his love for Celeste and through his several failed attempts at telling *her*, Margaret helped give him the strength needed to keep trying.

Because of this, Margaret remained a close friend to them both and was a loved member of their family. She was, as Celeste always said, their dear Margaret.

AFTERTHOUGHT

argaret sat in front of her vanity looking down at the worn portrait of Irene and sighed, her heart breaking almost all over again and her eyes threatened to fill with tears. All of those promises that they had made, all of the plans they had shared, meant nothing.

She pressed the picture to her chest and took a deep breath, remembering the warm embraces and tender words between them. How she wished she could feel that way again. How she wished she could–

She shook her head. But she could not. And it was futile to think otherwise. She gave another shaky sigh as she stowed the photograph away, hiding it under a stack of letters from other friends when there was a soft knock on her door.

"Miss Hepworth," came the voice of the housemaid.

Margaret quickly dried her eyes and pinched her cheeks to bring color to them. "Yes, Mary?"

"You've uh visitor, miss," the middle-aged woman said opening the door just a crack.

"Celeste?"

"No, miss, uh gentleman."

Margaret's heart dropped when the thought of it

being Doctor Digsby crossed her mind. He had been a frequent visitor as of late and, though she enjoyed his company, she did not feel equal to seeing him at the moment. However, she put on a smile and made her way down to the parlor where a man in a hunched posture, looking defeated, stood staring out the window, his hand bracing himself against the frame.

"Charles?" Margaret said tentatively. "I was not expecting you."

Charles turned to look at her, running a hand through his almond-colored hair to smooth it down. He seemed agitated. "Margaret," he replied with a short bow.

"Is everything alright?

He rubbed his mouth with his hands and sighed. "I am sorry to intrude on your solitude. Your maid seemed hesitant to allow me entrance."

"I cannot imagine why," Margaret replied. "It is only you. She should have nothing to fear." She held her hand out to one of the sofas. "Would you like to sit?" she asked him. "You seem out of sorts."

He shook his head. "No, thank you," he replied. He tapped his finger in the side of his leg. "I heard you and the doctor have been getting along well."

Margaret cleared her throat, her cheeks blushing slightly. "Yes, he is a very nice and interesting man."

Charles nodded. "I am glad to hear it. You deserve a someone who is such."

Margaret gave a small smile but could not bring herself to comment. "Should I order us some tea?" she asked. "It might be a little early for it, but I would not mind if it would calm our nerves."

Charles gave a soft laugh and shook his head. "No, thank you."

There was a brief silence between them.

"I was on my way to Celeste's, she having invited me to tea, when I found I could not go."

Margaret frowned. "Wherefore?"

Charles shook his head again. "My cousin Graham has recently come into town and they have—" He stopped himself and cleared his throat. "He just whips into town as he usually does and they just fall back into where they were before."

"It breaks your heart to see them together, does it not?" Margaret asked.

Charles looked up at her a little panicked.

"It breaks your heart to see her with, or think of her with anyone else, does it not?" Margaret continued. "Because you are in love with her, are you not?"

Charles moved back to the window. "How long have you known?"

Margaret smiled softly. "Charles, honestly?" she replied. "I have known you and Celeste long enough to understand the both of you. I know your moods and your reactions. And I have seen how differently the both of you interact with one another compared with anyone else. I see the way you look at her; hear the way you talk about her. I am quiet, but I am not blind."

Charles gave a small smile. "It appears so." He took in a deep breath and let it out in a huff. "Are saying you understand Celeste's feelings as well?"

Margaret regarded Charles for a moment, seeing the hopeful anguish in his eyes. "Celeste, as you know, is rather complicated," she started. "You of all people know she will go out of her way to do something she is advised she shouldn't do, or defy her father. Telling her directly your feelings, is not the correct course to take."

"Are you saying she does not love me in return then?"

Margaret shook her head. "Celeste is *scared* of her feelings," Margaret explained. "Scared of what they could mean and where they could lead. So, instead of listening to how she feels, she chooses to ignore it, repress it, pretend it does not exist."

Charles gave a slow nod. "Are you saying that she *does* love me then?"

"I am saying that she has yet to figure out that she does," Margaret concluded.

Charles frowned. "That is not encouraging," he mumbled.

Margaret walked over to Charles and took his hand, giving it a light squeeze. "We both know Celeste is quicker to act on others' emotions than she is to act on her own," she told him. "The only thing we can do is wait."

Charles sighed, discouraged. "Then I guess there is nothing I can do."

Margaret creased her brows pensively. "Do not go to tea," she told him.

"What?"

Margaret nodded. "In fact, ignore the next few invitations to anything for the time being," she added.

"You mean, stay away from her?"

"Yes, let her feel your absence. It might remind her what she will miss if you were no longer in her life. She loves you, but she will never realize it until she thinks she has lost you."

Charles smiled. "I have never seen this side of you Margaret," he replied.

"My romantic side?"

"Your scheming side."

Margaret gave a small chuckle. "I did grow up with

Celeste, you know?"

Charles nodded, unsure. "There is another issue, however," he confessed.

"Which is?"

"I am ruined."

Margaret frowned. "Ruined how?"

"My fortune," he began. "It has been squandered by my father. I have nothing to give her."

Margaret gave him a stern look. "Charles Pratt, if you think that would stop Celeste from doing what she wants, then you do not know her as well as I thought."

He shook his head. "It is not that. It is that I cannot give her what I feel she deserves."

Margaret's heart swelled at the love Charles had for Celeste. "Celeste does not need riches as much as you think she does," she reassured him.

He nodded. "But you truly believe she loves me?"

Margaret gave a small laugh. "I truly believe she loves you. But I know that if you do not let her come to you, she will only push you away. Have patience, Charles."

He gave a small smile. "Then I guess I will take you up on that tea you offered."

Margaret nodded. "I will also supply you with a piece of paper and ink to pen a letter with your regrets as to your last-minute change of plans."

"Thank you," he said genuinely. "You have always been a kind listening ear."

"You can always come here to talk out your problems and frustrations, Charles," Margaret told him. "I hope you know that."

"I think I shall have to," he replied.

Margaret smiled to herself when Charles left. She was glad her two most intimate friends were finally coming to terms with their love for one another and Celeste would have been proud to know it would be Margaret's scheming that brought them together.

www.ingramcontent.com/pod-product-compliance
Lightning Source LLC
Chambersburg PA
CBHW060537310726
48982CB00009B/1283/J

* 9 7 8 1 7 3 3 4 4 8 7 1 0 *